KILLING EMMALEE

A SONGS OF EXPERIENCE BOOK

ELLE WALLACE

THE BLUE DOOR BOOKS

Killing Emmalee. Copyright © 2026 by Elle Wallace.

All rights reserved. Published by The Blue Door Books, LLC

No part of this book may be reproduced in any form or by any electronic or mechanical means, including information storage and retrieval systems, without written permission from the author, except for the use of brief quotations in a book review.

All characters, places, events, and organizations presented within are entirely products of the author's imagination or used fictitiously.

ISBN: 978-1-972672-01-3

Cover Art by Ken Crossland

Dedication Art by Grayson Moore

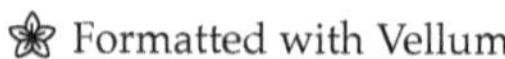 Formatted with Vellum

For my first and biggest hero,
my first and biggest fan,
my first and favorite teacher,
the reason I began —

For Mom.

Folly is an endless maze
Tangled roots perplex her ways;
How many have fallen there!

WILLIAM BLAKE

PROLOGUE

old.

That's all Emmalee knew. Everything was so very, very cold. And then there was the screaming. A guttural, keening wail. More animal than human. Piercing her ears, drilling through her skull.

She squeezed her eyelids tight and swallowed. Her throat was dry and hoarse. The screaming had stopped. Had she been the one screaming? She didn't have time to fully assess because the darkness took her again.

When the cold returned, the blood came with it. Her eyelids fluttered and she could see the thick, dark red of it pooling several feet from her. The metal tang of it in the air made her throat tighten, her stomach roil. The rhythmic dripping of more and more blood disturbed the glossy puddle. Whose was it? Was it hers?

Though the world was tilted sideways, her eyes followed the line of the drips, raked over shards of shattered glass and twisted metal. She tried to crane her neck to continue her search, to trace it to its source, but the movement ripped another scream from her already sore throat.

This was all her fault.

CHAPTER 1

The house was really more of a cabin. And "rustic" was generous, Emmalee thought, as she followed her mother's Tahoe into what served as a driveway, but was really more a bare patch in the side yard. She sighed as she turned off the ignition and stepped out of her beat up Ford Fiesta. She was glad to be done driving.

"Not too bad, huh?" her mom asked, smiling a bit too brightly.

"Yeah. Sure." Emmalee tried to return the smile, but the prospect of moving into yet another house – and especially this one – did not inspire joy. Her mother had rented this one sight unseen because they'd had to move quickly.

"I've lived in worse. Let's go take a look inside."

Emmalee followed her mother onto the rickety porch and into the A-frame cabin. The inside was worse than the outside. It was no wonder the listing had included no pictures of the inside, she thought, as she scanned what was supposed to now be home. A dilapidated green couch sagged against one wall with a dusty coffee table in front of it. The rest of the room was bare, except for evidence rats had been in there. Emmalee bit her lip to keep from crying.

In the kitchen, they found a working faucet and a chipped yellow formica table with two chairs. The cabinets held a few plates, cups, silverware, pots and pans. There was a banged-up 70s-era olive green stove and a matching refrigerator, but no dishwasher. And no microwave.

"It's not perfect, but this will work just fine for us," her mother said, nodding as she scanned the room. Emmalee suspected she was trying to be positive. There was no way her mother thought there was anything *just fine* about this place. Surely she wanted to have back the home – and the life – they'd had before.

Emmalee recalled the beautiful colonial home they'd lived in when her mother was stationed in Virginia, just outside Washington, D.C. The rooms had been expansive, with gleaming wood floors, windows that let in natural light, and comfortable furniture. And it had been filled with love. Family dinners at the solid oak table that had once been her grandmother's. She'd had two whole Halloweens there, watching scary movies and filling up on candy before dinner. Two Christmases in the big living room, wrapping paper everywhere, their yellow lab, Kobe, curled up in front of the fireplace.

She felt tears pooling in her eyes and turned to open the refrigerator, not wanting her mother to see her cry. She pretended the sticky drawers and cubbies for butter, lunchmeat, and cheese were exceedingly interesting.

"Looks like that will need a good scrubbing."

Emmalee jumped, not realizing her mother was so close behind her. She was good at that, her mother. Sneaking up on people was a specialty she'd honed over the course of a twenty-year career in special ops. Sometimes she was amazed her mother was an Army Ranger, and extremely proud of her, but most of the time, she wished her mother was just a regular mom, not Colonel Sloane.

It would be nice to just have Nikki, a normal mom who baked cakes and joined the PTA and drove carpool. Most kids wanted their parents to buy them a car the second they turned 16, but for Emmalee, there was no choice, even though she hated driving. She had to have a car because Colonel *Mom* was often whisked away at a moment's notice to God knows where for God knows how long on some top secret mission, and Emmalee had to fend for herself. And accept the fact that it was all her fault.

"You okay?"

Emmalee snapped out of her reverie. "Yeah, I'm fine," she lied. "Definitely needs scrubbing." Emmalee turned around, and her mother must have seen the disappointment in her eyes.

"I know it's not perfect, Em, but it's nothing a little elbow grease can't fix. Besides, it's just for a year, and then you'll be off to college."

Emmalee rolled her eyes.

"What?"

"Elbow grease? No one in this century says that." Emmalee grinned, showing her mom it was just like old times, just joking around.

"Well, I'm not from this century," her mother retorted, grinning back.

"That tracks." The familiar banter felt a little nice. A little like normal. She would try to make this move a little easier than the last. She was eighteen now. She shouldn't dwell on what once was. Time to focus on what is.

"I'm going to go unload my car." Emmalee shut the fridge door.

"I'll be right out. I want to see if the head is in working order."

Emmalee sighed. She's not a normal mom, she reminded

herself as she stepped out of the house. *Head* instead of bathroom wasn't that big of a deal.

Outside, she realized that the drizzle that had just started when they arrived had become actual rain, so she hurried to grab her backpack and suitcases out of the car and ran back inside in time to hear a toilet flushing.

"Thank God all of the plumbing seems to work!" her mother yelled.

"Where's my bedroom?" she called back.

"There's just the one. Down the hall on the left."

"Just one? How's that supposed to work?"

"You take the room. I'll take the couch." Her mom came back into the living room, drying her hands on her jeans.

"Mom! That's insane!"

"It'll be fine." Emmalee shot her a frown. "Look, honey, I'm gone a lot, so the couch will work just fine, and I'll just put an extra dresser in your room for my clothes."

"It's supposed to be like negative one billion degrees in Washington in the winter, isn't it? You can't work in that."

"I've worked in worse, kiddo." Nikki smiled and ruffled Emmalee's hair, a habit she'd had since Emmalee could remember. A habit that annoyed Emmalee to no end. "Now, go get that room set up. That's an order, soldier!"

"Yes, Sir," Emmalee said, attempting to annoy her mother.

"Move your boots, kid." Nikki turned to the kitchen. "I'm going to see what we can do with this."

Down the short hall, the bedroom was small and somewhat cozy despite the layers of dust. There was a twin-sized bed under a window that needed a good cleaning. Emmalee dropped her bags on the floor and climbed onto the bed, kneeling in front of the window and parting the yellow floral curtains. She gasped. The view was incredible — nothing but forest as far as she could see. The trees towered over the cabin, and she could see paths snaking through them in various directions. She could definitely see herself exploring out there, finding a stump or a rock to sit on and write on Saturday mornings when the weather was decent.

The rest of the room included a small desk and chair, nothing fancy, but they looked sturdy enough. Whoever had lived here before had left string lights hanging all the way around the room's ceiling. Emmalee flicked them on, using a chair to reach the cord, and was happy to find they were just a soft white, not a hideous pink or something.

A couple of framed photos hung on the walls as well. One that looked a lot like the view out the bedroom window. The other was harder to understand. It looked like the back of a head. She couldn't tell the age, or whether it was a male or female. They were captured just as they were falling out of an airplane, it seemed. Nothing but blue sky and a few cotton candy clouds through the opening in the airplane. The photographer must have been right behind them.

Interesting, Emmalee thought, wondering what it would feel like to just let go and fall. Then land. Then dark. She'd have to write a few lines about that in her notebook tonight. Maybe there was a poem somewhere in that idea.

Emmalee's eyes blinked open and she had a moment of panic, no idea where she was. She was cold, though, and the chill set her heart racing. Then, as her eyes landed on the photo of the woods, she remembered. Washington. Crummy cabin. New school today.

She could feel her heart start to pound even more. This was the worst part of moving, always being the new girl. It was like the movie Groundhog Day – she could never get out of this loop, it seemed. At least it was only the second week of school, not in the middle of the year like last time. She shook her head to clear the memory of last time.

"Up and at 'em!" Nikki barged into Emmalee's room. "School starts at 8:00, and I have to check in with my commander at 9:00. I also need to stop in town on the way to work and see about lining up some Wi-Fi for this place."

The door slammed shut again before Emmalee could reply. Reluctantly, she pulled herself out of bed, scrounging for clothes and a toothbrush. The shower felt great, like washing off the dirt of the house that was clinging to her. They'd spent the night before scrubbing the kitchen and bathroom and dusting the furniture, washing dishes, and sanitizing the refrigerator. She'd had a shower before bed, but she still felt gross. Something about living in someone else's dirt really creeped her out.

Freshly dressed and brushed, she appeared in the kitchen, where her mother was pouring coffee into two chipped brown enameled mugs. Nikki was in her uniform, hair pulled into a tightly-coiled bun. She turned and raked her eyes over Emmalee, head to toe, then back up again.

"You're going like that?"

"Not this again, Mom." She could feel her blood pressure starting to rise.

"The way you present yourself says a lot about who you are." Nikki stared at her over the rim of her coffee cup.

"Yeah, exactly. I'm dressed exactly the way I *am*." Emmalee gestured down to her oversized flannel shirt, baggy cargo pants, and combat boots. "You're not dressed all that differently. You have combat boots on, and pants with lots of pockets." Emmalee smirked.

"I'm dressed like an Army Officer, which I am. You're dressed like a—" Nikki paused.

"Like a what, Mom?" Emmalee could feel her face heating, turning red. She was sick of this argument.

"Your outfit just looks sloppy, like you don't care about how you look. Your boots are muddy. Your clothes are wrinkled."

"It's not like I had time to iron. I don't even know where the iron is." Emmalee spread her arms wide, gesturing at the ramshackle cabin.

Nikki lifted her coffee cup to her lips, nodding in the direction of the living room as she took a sip.

Emmalee glanced over to see the iron set up on the coffee table. "I can't do this today, Mom. I have enough to worry about."

Nikki sat at the table, patting the chair next to hers. "Sit down. We'll shelve the clothing talk, for now. What are you worried about?"

Emmalee sat, still annoyed, but she knew better than to ignore a direct order from Colonel Sloane. She wouldn't talk, though. Not yet anyway. Instead, she took a sip of her mother's very dark, very strong, black coffee.

"Out with it." Nikki stared at her, waiting.

Emmalee sighed. "You know what it is. I hate first days. Especially when it's not the first day of the school year."

Nikki scoffed. "Please. You're a pro at this. Besides, school's only been in session for a week."

"I'm not a pro. I may have to do it a lot, but that doesn't mean I like it. It's impossible to just waltz into a new school and make friends. I have to figure out what the school is like, what the other kids are like, how to fit in with them. Which I never do, by the way."

Nikki took a long drink of coffee, then sat her mug on the formica. "Em, you're amazing. You're a great writer, you're smart, you're funny, you're beautiful."

Emmalee started to protest, but Nikki interrupted. "Don't speak when I'm speaking. Anyway, your problem is a lack of confidence in yourself. You worry too much about what other people think. Just be you. They'll love you."

"They didn't love me at Edgewater." Emmalee's mom would have to agree with this one. Her last high school in Georgia had been a cesspool of wannabe influencers more worried about their TikTok likes than their grades, or anything else for that matter. Emmalee made a whopping zero friends during her year there.

"That's because people can smell lack of confidence a mile away, and let me tell you, it smells like crap. And we all know the only thing crap attracts is flies." Nikki grinned at her again.

"Great. I smell like crap. Gee thanks for the pep talk, Mom." Emmalee flashed a snarky smile back.

"The truth hurts, but it's the only thing that will set you free, Em." Nikki came forward, brushing hair out of Emmalee's face.

"I'm not one of your soldiers, Mom," Emmalee snapped, pulling away from Nikki's touch.

Nikki didn't let her go that easily. Instead, she leaned even closer, gripping Emmalee's shoulder. "Em, like one of my soldiers, I want you to be strong, ready for anything, and I'll do whatever it takes to help you get that way. Now, grab your gear, and let's go."

Emmalee was fuming inside, but stuffed that feeling down deep. She knew her mom had enough worries herself, and besides, it never paid to argue with Nikki when she was in Army mode. Instead, she loaded her backpack with her tattered copy of *The Perks of Being a Wallflower*, her notebook, and a couple of pens. Then she set out to face whatever horrors were in store for her that day.

CHAPTER 2

As she followed her mom along the dark forest roads that led to town, Emmalee gripped the steering wheel tightly and rehearsed her new girl, first day plan. She would keep her head down and her mouth shut, avoid eye contact, and stay focused on assignments during class. She'd find a quiet corner at lunch and read or write–alone. Being a wallflower was something she was good at. She could do this.

She took several deep breaths and finally pulled into a parking space in front of the small brick building. She breathed a sigh of relief as she shut off the engine. She hated driving even more than she hated new schools. She shivered and turned her attention back to the sign in front of the private school her mom had insisted on. She wanted to make sure Emmalee's education was top notch, never relying on public schools to do the job. So, here she was. Ravensville Academy. Nikki had insisted on a private school, reasoning it would provide a better education than public school. Emmalee knew better, after Edgewater.

She had to admit, though, the name, at least, was cool. Very Edgar Allan Poe. The town, and the school, were both much smaller than she'd imagined, which could put a damper on her plans. It was much easier to be a wallflower in a big school. As she scanned the building's facade and grounds, movement caught her eye. Several girls huddled in the entryway, making furtive glances at Emmalee's car. Time to face reality.

Luckily, the girls disappeared inside the entryway before Emmalee had to acknowledge them. Inside, Emmalee's fears of Ravensville being a small school were confirmed. The front doors opened into a common area scattered with overstuffed couches and chairs, gleaming side tables with brass lamps, and a few polished oak round tables with matching wooden chairs as well. Students were clustered together in small groups, most of them talking animatedly, a few poring over textbooks or scrolling on phones.

She'd seen this kind of school before. Rich. Old money. Small. Everyone had probably gone to school together forever and already had their friend groups set. Emmalee chewed her lip to keep from tearing up. She would just have to man up, as Colonel Mom would say.

In the main office, a friendly woman with a warm smile introduced herself as Mrs. Jenkins and handed her a freshly-printed class schedule. "Here you go, hon. Your first period will be Mrs. Smith's English class. Chase!" She called out to someone passing by the office door.

He immediately entered, smiling. "Mrs. Jenkins, how are you on this fine morning?" Emmalee sucked in a deep breath. Chase was very, very attractive.

Mrs. Jenkins grinned back, clearly doting. "Emmalee here is new. Could you show her to her first period? She has Mrs. Smith."

Chase turned around. When his eyes fell on her, Emmalee could almost feel them, her skin burning everywhere they landed, even through her baggy clothes. He smiled. Welcome to the Raven, Emmalee." He beamed that perfect smile at her, and it felt like sunlight.

Emmalee nodded and gave a little wave, letting her hair fall in front of her face, hoping to hide the redness she could feel warming her cheeks. "Thanks."

"Well, it just so happens that I also have Mrs. Smith for first period. Come on, I'll take you there." He nodded his head in the direction of the hallway, arm extended, welcoming her to go first. He flashed her that incredible smile again, his teeth far too white and his blue eyes far too sparkly for an actual human.

Emmalee tried to avoid crushes because they were rarely returned, but sometimes it was just impossible not to fall for a guy this obscenely attractive. What could she say? She was a sucker for the blond, blue-eyed, muscular type.

She could feel eyes following them as they walked the halls, but Chase stayed focused on her, pointing out the library, the gym, the cafeteria, and then led her upstairs to a cozy, wood-floored classroom on the second floor.

When they entered the room, a stern-looking woman with a long, white braid down her back swiveled her head away from the chalkboard, looking directly at her. Mrs. Smith, Emmalee presumed.

"Mrs. Smith," Chase confirmed, "we have a new student. This is Emmalee. She's coming to us from...?" He looked at her, eyebrows raised.

"Georgia," Emmalee offered, smiling at the teacher.

"Hello, Emmalee. I do recall an email last week about a new student. I hope you're well-prepared. Our Senior English class is not an easy A."

"Well, English is my favorite subject," Emmalee offered, smiling, hoping to earn early favor with Mrs. Smith.

The older woman looked her over, then nodded. "Well, welcome. We'll need to find you a seat." She began shuffling some papers on her desk, but Chase interrupted.

"She can sit by me, Mrs. Smith. I'm kind of showing her

around today." He smiled at Emmalee again, and she could feel her heart skip a beat.

"Very well." Mrs. Smith pulled out a textbook and a syllabus and handed them to Emmalee. "Get the syllabus signed before tomorrow."

Emmalee nodded and took the seat Chase pointed out. When she looked up again, he was heading for the door.

"I'll see you in a few minutes for my favorite class, Mrs. Smith!" He rolled his eyes at Emmalee, who grinned while the teacher's back was turned.

"Bye, Dear," Mrs. Smith called. She had already resumed writing on the chalkboard. From what Emmalee could tell, today's lesson was going to be diagramming sentences.

Wonderful, thought Emmalee. She'd hoped to find refuge in her English class. She loved reading and writing, but this activity, at least, would be more about punctuation, spelling, and grammar, all the easy but boring stuff.

She pulled out her schedule to start familiarizing herself with it, noticing that she'd been enrolled in the Creative Writing class her mom had requested. She was glad to see that she had a different teacher for that class. Maybe Mrs. Smith would prove her wrong and be amazing, but Emmalee wasn't holding out hope for that.

The bell rang and students began filtering in. Mostly, they appeared to be normal suburban teens – trendy clothes and shoes, nice haircuts. The girls all sported professionally manicured nails and expensive water bottles in pastel colors.

She took a deep breath and watched them, but they didn't seem to notice her at first, and she was okay with that. Her invisibility ended, though, as a petite blonde girl took the seat in front of her. "Who's this?" she asked, nodding at Emmalee.

The linebacker-sized brunette guy who had walked in with her looked up from his phone and surveyed Emmalee, his eyes lingering on her chest a beat too long. He shrugged. "No idea." Then went back to his phone.

Emmalee felt like crawling inside her bag and hiding for the rest of the day, but the blonde girl grinned at her. "Hi. I'm Britney. This is my boyfriend, Bryce." She pointed at the pervy linebacker next to her. "You must be new?"

Emmalee nodded, smiling back. "Yes. Emmalee. Nice to meet you."

Britney scrutinized her a moment longer, eyes roaming over her hair and clothes. Emmalee had to admit, they were different from Britney's very short denim shorts, cropped tank, and strappy sandals, not to mention her sleek blonde bob.

Just as she was about to feel even more uncomfortable, Chase arrived again and sat between Emmalee and the window.

"Hello again, Emmalee."

Britney's eyes snapped to him.

"Hey," Emmalee replied.

"How have you fared in my absence?"

She was trying to figure out how to respond when Britney piped up. "You know her?"

"Sure. We're old pals. We go way back to, when was it, Emmalee, five minutes ago?" That incredible smile lit up his face again, setting Emmalee's nerves even more on edge.

Britney nodded and turned back toward the front of the room.

"Chase, what happened to the desks?" A tall, slender girl with long, shiny red waves that fell perfectly over her shoulders, frowned at Chase.

"We have a new friend, Babe. Meet Emmalee." Chase smiled at the gorgeous redhead.

"Hi." She flashed a clearly disingenuous smile at Emmalee. "But I usually sit by you," she snipped.

"Oh! No problem. I can move." Emmalee started to stand up, but Chase put his hand on her wrist, squeezing gently.

"Stay, Emmalee. I know it's your seat, Gretchen, but it's okay. Mrs. Jenkins asked me to show her around today. I figured this is better than putting her next to Bryce." He narrowed his eyes a bit, an unspoken message clearly passing between them.

The redhead nodded slowly, then took the empty seat next to the brunette guy who was obviously Bryce, who was obviously known by all as a bit of a perv.

"I assumed this seat was empty?" Emmalee raised her eyebrows at Chase.

He shrugged. "Mrs. Smith is too old to notice. Or care."

"Everyone, get your notebooks open and be ready to begin class when the bell rings." Mrs. Smith's voice was loud and sharp.

Students started digging in bags, opening notebooks, scrounging for pens. Emmalee pulled her own pen out and waited, hearing but not really listening to the chatter around her. Instead, she was just happy that she already knew several names. In spite of a few tense moments, the day was starting off better than she'd expected.

When the tardy bell rang, Mrs. Smith directed them to start copying down the sentences from the board and diagramming them while she circulated through the room. Emmalee was trying her best when she heard the older woman shuffle up behind her, peering over Emmalee's shoulder.

"Ms. Sloane, are you familiar with diagramming sentences?"

"Ummm, no–" Emmalee could feel her face reddening.

Mrs. Smith clucked her tongue. "That is unfortunate. If you come by after school every day for the next few days, I can get you up to speed. Everyone should know how to parse their native tongue."

All heads were turned, staring at her. A couple of boys Emmalee hadn't met yet were silently laughing and shaking their heads at her. Emmalee could feel her face burning.

"I might be able to come by–" Emmalee's voice trailed off when Chase interrupted.

"Don't worry, Mrs. Smith. I'll get her caught up." Chase's voice sent thrills of relief coursing through Emmalee. Anything to have the focus off of her.

Mrs. Smith nodded. "Very well. If you have any questions or need any help, let me know, Ms. Sloane."

Mrs. Smith moved on, heels clicking, peering over other shoulders, and Emmalee breathed for the first time in minutes it seemed.

Chase leaned close to Emmalee. "Don't worry about her. She just thinks her class is the most important thing in the world," Chase whispered. Emmalee could feel his breath on her ear and neck, and felt herself blushing again.

"Thanks," she whispered, smiling at him.

"No worries, Em. Can I call you Em?"

"Yeah, sure." Emmalee didn't think a boy had ever paid this much attention to her, especially one this cute.

Gretchen noticed, too. When Emmalee turned to see where Mrs. Smith had wandered, she saw Gretchen's eyes assessing her cooly. "So, Em, where are you from?"

"Georgia," Emmalee replied, taking care to smile and sound extra friendly. She did not need enemies on day one.

"Ah, a cowgirl, then?" Britney piped up, turning as well. "Or, maybe not, given your–" she gestured to Emmalee's outfit "aesthetic."

Emmalee felt her face heating up again. Was that a dig, or just an assessment? "Nope. Not a cowgirl. Just a girl."

Britney's lip curled up on one side in a smirk. "Just a girl. Cute." She turned back around facing the board, leaving Emmalee to wonder what she'd meant by that–compliment or shade?

Chase leaned in again, closer this time, and his voice was even quieter. "Don't mind Britney, either. She can come off as somewhat of a bitch, but don't tell her I said that." He chuckled, the feel of his breath on her skin sending electric tingles through her.

She did not understand what was happening. He was clearly involved with Gretchen, who clearly seemed annoyed with his attention to Emmalee.

Emmalee bent over her work, trying to separate herself from Chase physically. Yes, he was clearly attractive and clearly trying to flirt. But, she was not interested in earning any enemies on day one. Whatever was going on between this perfect couple could stay between them.

CHAPTER 3

When first period ended, Emmalee hurried to gather her things and get into the hallway, where she could hopefully blend into the crowd and breathe. As soon as she exited, though, she felt a hand on her elbow.

"So, Em, where are you off to next?"

Emmalee opened the wrinkled schedule in her hand. "Ummm, Spanish?" She looked up at Chase, who pointed down a short hallway. "Down there, turn left. Gretchen and I have a free period. Enjoy Español." He smiled at her again. Gretchen did, too, but it was more scary than friendly.

Emmalee smiled back anyway, hoping to start earning a place on the girl's good side, then watched the two walk off, Chase's arm slithering around Gretchen's waist, pulling her close to his side, his lips brushing her cheek before whispering something into her ear.

Emmalee sighed and shook her head, hoping her next class would be less dramatic.

It wasn't. Inside the small classroom, Emmalee found herself accosted visually by a rainbow of colorful piñatas, posters, God's eyes, sombreros, maracas. A feeling of dread settled in her stomach. Just the visuals implied that this would be a high energy, high involvement class. She was not interested in that. She was also accosted by an exuberant young woman with long, black hair, a long, flowing skirt, and a gauzy top with sleeves that fluttered from her wrists.

"Hola!" the woman gushed, a genuine smile lighting up her face. "You must be our new student!"

"Yes, I'm Emmalee," she responded, smiling nervously as the woman put her hand on Emmalee's back and ushered her to a seat.

"Join us, join us. Class, let's welcome our new student, Emmalee." Emmalee was happy to meet a nice teacher, but hated the attention zeroed in on her.

"Hola," the other students droned. Her plan to blend in and fade into the background crashed and burned. Her stomach clenched at that image, and she swept it from her mind.

The class period went by at a snail's pace. The teacher was Señorita Cambridge, and Emmalee was re-christened Juana, an unfortunate fact as a boy Emmalee recognized from her English class leaned forward and asked, "Juana Mi Banana?" as he grabbed his crotch. Nearby students chuckled, but Señorita Cambridge was oblivious, conjugating the verb *molestar* on the board.

Finally it was over, and Emmalee spent the rest of her morning enduring science with Mr. Pittman, followed by history with Coach Wideman, an unfortunate name given the way several of the students made fun of his size. In both classes, she was thankfully able to recede into obscurity. Neither man seemed interested in the fact that a new student had enrolled. They simply pointed to empty seats near the back of each room and went on about their business.

As far as Emmalee could tell, Mr. Pittman's business was amusing himself with Chemistry jokes, and Mr. Wideman's was amusing himself with his unasked-for political opinions on how the "women's lib" movement ruined the American family. She doodled in her notebook to keep him from seeing the daggers shooting from her eyes.

According to her schedule, Emmalee had Creative Writing next, but when she arrived, the room was dark and empty.

A passing student said, "You must be the new girl everyone's been talking about. Are you in Creative Writing?"

Emmalee turned to see a short girl with brown hair, straight bangs, black eye makeup, and an Aerosmith tee shirt grinning at her. "Yeah. But there's no one here."

"We have first lunch period. You can eat with us if you want? I'm Mekayla, by the way." The girl's smile was genuine, and Emmalee felt an instant liking for her.

"I'm Emmalee, and that'd be great." Emmalee smiled back and followed Mekayla to the cafeteria, where they stood in line for limp-looking chicken patty sandwiches and nearly expired milk cartons.

"This food is so gross," Mekayla said, wrinkling her nose.

Mekayla sat down at a table in the far back corner of the cafeteria, where a thin, curly-haired boy with glasses was sitting. "This is Marshall."

He raised his eyebrows in question as Emmalee sat down as well.

"Marshall, meet Emmalee. She's new here, and she's in Creative Writing with us."

"Cool." Marshall stuffed another bite of breaded chicken in his mouth and started chewing.

"Ugh, have some manners, Marshall. We close our mouths when we chew, remember?"

His face reddened, highlighting his acne, and he snapped his mouth shut and grinned sheepishly.

"Marshall isn't used to human company." Mekayla gestured

to an open graphic novel on the table. "He's more interested in his books and notebooks."

Emmalee smiled. "I get that."

Marshall went red again. "He's also not used to talking to girls," Mekayla teased.

"I talk to you," he protested.

"I'm not a girl." Mekayla glared at him.

"Here we go again." Marshall rolled his eyes. "Mekayla, I didn't mean it that way."

Mekayla faced Emmalee to explain. "Marshall says I'm not a girl because we've been friends forever."

Marshall sighed. "I just meant that we're almost like siblings, you know?"

"Yeah, sure, I know." Mekayla rolled her eyes again, but it was friendly. Emmalee was a little jealous of their easy friendship, the way they knew each other well enough to tease each other and not have it feel mean. She hadn't been in one place long enough to have a friendship like that. Not since Lilly, her best friend in Virginia. Just the thought of it had her blinking tears back.

"So, Emmalee, tell us about you." Mekayla waited expectantly, picking at her sandwich.

Emmalee swallowed the lump forming in her throat. "Well, not much to say. I came here from Georgia." Emmalee shrugged.

"Yeah, but what about hobbies, hopes, dreams?" Mekayla smiled, crinkling her nose. "That sounds so cringe."

Emmalee laughed. "Maybe a little cringe. But, yeah, I like to write."

"What do you write?"

"Oh, random stuff. Poetry mostly."

"Cool. I'd love to read some."

Emmalee didn't want to share too much. Her writing was private. She didn't even share it with her mother. She hadn't shared it at all since her dad died.

"Oh, it's not that good." Emmalee blushed again. She hated that about herself, the way she wore her emotions in color on her face, for the world to see.

"Pffft." Mekayla smiled and waved her hand. "None of us are professionals or anything, but it's fun, and it keeps us out of art."

Emmalee laughed. "Yeah, I can't even draw a stick figure."

"God, me either. And Mr. Denney is a real weirdo. He's all 'feel' where the art is taking you, crap like that."

"Oh, God," Emmalee commiserated, but inside she knew what this Mr. Denney meant. She did that with her writing. Her dad had always told her to just let it flow. He was always writing, and she'd love to climb into the overstuffed chair in his office with her notebook, even when she was four or five. She would scribble while he worked on his latest news article, tap-tapping on his keyboard, glasses perched on the end of his nose, eyes squinted in concentration. She pushed the memory away before tears could come.

"You should also join the newspaper staff." Mekayla stared at her intently. "We could use another writer."

"Oh, yeah?" Emmalee wasn't so sure about that. The idea of interviewing people sounded terrifying.

"Yeah. We had several seniors leave last year that we weren't able to replace. And Wideman is the advisor, but it's okay. He kind of lets us do what we want. We have a staff meeting tomorrow after school."

"Come on." Marshall stood and began gathering his bag and tray, saving Emmalee from replying right away.

Mekayla sighed. "Marshall likes to get to class early."

"If we go now, we can avoid the annoying people making out in the hallway." He directed his eyes at a table behind Emmalee's head.

She turned around. "Oh. I met them in my first period class. Chase, Britney, Gretchen at least." There were a couple others at the lunch table she hadn't seen.

"You met them?" Mekayla looked curious.

"Yes."

"And?" Mekayla's eyes narrowed.

"And what?"

"What did you think?"

She wasn't sure what Mekayla was fishing for, but it felt like a test. "They were okay. We didn't really get to talk much."

Marshall nodded. "They do a lot of making out in the hallway."

"You're not wrong." Mekayla stood and lifted her bag to her shoulder. "You didn't eat anything." She looked down at Emmalee's tray.

"I'm not hungry." Emmalee looked down at her untouched food as well and shrugged.

"I get that. The food here would ruin anyone's appetite, but you get used to it." Mekayla smiled and bounced away, trailing Marshall.

Emmalee followed them through the line to return their trays, dumping her food in the trash under the disapproving eye of one of the cooks.

Inside the Creative Writing room, it was still dark, but the teacher was seated at the front of the room.

"Hey, guys." The teacher didn't even look up from her laptop. "How's your day been?"

"You know. The usual."

The teacher nodded at Mekayla's words, obviously distracted by something on her computer.

"Well, no worries. Your favorite students are here now," Mekayla quipped.

She and Marshall took seats next to each other at a rectangular table. Emmalee remained standing, unsure where to sit until Mekayla pointed to an empty spot at their table. Emmalee sat, taking her notebook and pen out of her bag.

"Is this it?" She looked around, wondering if anyone else would be arriving.

"There are a few more of us," Mekayla whispered back. "Most people here at the Raven aren't creative types."

A few more students entered, none she recognized from earlier classes. Then the projector screen lit up, and Emmalee saw a picture of a dark forest road, enveloped in fog. "There you go," Mrs. Murray said, opening a notebook. "Let's write for five minutes to warm up. Emmalee, you can just write whatever you're inspired to write."

Emmalee nodded, unsure how to fade into the background with so few people. She looked back at her notebook, not quite sure what to do. She'd never had a Creative Writing class before, but the other students and Mrs. Murray were busy writing, so she put her pen to the paper, staring at the image. It called to mind not a place, but a feeling. She wrote, and the words flowed.

Suddenly, she wasn't at a new school. She was in her own world, the place she always went to when she wrote. She could hear nothing, see nothing, feel nothing but words flowing through the pen and onto her paper.

> *The cold was a lullaby*
> *sung heavily in her bones*
> *making her want to stop and lie*
> *in the drifts of falling snow*
> *to say goodbye to memories*
> *fading slowly under downy flakes*
> *She closed her eyes, beneath the trees...*

The words kept coming and she lost herself in them, knowing they weren't perfect, not by a long shot. Knowing they didn't make sense, but okay with that. It was hers. All hers.

"Earth to Emmalee." She was startled, pulled from the safety of her inner sanctum into the reality of the classroom. Mekayla was smiling at her. "That must have been good. Let's hear it."

"Hold on, Mekayla, she may not want to share on day one." Emmalee snapped her notebook shut and looked at Mrs. Murray gratefully. "But, since you volunteered her, you know my rule — now *you* have to share."

"Okay." Mekayla began reading, and Emmalee listened, enthralled by the tale Mekayla wove about a young boy lost in the dark woods, helped by a stranger, a woman, who showed him to a cabin hiding in a clearing lit only by the moon.

"That's all I got so far." Mekayla shrugged.

"Nice. I just wrote a few lines about how this picture reminds me of Boy Scout camp." Marshall shuddered, but everyone else laughed.

"It was traumatizing, thank you very much, all of you." Marshall feigned insult, but then laughed it off. "I think we all know I'm not meant for the outdoors."

"Not with that pale skin. You burn too easy," Mekayla replied, and everyone laughed again.

Emmalee watched Marshall. He was red, but his smile seemed real. This was a group he felt comfortable in.

Mrs. Murray put a stop to the fun. "How about we focus on our mission today and continue plotting our short stories? Emmalee, here's an outline template." She crossed the room, holding out a stapled packet of papers. Emmalee took it and skimmed over it. She'd never really written fiction and wasn't sure what to do.

"What should it be about?" Emmalee asked.

"Whatever you want," the teacher replied. "Mekayla, Marshall, can you tell Emmalee what your stories are about so she can get some ideas?"

"Mine's about an alien who finds himself here in Ravensville.

His ship crash lands in the square, and it turns out he's related to Mr.

Cobb, the—"

He was interrupted by Mrs. Murray. "No spoilers," she laughed. "Mekayla?"

"Mine's about a boy who gets kidnapped by his own aunt, and she cooks him."

Emmalee must have looked confused because Mrs. Murray said, "It's disgusting, isn't it? I love it!" and smiled. "If no one else wants to share, you guys can work on your story outlines for the rest of the period. If you have any questions, don't hesitate to ask."

Emmalee nodded and stared down at the template. She needed to think of a character. This was out of her depth. She usually just wrote poems about whatever she was feeling at the moment. She didn't create characters and settings and storylines. She looked around, and the others were all absorbed in their work, so she just wrote the first thing that came to mind.

Name: Chase

Her face turned red. Scratch that.

Name: ~~Chase~~ Calvin

Better.

Age: 17.
Occupation: Quarterback.

She thought about writing down *being gorgeous* and grinned. Better not.

Special Skills: Winning football games

Then, thinking back to his arm around Gretchen, she added *being a player* to the list. This was fun.

Job:

Hmmm.

Job: None. Mommy and Daddy pay for everything.

Appearance: Muscular, tall, blond, blue eyes.

She thought for a moment. Scratch that. She didn't want to be too obvious.

Appearance: Muscular, tall, blond, ~~blue~~ green eyes.

She continued on, brainstorming quite the story for Mr. Calvin, including him falling in love with a new girl at his school and giving up his player life for her. Wishful thinking on her part? Probably. A girl could dream, though, couldn't she? Emmalee sighed.

"Everything okay, Emmalee?" Mrs. Murray asked, looking at her with genuine concern.

"Yes. Fine, thanks." Emmalee smiled and Mrs. Murray smiled back, then bent her head back to her own writing.

The rest of the period zoomed by, and when the bell rang, Emmalee was disappointed. She did not want to leave the quiet, friendly safety of this room and these people.

CHAPTER 4

The rest of the afternoon was excruciatingly slow. First, there was P.E., taught by a very serious Coach Taylor. He sighed loudly when Emmalee said she didn't have any gym clothes that day and made her do sit-ups, pushups, and laps with everyone else anyway, just without her boots on. Instead he'd made her choose from a pile of disgusting old shoes left behind by previous students. Thankfully, Chase wasn't in this class. But Gretchen was. She took long, lean strides, her flawless pony tail streaming behind her, careful to pass very closely by Emmalee as she lapped her. Careful not to touch her, though, or to talk to her. Ugh. She'd really wanted to avoid drama at this school. It seemed nothing good ever came from getting involved with people.

After that was Trig, a singularly boring class with a very old, very bored Mrs. Hensley, who worked problems on the white board while muttering to herself all hour. The students didn't even try to keep up. Chase was in this class, seated behind Emmalee, and leaned forward, whispering, "Don't worry about trying to take notes. We all just look up the problems online and get the answers. She has no idea."

Emmalee couldn't help thrilling a little at the quiet, conspiratorial whisper in her ear, the way it rustled her hair. Still, she tried to discreetly write the notes. She wasn't big on cheating, but she also didn't want him to think she was a try-hard.

When the last bell of the day rang, she made a beeline to her car, waiting several minutes for the lot to clear so she could back out of her space. Just as she put the car in reverse, she noticed Chase and Gretchen approaching a shiny black sports car several spaces away. Chase took Gretchen's bag and tossed it with his into the back. Then, he grabbed Gretchen's hips and pinned her to the passenger side door, leaning down to kiss her. Gretchen's arms went around his neck, and he pressed his body to her.

Emmalee could feel herself blushing, with both guilt and a bit of jealousy. Ridiculous, she thought. He's got a girlfriend, and he's *so* not my type. Then his eyes wandered over and caught hers staring back. He winked at her, and she nearly screamed. Hurriedly, she backed out of the space and sped to the main road, needing to get anywhere but there.

At the house—she wouldn't call it home—she opened the refrigerator and found nothing but a few water bottles. In the pantry cabinet, she found a half-eaten bag of Cheetos from the road trip. She took a water, Cheetos, and an old blanket out back. After hiking just far enough that she was really in the trees but could still see the cabin behind her, she spread the blanket, plopped down, leaning against a tree trunk, and munched on Cheetos, absorbing the infinite calm of being utterly alone.

She thought back over the day and shuddered. So much of it had been humiliating—like doing P.E. in nasty old shoes. But some of it hadn't been as bad as she expected. She sighed with relief. She just wasn't built to be around people. Out here, in the woods, this was where she belonged.

She crumpled the Cheeto bag and stuffed it in her pocket, then stretched out on the blanket, staring up at the branches and bits of grayish sky peeking out between them. Weren't there bears in Washington? She imagined what it would be like to see a bear approaching. To just sit and watch it get closer and closer and...After a few minutes, she closed her eyes and listened to the birds and the breeze rustling the leaves.

When her eyes next opened, it was nearly dark and very cold. Her heart started racing, and she could feel a scream threatening to rise from her core. But then she remembered. It was just the woods in Washington. She scanned the area and saw the faint glimmer of moonlight on the cabin windows.

Inside, she found her mom asleep on the crappy sofa, a thin blanket pulled up to her chest and a soft snore emanating from her open mouth. She hadn't even changed out of her uniform all the way, having collapsed, Emmalee assumed, in her camo pants and brown tee shirt. An open bottle of Crown Royal sat on the coffee table next to an empty glass. Emmalee's heart clenched at the sight that had become really common ever since that night, two years ago.

Nikki's boots were set neatly by the front door, along with her go-bag. She always had to be ready to leave at a moment's notice. For now, though, Emmalee felt good seeing her sleeping there. Colonel Sloane did not get enough sleep.

She crept back into the kitchen and peeked in the refrigerator again. There was now a box of leftover pizza. Emmalee grabbed a slice, as well as a can of soda — also new — and went back to her room where she unearthed all of her homework from her backpack. It was a lot for a first day, but she reminded herself it was only a first day for her, not for the rest of the school. Sighing, she used her phone to Google how to diagram sentences and set to work.

It was after 3:00 am when she finally crawled back into bed and closed her eyes, this time not falling right to sleep. Instead, she tried to shut out the visions of blood and death hanging out there on that lonely forest road. Emmalee screamed, but only on the inside.

The next day dawned bright and early with Colonel Sloane sounding the wake-up call. "Up and at 'em, Troop!" she yelled. Emmalee knew it was her mother's way of making a joke, but she groaned inwardly. She hated being referred to as *troop* or *soldier*.

"I'm coming!" she shouted, hoping her mom would stay out of her room. No such luck. The door banged open.

"What's all this?" Her mother scanned the room then looked at her accusingly.

Emmalee scanned the room as well, taking in the crumpled Cheetos bag, empty water bottle, discarded clothes, books, papers. Crap. "I was doing homework."

"You know you're not supposed to eat in your room, and you're supposed to pack your bag and put your things away before bed."

"I know, I know." She hated her mother's rules. Normal kids could eat chips in their room and leave clothes all over the floor. Not in Nikki's house. Nikki ran her home with the military efficiency and strictness with which she ran her troops. It had long been a source of contention in the family.

"Clean this up, make your bed, and get dressed. You have fifteen minutes." The door shut with a bang, and Emmalee jumped.

Fifteen minutes later, she was showered and dressed, hair still wet, bed made, bag packed, trash cleared, and waiting in the kitchen for her mother to pour her a cup of coffee.

"Sit," her mother ordered.

She sat, dreading what she knew was coming. Nikki set a mug in front of Emmalee, then took a seat across the table.

"I was surprised you weren't in the house when I got home last night." Nikki let the words hang in the air when Emmalee didn't respond right away.

Emmalee caved. "I just went out back for a while and accidentally fell asleep."

Nikki stared at her for a moment. "I know. I did a little recon." She grinned, then turned serious. "But, I'd prefer it if you stayed close to the house. It's not safe to be in the woods alone."

Emmalee rolled her eyes. "There's nothing back there." She thought about the bears and wondered.

"Maybe so. But still. If you want to explore the woods, don't go alone. End of discussion. Now, let's have a little after action report. How'd your first day go?"

"It was fine." She picked up her cup and took a much-too-hot sip, hoping against hope her mother would let it go.

No such luck. "Fine? Elaborate."

"I made it through all of my classes. I met a few people." Please let her stop.

"What kind of people?"

Emmalee sighed. "Just people. You know, students."

"There are a lot of different kinds of people in the world, Em. What kind were these?"

"Seriously, Colonel Sloane, just kids." Nikki shot her a warning look, and Emmalee huffed. "It's been one day. I don't know anyone well enough to psychoanalyze them yet."

"Give me something, kiddo." Nikki's eyes were dark, narrowing in concern.

Emmalee sighed another heavy sigh. "They're okay. Mostly they seem like they have a lot of money. I met a couple of nice kids in my Creative Writing class."

"Hey, that's something. They sound like your type. Do they have names?" Nikki grinned at her, and Emmalee wanted to say something snide, but opted for a half smile instead.

"Mekayla and Marshall, Mom." Do you want their birthdates and social security numbers, too? Emmalee knew better than to voice that though and instead chugged more coffee, letting it burn her tongue.

Unruffled by Emmalee's bad mood, Nikki stood up. "Come on, soldier, let's get a move on. I hope to be home earlier tonight.

Oh, that reminds me. Here's some cash," Nikki handed her a wad of bills. "Pick up some groceries on the way home? It'd be nice to have a home cooked meal for once."

"Okay. What store?"

"No idea. You can do some recon at school, can't you?"

"I guess. What do you want?" Another thing she hated about having a soldier mother. No home cooked meals waiting on her.

"You decide." Nikki glanced at her watch. "I better go, and so had you. On time is late, you know."

"I know." Emmalee silently retorted, *on time is on time,* as she grabbed her things for school. On the way out the front door, she noticed that the Crown Royal bottle and empty glass had disappeared. She thought about saying something, then thought better of it. No sense opening a box when she wasn't sure if she really wanted to know what was inside it.

CHAPTER 5

The second day of school at Ravensville, or the Raven as everyone called it, started better than the first. At least she knew where she was going, and a few kids waved or said hi as she made her way to class.

After first period English, Chase was waiting for her by the door. "Hey, Em. I just wanted to make sure you had a good day yesterday?"

"Yeah, sure. It was fine." Emmalee's face reddened again. God, she hated that about herself.

"Great. I would have asked you this morning, but, as you know, I was a bit late." She just shrugged, not wanting him to know she had very much noticed him waltzing into class five minutes late, Gretchen trailing behind him. He flashed her that award-winning smile and sauntered off, pulling Gretchen in close to him. Emmalee took a deep breath and headed reluctantly toward Señorita Cambridge and her endless excitement about the Spanish language.

By lunchtime, she was exhausted and ready to go home. Pittman had droned on and on about the periodic table, and Wideman was lecturing them on the decline of the American family and the rise of single mothers as the bane of society. Emmalee forced herself to just copy the notes from the slides and keep her face from showing any emotion, but by the time the bell rang, she was too nauseous to eat.

"Hey Emmalee!" Mekayla fell into step beside her. "It's a great day to be a Raven, huh?"

Emmalee grinned at the sarcasm in Mekayla's tone. "Yeah, fantastic."

They parted ways as Mekayla headed into the kitchen to pick up a tray, and Emmalee looked for the back corner table. Her search was interrupted by a hand on her elbow. "Hey there, Emma, right?"

"Ummm, Emmalee." Emmalee looked up to see Britney, the petite blonde from English.

"Emmalee, right! I assume you remember I'm Britney?" The blonde beamed a bright smile at her. "Come sit with us. We were going to invite you yesterday, but they got to you first." She nodded toward the back of the room, where Marshall's head was swiveling, likely scanning for Mekayla, and maybe even Emmalee. Britney grimaced. Part of Emmalee wanted to say no and just head toward Marshall, but another part of her was really overwhelmed by the idea that the popular kids wanted her to eat with them.

"Come on!" Britney put her hand on Emmalee's elbow and steered her to a table in the middle of the cafeteria where Chase, Gretchen, and Britney's boyfriend were sitting.

"Hey, everyone! Say hi to, ummm, Emmalee, right?" Britney looked at Emmalee, confirming.

Emmalee nodded. "That's me." She gave a little wave.

Everyone at the table stopped talking and looked up, silent for a moment.

"Hi, Em." Chase broke the silence.

"Hey," Gretchen said with a frown.

"Hi there," said Britney's boyfriend, the perv. "Bryce." He

extended his hand, and when Emmalee took it, he gave it a little squeeze. "Sorry we haven't done a better job welcoming you. We've just had a little drama unfolding."

Britney, who'd sat next to Bryce, put her hand on his thigh and squeezed. "Shut up, Bryce. Emmalee doesn't want to hear about that."

Oh, Emmalee thought it might actually be interesting to hear what kind of drama could plague such perfect specimens of human beings.

"No, go ahead, don't mind me." She offered up a smile again, but noticed Britney didn't return it. Interesting. She sat down by Britney, leaving two empty spaces to her left.

"We were just talking about a benefit coming up for our dear friend Audrey." Bryce smirked in Britney's direction. "Right, Brit?"

Britney glared at him. "Right. Oh, hey, you two!" Britney waved at an approaching couple who took the empty spots next to Emmalee. The guy looked at Emmalee and then raised a questioning eyebrow at Britney.

"Tyler, Kristina, this is Emmalee, our new friend." Britney emphasized the word friend, giving Emmalee a moment of pause, but she was quickly distracted by Tyler's extended hand.

"Welcome, Emmalee. It's lovely to have another beautiful woman in our midst."

Kristina elbowed him in the side. "Give it a rest, Ty. Sorry, Emmalee." Kristina flipped her long, jet black hair over her shoulder and flashed Emmalee a perfectly white smile, framed by perfectly lined and stained lips.

Emmalee smiled back. Was this real? She felt so out of her depth in the middle of these beautiful beings. She couldn't imagine putting so much energy into her appearance, but she had to admit, they looked good.

"No lunch?" Britney asked as she crunched into a celery stick.

"Not hungry."

"I wish I had that problem." Britney sighed.

She didn't know what to say. Britney was obviously thin, thinner than Emmalee, so she just sat quietly, listening to them chat about classes, gossip about other students, and was really just letting it wash over her, when she felt her arm being shaken.

"Em?" Kristina's brows furrowed together. "You ok?"

"Yes. Sorry. I was just thinking."

"Hopefully about whether you're coming?" Britney closed up a bag of half-eaten carrots

"What?" Emmalee must have really zoned out.

Kristina laughed, looking at her friends each in turn. "We just invited you to the party Friday. At Gretchen's house?" They all stared at her, expectant.

"I'm not sure. My mom–"

"You have to come!" Britney insisted. "It'll be so much fun! Gretchen's parents are in Paris this weekend. We'll have the place to ourselves."

Emmalee hadn't been to a party since elementary school. She thought about the last party she'd wanted to attend–that night two years ago–and swallowed a lump in her throat.

"I don't know if I can." It was a lie. Colonel Sloane would allow her to go to a party. In fact, she'd love it if Emmalee started showing interest in a social life.

"Well, you better try." Chase's blue eyes stared at her intently across the table. "We'll miss you if you don't."

Both Britney and Gretchen snapped their eyes toward Chase, looking irritated. Emmalee blushed. The bell rang just then, saving her from any more embarrassment, and she made a quick escape.

She was met with silence when she entered the Creative Writing classroom. Everyone had their heads bent over their notebooks. Mrs. Murray was doing something on her computer. Emmalee took her seat and stared at the screen: "Write about your main character's biggest fear."

She thought about Calvin/Chase, and wrote, imagining him getting to know New Girl/Emmalee. Realizing he was falling for her. Worrying his friend group wouldn't approve. When they finished writing, she declined to share, again, and listened in awe as Mekayla and Marshall shared stunning, weighty backstories for their characters. They were serious writers, and Emmalee felt bad about ditching them at lunch. Not that she'd promised to eat lunch with them every day or anything. It just seemed a little rude to abandon them on day two.

"Sorry about lunch. Britney asked me to sit at her table before I got back to your table," she said as they waited for Mrs. Murray to hand out some papers.

Mekayla looked a little confused. "It's no big deal. Not like we own you or anything."

Emmalee felt relieved, enjoying idle conversation with Marshall and Mekayla until Mrs. Murray set the timer and they all worked on their stories until the bell rang.

"Have a great day, you guys, and don't forget, open mic at the Blue Note Friday at 7:00. I hope to see you all there."

"What's the Blue Note?" Emmalee asked as she walked into the hallway with Mekayla.

"A café downtown. Normally on Friday nights, they have jazz and blues bands from Seattle in to play, but once a month, they let us locals read our writing or play our songs. We're not winning any awards, but we support each other. It's fun. You should come along."

"Oh, I could never do an open mic night." Emmalee could feel her heart starting to hammer in her chest, suddenly feeling a bone-deep cold settle over her.

Mekayla reached out and squeezed Emmalee's arm. "No worries! You don't have to read. But you could be a friendly face for Marshall and me. Plus, it's fun to listen to all the other performers. There are some really amazing writers and musicians around here."

Emmalee could feel herself relaxing. She could handle coffee and just listening and supporting. "I'm not sure my mom will let me, but I will if I can." Of course her mom would let her. She just needed some time to decide if she was up for going out in public and socializing.

Mekayla smiled and headed off to her next class. Emmalee thought she'd be much more likely to be "allowed" to go to the open mic night than a party. She smiled to herself, shocked that it was only day two, and she already had multiple invites for Friday night. Maybe Ravensville wouldn't be so bad.

She recognized that warm feeling of hope, and it was immediately followed by cold, even though it was seventy-five degrees outside and the school's AC wasn't on. Shivering, she shoved the excitement out of the way and hurried to her next class.

CHAPTER 6

When she pulled into the driveway Friday afternoon, she wasn't too bothered by the fact that her mother's car wasn't there. After all, it was only 4:30. As she juggled her backpack, keys, and two bags of groceries, though, she realized her mother's go-bag was no longer in the entryway either. Her heart sank.

She set the groceries in the kitchen and found a note on the countertop:

> Had to deploy. Don't know how long. Cash and credit card are in my sock drawer. Keep the doors locked and stay out of the woods. Call Uncle Dan if you need anything. Love you, soldier.

Emmalee wanted to cry. Instead, she put the groceries away and tried not to think about what might happen to her mom in God-knows-where she was off to this time. She was glad they didn't have their TV hooked up yet, or she'd be tempted to scroll news channels all night looking to see where in the world there was conflict, not sleeping because she was imagining the worst.

Sighing, she took her notebook out back and sat on a grungy deck chair, a begrudging nod to Nikki's orders not to go out in the woods alone. She was completely engrossed in writing her Creative Writing story when her phone pinged. A text from Uncle Dan.

> **UNCLE DAN**
>
> Hey, Emma Bee. Your mom told me she had to deploy for a while. I'm in LA this week, so let me know if you need anything. I can catch a flight any time. And check in at least once a day so I don't have to call in a search party for you 😉

Emmalee smiled. She didn't mind the pet name from Uncle Dan. Her mom's younger brother, Dan was everything her mother wasn't. Maybe not everything. When he wasn't at his very cool loft apartment in New York, he was traveling the world as a photojournalist, so he definitely had her mom's sense of wanderlust. But, he was also fun and believed in breaking rules – sometimes – and enjoying life. He cared about her. But he also knew you didn't have to make your bed with perfect corners or iron your clothes to be a good person.

She was so glad she was a senior and eighteen. Last year, she'd had to stay with a neighbor every time her mom had deployed. When they moved, she'd begged to be allowed to stay by herself. She'd enlisted Uncle Dan's help, and he had offered to check in on her by phone.

Emmalee was thrilled when Nikki agreed. She had made Emmalee promise, however, to respond to Dan's texts immediately, answer the phone every time he called, and stick to certain rules, like only spending the cash on school and food, using the credit card for emergencies only, and having absolutely no parties. She smiled and tapped out a reply.

> Got it, Uncle Dan 🙂

She was just getting back into the story when her phone pinged again. She wondered what he wanted already. It wasn't like Dan to invade her space too much.

MEKAYLA
You coming tonight?

> ???

Open mic?

Ah, right. She'd forgotten about that when she'd gotten home and found her mom gone.

> Sorry not feeling up to it tonight

Come on! Don't make me go alone!

> You won't be alone.

Marshall doesn't count! jk but seriously.

> Murray will be there?

Murray's a teacher!

> Fair point.

So you're coming? 🩶

Emmalee thought about it. Her mom was gone. No one was here to wait around for, and no amount of pouting would make her feel any better. She was a little low on cash, but since Mrs. Murray was going, technically it was a school thing – kind of.

> Sure. See you at 7

Yayyyyyyyy!!!

Wait what do I wear?

Whatever you want.

She looked at her watch. She had an hour. She heated a can of Spaghettios, glad she'd grabbed some extra food at the store. After she ate, she ran a brush through her hair, swished some mouthwash, and took a deep breath. This was her first non-family outing since her failed attempt that night two years ago. She shuddered, then shut the light off and left.

Parking in downtown Ravensville, she was shocked at how full the streets were. Apparently downtown was the place to be on a Friday night. She scanned the storefronts, her eyes landing on a large blue music note. That had to be the place.

Inside was an eclectic crowd. A group of older women sat at the bar, sipping white wine and chatting animatedly. Some college student types filled several tables near the stage, nursing bottles of IPA and sporting UW shirts. Okay. Not just a café then.

Emmalee searched the room again, worried for a minute that it was all a joke and Mekayla and Marshall had stood her up, payback for ditching them at lunch today. Then her eyes landed on Marshall's shock of curly red hair bent over a notebook in which he was writing furiously. Just as she approached, she felt hands grab her shoulders from behind and jumped.

"Gahhhh! You made it!" Mekayla squealed. "I was so afraid I'd be alone."

"Thanks a lot, Mekayla." Marshall looked mock-offended and then nodded at Emmalee. "Glad you could make it."

"Is Mrs. Murray here?" Emmalee took a seat, careful to leave her notebook in her bag, which she slipped to the floor between her feet.

"Nah. Her kid had something else tonight, I guess. She emailed a few minutes ago."

"Oh. Just us then?"

Mekayla nodded. "Just us. Cozy." She smiled at Emmalee and then Marshall. "Three peas in a pod."

"I thought you said this was a café?" Emmalee asked, gesturing toward the bar.

Mekayla shrugged. "They serve coffee, too."

"But, aren't we too young for a bar?" Emmalee had a little alarm bell in her brain telling her she should leave.

"Nah. Everyone's welcome here." Mekayla pointed to a table near the door where a couple about their age was deep in conversation. "Anyway, they should be starting any minute."

"A waitress will be by soon if you want to order something." He nodded toward his glass of what looked to be soda. "Nothing harder than Coke or coffee for us youngsters, I'm afraid. This town's too small for a fake ID to work. Everyone in here knows everyone's mom or dad or grandma or teacher." Marshall shrugged.

"Ah, okay. So, I shouldn't ask for a Jack and Coke, then?" Emmalee joked, then cringed, thinking about her mom's open bottle of Crown hiding somewhere in the cabin.

"Definitely not. Unless you want to do it for our benefit, give us something to write about in the school paper?" Marshall laughed, but Mekayla shot him a look.

"Nah. I'll pass." Emmalee laughed.

Just then, the lights went down, and a thin man of about thirty took the stage, wearing a wrinkled button-up shirt over baggy khaki pants and a beat-up pair of Doc Martens. He welcomed everyone and asked for the first volunteer. Emmalee watched Marshall and Mekayla exchange glances, both nervously smiling.

Fortunately, a twenty-something woman took to the stage in a long, flowing dress and strappy sandals, and read to them a spoken word poem about her menstrual cycle and the power of the sacred feminine. Emmalee kind of wanted to laugh, but it was actually kind of good. This place felt nice, like somewhere she could fit in.

Two singer-songwriters later, there was a brief intermission, during which Mekayla and Marshall ran for the bathrooms. Emmalee pulled her phone out, hoping her mother might have texted. Funny how she always wanted Nikki to leave her alone. Until she did. There was nothing from her mother, but there was a text from an unknown number, a different one this time.

UNKNOWN

Where are you?

Her heart jumped. She'd only given her number to Mekayla so far.

She sent back a single question mark, her tried-and-true method of getting more information before revealing too much.

I think the question speaks for itself. Where are you?

Who is this?

Your destiny.

Emmalee's heart sped up even more.

????

How can you have a date with destiny if you won't let him know where to pick you up?

She could feel adrenaline coursing through her veins. She couldn't help but think this was Chase. But, maybe Mekayla had given her number to Marshall and they were messing with her. She raised her eyes and looked around. Her two classmates were standing across the room, talking to a couple older kids. It definitely wasn't them.

Well? I'm waiting.

She wasn't entirely sure what to feel, but she had to admit, it was a little exciting being pursued, even if it was by a possible stranger.

Busy. And I don't give my location to strangers.

I see.

There was nothing else. She waited, hoping the three dots would show up, but after a couple of minutes, she gave up, annoyed with herself for feeling disappointed. Mekayla and Marshall had come back to the table by then anyway, so she tucked her phone in her pocket and smiled at them, trying to jump back into their casual conversation.

After two more readers shared spoken word poems, Mekayla worked up the courage to read. Tonight she wore a black leather miniskirt over hot pink tights and white tennis shoes. Emmalee couldn't quite make sense of what style Mekayla was going for exactly, but it was her own. Emmalee envied that. There was something beautiful about her up there, reading a story about a child-eating woman in some bizarre modern take on Hansel and Gretel and loving every second of it. Marshall and Emmalee snapped loudly when Mekayla finished reading and bounced down off the stage.

"Your turn!" Mekayla leaned down and squeezed Marshall's shoulders.

"Oh, I don't know." Marshall's face turned red.

"Get up there! That's the deal. If I do, you do!"

Marshall groaned but got up and walked slowly to the stage. His hands were shaking as he adjusted the microphone, but then he closed his eyes, took a deep breath, and a stillness settled over him. He became someone else as he opened his mouth and recited a beautiful poem to them. His reading was hypnotic, rhythmic, the words beautiful, his voice tender but strong. She loved the line he kept repeating, "Reverberations in the rain, my image of you slain."

She could feel that, transported back to that night on the highway, the way the rain fell, distorting her view from the ice cold ground on the side of the road, the view of her father's blood, thick red rivers of it running into muddy pools just inches from her. Her eyes were glistening by the time Marshall retook his seat.

"That was great, Marshall," she croaked out, her throat throbbing with a sob she refused to let out. "You two are great. Wow." Emmalee was shocked at how the honest feelings just came pouring out of her.

Marshall blushed, and Mekayla smiled. "Your turn?"

"Me? No. I can't. I didn't bring anything." Emmalee could feel heat rush to her face.

"Bullshit. I'll bet it's in your bag." Mekayla was grinning, but there was a hint of disappointment in her eyes. "But I suppose you can sit it out this time. Seeing as it's your first time here." She stuck her tongue out at Emmalee, then took a long drink of her Diet Coke.

Emmalee felt relief flood through her body. There was no way she could stand up there and share her writing, herself, like that. She shivered, wrapping her arms around herself, and tried to focus on the next reader.

CHAPTER 7

"You broke my heart, Em!" Chase clutched his chest and gave her puppy eyes as she took her seat in English.

"What?" She could feel her face heating as all eyes turned to her and Chase.

"You ghosted me when I texted you last night. I'm hurt." Chase's eyes twinkled, but Gretchen and Britney were scowling.

It was him! "Oh, that was you."

"Obviously. Who else could possibly be your destiny?" He ran his index finger along his jawline and grinned suggestively at her.

"Chase!" Gretchen snapped. "Don't mock her."

Emmalee wanted to disappear inside her book bag, but instead, she took her time pulling out her notebook and pencil and turning individual pages until she got to a clean sheet.

"I think what Chase is trying to say, Em, is that you blew us off last night," Britney huffed.

She looked up. "I'm sorry. My mom wouldn't let me go." Emmalee almost felt bad about how easy it was to lie.

"But she let you go to The Blue Note?" Britney's eyebrows arched.

How did Britney know about that? Weird.

"Well, yeah. It's in public."

"Right. Okay. Well, I really hope you'll come next Friday. Gretchen's parents are out of town again. Give me your mom's number later, and I'll have my mom call her and assure her we're trustworthy," Britney grinned.

The bell rang, saving her from having to hand over her mom's number or attempt to make up another lie. Fortunately, the rest of the day went smoothly, and Mekayla even invited her to attend the school newspaper's staff meeting. Even though she had to meet new people, Emmalee was excited to have something new to do after school.

She found the newsroom in what used to be the computer lab before everyone had their own laptop. Several students were scattered around the room in rolling chairs, staring at their phones. At the podium, Wideman looked up and stared at her for a moment over his glasses.

"You lost?"

"No," Emmalee stammered. "Mekayla and Marshall invited me to see if working on the newspaper is something I'd be interested in."

"You will be," Mekayla responded as she bounced in the door with Marshall. "The meeting can start now."

Mekayla sat in a chair behind the instructor desk and pulled out a reporter's notebook.

"I have a new story idea." She raised her eyebrows and grinned.

"Mekayla here plans to get the paper shut down," Marshall said with a bit of acid in his voice, which was new for him, in Emmalee's experience anyway.

All eyes lifted from phones to stare at Mekayla. Wideman groaned. "Mekayla, let's not do this again."

"I'm not doing anything but suggesting that if we're going to run a newspaper, it should be actual news, more than just fluff pieces to make the school look good!" Mekayla's face was starting to turn red.

Emmalee looked to Wideman, who had taken his glasses off and was pinching the bridge of his nose.

"As you can see, Emmalee, we have a very passionate news crew. Go ahead, have a seat."

Emmalee grabbed a chair near Marshall.

"Here's the thing," Mekayla started again. "And Marshall, do not interrupt me." She held her hand up as a warning, and Marshall's mouth snapped shut. "Anyway, I want to do some investigative journalism."

Wideman groaned. "Mekayla, let's not have a repeat of last year's cafeteria exposé, please."

"Hang on, we need to catch Emmalee up." Mekayla turned back to Emmalee. "There's a student who had an accident a few weeks ago. She's in a coma and will likely never gain consciousness again."

"That's horrible!" Emmalee felt an immediate sense of sorrow for this person she'd never even met. She may not know them, but she could feel like it was yesterday the pain, confusion, and horror of her own accident. The accident she'd caused.

She looked around the room, but no one was looking back or making a sound.

"It is horrible," Mekayla resumed. "I mean, Audrey wasn't exactly my friend. To be honest, we barely tolerated each other. But that doesn't mean I wanted her–"

"Wait a minute," Emmalee broke in. "Audrey? As in Britney's friend?"

Mekayla's eyes narrowed. "You know her?"

Emmalee shook her head, questions forming. "No. Bryce mentioned her at lunch the other day."

"Really?" Mekayla sat up straighter, eyes large. "What did he say?"

"Not much. Something about a benefit, but then Britney cut him off."

Mekayla bit her lip and squinted her eyes. "Of course she did."

"Mekayla, try to keep your bias out of it," Wideman warned.

"I'm not biased. I just know something's not right, and I'm pretty sure Britney has something to do with it. I have my reasons."

"What do you mean?" Emmalee was intrigued. Sometimes there was a look in Britney's eyes that seemed not quite so nice, but so far she really had been nice to Emmalee. She couldn't really see Britney hurting someone.

"I want to investigate," Mekayla replied. "Find out what really happened, but I can't just go up and ask Britney if she put her friend in a coma."

"Agreed. You should drop this, now," a girl with short brown hair offered. "You don't want to be on Britney's bad side."

Bad side? She was definitely outspoken and outgoing, even assertive, but Emmalee had a hard time seeing her as dangerous. She was just a teenager.

"I'm not going to drop it, Becks. And I'm not going to investigate it." Mekayla turned a huge, cheesy grin toward Emmalee.

"Me?" Emmalee's voice squeaked.

"Yes, you. You're the perfect person." Mekayla's smile got even bigger. Emmalee could see her excitement.

"Hang on," Wideman interrupted. "I've let you explain your idea, Mekayla, but there's no way we're going to actually run an investigation like this. Let alone publish it in the school paper."

"But–" Mekayla's eyes flashed.

"No buts." Wideman's voice was firm. "It's a school paper. We can and will be censored by the administration."

Mekayla sighed. "Then what's the point if we're not even reporting real news?"

"We can have real news. We just can't be accusing students of attempted murder. It's a fine line." Wideman attempted a half-hearted smile, but Mekayla's jaw was tense.

"Right. Well, let's talk about what we can write." Mekayla sat back in her chair, arms folded across her chest, with a suddenly placid smile.

"Uh oh. She's got that look." Marshall shook his head again.

"No secret plans, Mekayla," Wideman warned.

"You want me to do what, exactly?" Emmalee wasn't sure she'd heard Mekayla right. They were sitting at a small table in the back of Café Vibes, a coffee shop Mekayla had insisted the three of them head to after the staff meeting.

Mekayla looked at Emmalee with wide, innocent eyes. "I want you to infiltrate Britney's crowd and find out what happened to Audrey. Simple." She smiled. "And this shouldn't be news. I already mentioned it in the meeting." Mekayla shrugged and her skeleton earrings tinkled.

Emmalee was speechless. She picked up her latte and took a long sip. "The meeting where Wideman said absolutely not."

"Mekayla, Wideman will kill you," Marshall implored. "I might even kill you."

"Right." Mekayla cut Marshall an *as if* look. "The only thing you're killing is zombies on Minecraft."

Marshall nodded and shrugged his shoulders. "True, but still. This isn't like when you tried to uncover the truth about what was in the noodle bowls the cafeteria served last year. This is legit crazy."

"Marshall, Audrey is in a coma!"

"Quiet!" Marshall's head swiveled as he scanned the room. "Do you want the whole world in on your insane scheme?"

"Okay, okay." Mekayla leaned in toward the center of the table and whispered, "We might not be able to investigate for the school paper, but if we find enough information, we can break it to the local news."

Emmalee stared at Mekayla, eyes huge. "Why are you so insistent on investigating this? We're only high school kids."

"Something just isn't right about the whole thing." Mekayla leaned forward, whispering. "There were all those rumors about Audrey being assaulted, and then suddenly, she just falls down the stairs at a party and ends up in a coma? And the only people at this party are Britney and her crew? I just think there has to be more to it."

"Audrey was assaulted?" Emmalee couldn't believe this. The poor girl had been through so much.

"That's the rumor. She and Gretchen were really close, and Marshall here overheard them talking about something that happened the weekend before. Something bad." Mekayla paused and gestured for Marshall to continue.

Marshall took a deep breath. "They were saying that Audrey needed to report it to the police."

"Then, we started hearing rumors around the school about Audrey cheating on Chase."

"But Gretchen is Chase's girlfriend!" Emmalee practically shouted.

"Shhh!" Marshall had his finger to his lips, head swiveling again.

"She is now. She wasn't then." Mekayla raised her eyebrows in a knowing look.

"So, wait, this is all confusing." Emmalee didn't even know how to start sorting it out in her head.

"Yes, it is. That's probably why the police just accepted the whole accident story last year. Well, that and the fact that Britney's dad is the Governor." Mekayla rolled her eyes.

"Like, of the state?" Emmalee couldn't believe what she was hearing.

Mekayla scrunched up her face. "Yes, of the state. What else?"

"Look, I don't really see how I fit into this exactly. Why don't you investigate? You know all of these people better." Emmalee was at a loss.

"First, there's no way they'd let me near them. Britney and I have been mortal enemies ever since she blamed me for letting the pet turtle loose in 1st grade. But you. They invited you to sit with them at lunch the other day, right?"

"Well, yes. But–"

"What did they want?" Mekayla interrupted, leaning forward with interest.

"They invited me to a party."

Mekayla squealed. "What! They invited you to one of their parties?"

"Yes." Emmalee didn't understand what the big deal was. "So?"

"So? Are you kidding me? They never invite anyone into their little clique. This is perfect. Did you go?"

"No. I went to the open mic night with you two." Emmalee felt worry tug at her, worry about potentially going to a party with Britney and her friends. She'd sworn off parties.

Mekayla looked deep in thought for a minute, tracing her finger around the rim of her mug.

"Okay. Here's what we do. Well, what you do. Apologize for not going to the party, and then ask for a rain check."

"I don't have to apologize. They already invited me to another party next Friday." A chill went through her at the thought of actually going. "But I'm definitely not going."

"Emmalee, a girl is in a coma. Don't you think her family deserves to know what happened to her? Her life has been altered forever. It's basically over." Mekayla stared at Emmalee with a fierceness she couldn't ignore.

She flashed back to two years ago again, when she realized she'd made a very, very big mistake. Realized she could never take it back. It was thinking of only herself that landed her there in the first place.

"Okay. I'll help."

CHAPTER 8

Emmalee took a deep breath and approached Britney at her locker. She'd been lurking at her own locker, waiting for Kristina to leave.

"Britney?" She hated that her voice sounded so timid and whispery. She cleared her throat and forced herself to speak louder. "Do you have a sec?"

Britney turned and stared at Emmalee for a moment, her eyes traveling up and down Emmalee's body. "I'm on my way to practice. What do you need?"

Emmalee took another deep breath. "I just wanted to apologize."

"For?" Britney turned to the mirror in her locker and ran a brush through her blonde bob.

"For not making it to the party last week. I should have been more clear about not being able to go." Emmalee really wanted to tell her she just didn't like parties. But that wouldn't be entirely true, would it? Part of her really wanted to be part of the popular crowd.

"Right. Well, things happen. No need to apologize." Britney

pulled a duffel bag out of her locker and swung it over her shoulder.

"If the offer still stands, I'd love to go this Friday." Emmalee swallowed down the lump of fear she felt and tried to smile.

"Oh?" Britney's face lit up, and Emmalee felt a stab of something. Excitement? Fear? Maybe both.

"Yeah." She choked out the word.

"Cool. Well, we actually moved it up to Thursday night because her parents are coming back early."

"But, we have school tomorrow?" Emmalee frowned.

"Yeah, so? Fridays are chill." Britney looked confused. "Anyway, you can meet us at Gretchen's house early so we can get ready together. I'll text you the address."

"Awesome!" Britney's eyes shone brightly, which gave Emmalee a moment of pause. Britney really wanted to be Emmalee's friend. She felt a little bad that she was only going to snoop. Well, mostly to snoop.

As soon as the last bell rang on Thursday, Emmalee passed a couple of hours at home, doing homework and laundry and straightening up her room. Finally, it was time to head to the address Britney had sent her. She drove ten or fifteen miles outside of town, through the woods, continually questioning her own decision-making power. What was she doing here? She was nervous about letting Mekayla and Marshall down if she couldn't get any information on Audrey. And she was even more nervous about Britney and her friends finding out that she was snooping. To be completely honest, though, part of her was a little thrilled at the thought of danger, too.

When she stopped her car in front of an enormous house at the end of a long, winding driveway, Emmalee gawked in disbelief.

The door opened moments after she rang the bell. Gretchen stared at her, waiting for her to say something.

"Wow," Emmalee finally croaked out. "You have an incredible house."

Gretchen just stared at Emmalee for a second. "Oh, yeah. It's a bit much, I know, but it's home." She flashed a smile.

They entered the house through the enormous double doors that opened into a massive foyer, all white and shining marble and glass. Two staircases snaked their way up either side to a second floor with a balcony overlooking the tiled entry.

"This is beautiful," Emmalee whispered.

"Thanks, hon." Gretchen smiled at her as she might at a toddler, and Emmalee felt herself bristle but forced herself to smile back. Maybe that was just Gretchen's personality.

"Here, come with me. We'll go find you something to wear." Gretchen's eyes were taking in Emmalee's attire with barely hidden disgust.

"I'm fine, really."

"Really, it's no trouble." She smiled and dragged Emmalee upstairs to an expansive bedroom with an ensuite bathroom. Emmalee took in the lush cream and blush fabrics, the ornate canopy bed, and the thick carpeting, and worked really hard not to drool. Their family home in Virginia had been beautiful, big even, but not this massive or this opulent.

"Your room is gorgeous." She thought about her tiny room with faded curtains and used furniture.

"It does the job," Gretchen retorted.

Oh please, Emmalee thought. It does a whole lot more than that. Out loud, she just murmured, "Mmhmm."

"Kris, Brit, can you get Em here ready for the party?"

"Uh, yeah. I'm sure we can find you something." Britney grinned at Emmalee.

"Okay, I'll leave you to it. I'm going to set up the refreshments. Speaking of which, I restocked the mini fridge." Gretchen swept out of the room, Emmalee watching her leave.

It was a little overwhelming. These kids all seemed so grown up and sophisticated. Gretchen breezed through the house like she owned it, like she hosted parties and served refreshments instead of drinks and snacks. Emmalee's idea of a party was a cake and little pointy cardboard hats with rubber band straps to hold them on.

"I think she's an 8." Emmalee realized the other girls were talking about her.

"No, definitely a 10."

"No way." Kristina flounced her way to Gretchen's closet, a pale ivory robe billowing behind her. "Absolute 8, so a 6 could work, but there's no way Gretchen has anything over a size 2. I'll check Miranda's closet."

When she left, Britney sat at the vanity and stared into the mirror, touching up her eye makeup.

"Who's Miranda?" Emmalee thought maybe Gretchen had a sister.

"Gretchen's housekeeper." Britney smirked at Emmalee through the mirror. "No worries, though. She has some cute stuff that Gretchen's parents bought for her."

Emmalee felt the sting of the comment, but offered up a meager smile. While she waited, she began walking the perimeter of the room, passing over the expensive-looking decor for a bulletin board with photos tacked to it. There were pictures of Gretchen with Kristina and Britney and some other girl, all in bikinis, posing on what looked to be a California beach.

Others showed Gretchen and Chase in formal wear, clearly headed to some kind of dance. They both looked like grownups attending a fundraiser instead of two kids heading to a school dance. In them all, Gretchen was smiling. Joy glowed from her eyes when she was surrounded by her friends, by Chase.

Those pictures were much different from the ones of her on a stage in what appeared to be pageant photos. In these, she smiled, but the smile didn't reach her eyes. It looked forced. In one of the photos, Britney and that same unknown girl flanked

Gretchen, who was being crowned. Britney was obviously a runner-up. Interesting.

Emmalee pointed to the mystery girl. "Who's this?"

Britney crossed the room and stood behind Emmalee, peering over her shoulder. "That is Audrey. Poor, sweet Audrey." Britney's voice was dripping with sarcasm.

Emmalee played dumb. "Poor?"

Britney sighed. "Yes, poor. She had a terrible accident at the end of the summer. She's been in a coma ever since."

"Oh my God! What happened?" Emmalee was surprised at how easily she feigned ignorance.

"Day officially saved." Kristina breezed back into the room, carrying three hangers holding various shades of silky fabrics. Very little silky fabric, Emmalee noticed. Her heart started beating faster.

"I'm fine, really," she stammered. "You don't need to go to all this trouble."

"Whatever. You can't wear that tonight." Britney gestured, encompassing all of Emmalee's body in one fell swoop of her pointed finger.

"Yeah, the 90s grunge vibe is not it." Kristina shook her head. "Here, try on this red one first. It'll look good with your dark hair." She held out a hanger with a very short red dress slinking from it.

"Oh, no, that's definitely not my style."

"Come on. It'll be fun, like a makeover." Britney grinned at her, taking the dress from Kristina.

Emmalee felt anger rising in her cheeks. "I don't need a makeover. I'm happy with my style."

"Oh, we're just kidding. Your style is great, very you. It's just that we usually dress up for these parties, and we thought you'd want to join us." Britney shrugged, laying the dress on the bed.

"Em, come on. Just try it on. Trust us." Kristina grabbed

Emmalee's arm and the dress off the bed and escorted her authoritatively to the bathroom.

Inside, Emmalee shut the door and locked it, hearing the other girls whispering quietly outside the door. She looked in the mirror, mortified at the red blotches on her cheeks and the tangles in her air-dried hair. Normally, she didn't care. But nothing about this place, or this night, was normal.

She slid off her boots, then her pants and shirt, replacing them with the red dress that clung to her way too much. She preferred to be swallowed up by her clothes. They were like an extra layer of protection between her and the world. This was definitely not that.

"Come out and let us see," Kristina called.

"Just a second." Emmalee's heart raced.

"We don't have a lot of time. Let us see!" Britney yelled this time.

Emmalee's hand trembled as she opened the door. The girls looked at her, both of their jaws dropping in unison. Emmalee was trying to decide if this was good or bad when the girls turned to each other and broke into huge grins.

"Stunning. That definitely works for you," Kristina said, her shiny black hair falling over her shoulder as she nodded. "Right, Brit?"

"Yeah. It's perfect." Emmalee sensed something in Britney's tone, but she couldn't quite tell what. It felt calculating, like maybe she was thinking of something else. Before she could think more on it, Kristina's hands were on her again, this time turning her toward a full-size mirror next to the closet.

"Look at you, Slut." Kristina laughed. Emmalee must have frowned because Kristina immediately followed it up with, "I mean that as a compliment."

Emmalee focused on her reflection in the mirror and was shocked. The dress outlined curves she'd never really paid attention to before, curves she'd always kept covered up. They were all front and center, the neckline of the dress dipping to reveal cleavage she normally kept covered, cinching at the waist just to snake down over her hips. It stopped just above mid thigh, leaving her legs almost entirely exposed. Thank God she'd shaved recently.

"I would ditch the socks if I were you." Kristina smirked and handed her a pair of strappy silver-heeled sandals. Put these on in a minute. First, we have to do something with your hair.

Emmalee felt like a mannequin. Britney joined Kristina in maneuvering her to the seat at a silver vanity with a large mirror framed in Hollywood-style bulbs.

Kristina ran her fingers through Emmalee's hair. "Don't you ever brush this mane?"

"Yeah, of course—"

"Just kidding. Lighten up, Em. Your hair is gorgeous, in a wild, natural kind of way." Kristina started squirting gels and sprays into her hands and rubbing them into Emmalee's long strands of hair, then tugging a comb through it, taming and curling individual sections with a styling iron.

Emmalee watched in fascination. She'd never had the patience or interest to worry about how to style hair. She just washed it and let it dry, occasionally pulling it out of her face with an elastic. She couldn't believe the transformation happening before her eyes.

Then Britney blocked her view, hopping up on the vanity, perched in position to work on Emmalee's make-up while Kristina finished tending to the hair.

"A little makeup will polish you up nicely."

Emmalee must have looked offended because Britney added quickly, "No offense."

"I don't usually wear make-up."

"I know, Babe." Emmalee just let the other girls take over, opening her eyes, puckering her lips, turning her head this way and that, whatever they told her to do.

Finally, they pronounced her ready, stationing her in front of the full-length mirror again, shoes on this time. Emmalee was stunned. Her feet hurt, and she wasn't even sure she could ever do this herself, but she had to give them credit. She looked ten years older, and almost beautiful, a word she'd never imagined using about herself.

"Wow."

"Yeah. Wow." Kristina smiled over Emmalee's shoulder, proudly taking in the results of her work in the mirror.

"It'll do." Britney grinned. "Let's go, Bitches."

Emmalee took a deep breath and followed them out the door, both excited and nervous about what the night would bring.

"Damn, Em! You are smokin' hot!" Bryce hooted when Emmalee reached the bottom of the stairs, his eyes blatantly roving over her body. "Who knew you had all that under those homeless clothes you wear?"

"Bryce! Shut up! Ignore him, Em, he's still in his pre-pubescent phase."

"I most certainly have pubes, Krissy, wanna see?"

"Ugh. You're a pig." Kristina rolled her eyes.

"I may be, but I've heard how much you love your pork." Bryce snorted and made an obscene gesture with his pelvis, apparently very proud of that insult, but Tyler just punched him in the shoulder.

"She's right. You're disgusting, Bryce. Go get us some more beers, why don't you?" Tyler rolled his eyes at Emmalee as Bryce exited. "Sorry. We're not all like that."

"No problem," Emmalee murmured. It was actually really weird. She was used to being in school hallways and cafeterias with teenagers cussing and making lewd gestures. She just wasn't used to being around them in a party. At one of their homes. With no adults around. She couldn't believe this was her life. Tonight at least.

"Oh, quit being such a prude, Tyler. At least Bryce knows

how to have fun." Britney looked at Emmalee pointedly. "From what I hear, Tyler's lacking in the pork department." She snickered when Kristina's jaw dropped.

"Fuck off, Brit." Kristina was smiling, though. "You're just jealous you're stuck with Bryce while I have a real man."

"Ah, that's what we're calling him, now?"

"Okay, okay ladies. Let's do less talking and have more fun. When's everyone getting here?" Tyler put his arms around Britney and Kristina's shoulders, looking back and forth at them.

"Everyone?" Emmalee was struck dumb listening to all of them eviscerate each other for sport. She couldn't imagine more of them.

"Everyone coming to the party." Britney looked at her like she was a moron.

"Ah." Emmalee clamped her mouth shut. Note to self: shut up.

"Bryce is right about one thing, though, Em. You do look great." Tyler kept his eyes on her face, and she blushed and smiled in return.

"Thanks." ·

"Thanks for what?" Chase walked into the room and stopped dead in his tracks.

"Wow. You look–" He ran his hand over his stomach, nervously smoothing his black quarter zip sweater. Gretchen walked up behind him and slid her arm around his waist, reaching her other one up to fix a stray hair that had fallen into his face.

"She does look great, doesn't she?" Gretchen sounded a little too chipper.

"Ummm, thanks." Emmalee had never felt so out of place.

Bryce entered with two beers, handing one to Tyler. "Here you go, man."

"Thanks." Tyler took a long pull from the bottle. "I think I heard car doors."

"And the night begins." Gretchen headed for the door.

"Emmalee, let's go get you a drink." Chase held his arm out to her. She took it and followed him toward the back of the house into a huge kitchen designed for entertaining. Everything was granite and steel and gleaming. A massive curved island was covered in bottles of beer, wine, and harder options. She recognized her mom's whiskey of choice.

"What'll it be?" Chase beamed that smile at her.

"Water's fine." She shrugged.

"Not tonight. We're here to have some fun."

"Really, just water."

"A compromise then." He pulled out a tall glass, opened a bottle of gin, and poured it liberally in the glass, topped with tonic water and a slice of lemon.

"Basically water – just better." He smiled and handed it to her. When she reached out to take it, he held on, leaning close. "You do look amazing, by the way." Again his breath tickled her ear, and she could feel her face heating.

"Thanks. For the drink." She stared at the glass in her hand and tipped it up, taking a long drink. She hadn't planned on drinking, but maybe she needed it. When she swallowed, the cold liquid cooled her burning throat at first, but then felt like fire. She coughed, and Chase chuckled. "That's my girl. Let's get outside."

He led her to a set of French doors that opened onto what could only be described as a magical fairytale kingdom. A crystal blue pool, lit from under the water, took center stage. Even in the cool night air, it looked inviting. Fairy lights were strung between white trellises and gazebos that dotted a huge manicured lawn, accented with clusters of gorgeous plants and flowers. It was paradise.

When she looked at Chase, he was staring at her, grinning. "Nice, isn't it?"

"Nice is not the word," she breathed out.

"Well, that's why we love a party at Gretchen's." He sighed.

Suddenly, music started pulsing from somewhere –no, from everywhere. There was obviously an outdoor sound system.

"Let's dance, Bitches," yelled Britney as she came up behind Emmalee and threw her arms around her. "Time for a party!"

Chase smiled at Emmalee, a little sadly, she thought, but she followed Britney out toward the center of the patio, Kristina trailing behind them.

Dancing wasn't really her strong suit, but she tried to follow the other two girls as they moved to the music, shutting her self-consciousness out and just enjoying the moment. Here she was in heels and a gorgeous dress, her hair swirling around her, her skin damp with sweat, feeling part of something fun and young for once.

Their group got larger, more people gathering around them, pulsing with them to the beat of the music. Emmalee looked around and saw Chase watching from across the patio, leaning against a raised flower bed, drink in his hand. His eyes were on her, following her as she moved. She could feel her skin flush, enjoying his eyes on her, but she reminded herself that he had a girlfriend and closed her eyes again.

Suddenly, she felt a hand on her lower back. She stopped and turned to find that Chase had made his way across the patio to her. He leaned in, trying to be heard over the loud music.

"Have you seen Gretchen?" His lips brushed Emmalee's ear.

"Umm, no," she stammered. "Not since we came out here."

He nodded. "Sorry to interrupt." He raised his glass toward her, then retreated.

Emmalee felt an immediate hot streak of regret. She was supposed to be investigating what happened to Audrey, not partying.

She leaned over to Britney. "I'm going to get another drink," she yelled. "Want anything?"

"We could use a couple more drinks!" Britney yelled back, grinding her hips into Bryce's.

She slipped across the patio and inside the house, planning to find her way back to Gretchen's room. Gretchen was dating Chase, after all, and that started very soon after Audrey's supposed accident. It seemed more likely that Gretchen had something to do with it, if anyone did, instead of Britney, who seemed perfectly happy with her own boyfriend.

Upstairs, she quickly recognized Gretchen's door and tiptoed toward it, putting her hand on the doorknob and pausing momentarily. She was glad she hadn't just turned the handle because she heard quiet talking coming from inside the room. Gretchen's voice.

"I was drunk. It was a mistake. I should never have gone there." Gretchen's usual confidence was replaced by a softness, a sadness. Maybe she was right, and it had been Gretchen who caused Audrey's fall.

"What are you doing?" A sharp male voice interrupted her eavesdropping, making her jump.

"I'm just, I got lost," Emmalee stammered.

"You got lost looking for drinks? Upstairs?" Bryce's eyes were narrow and dark. "I doubt it." She didn't like the wicked glint in his eyes.

"Well, I just wasn't sure where–"

"Save it," he cut her off. "I'm not your daddy." He smirked.

Emmalee's heart dropped.

The bedroom door flew open. "What is going on out here?" Gretchen's voice was hard now. Gone was any trace of the softness Emmalee had heard a few moments before.

"Emmalee here got lost. Looking for drinks. Right, Em?" Bryce cocked his head sideways, daring her to argue.

"Were you snooping?" Gretchen asked, scowling with disgust. "Who does that?"

"I wasn't snooping. I just–"

Gretchen scowled back at her. "Just stay downstairs with everyone else. This isn't your house."

"Don't be rude, Gretchen." Britney's voice behind them was a welcome relief. "Emmalee's our guest. She's new, and she obviously just got lost. Don't be such a bitch. You should apologize."

The two girls stared at each other, something passing between them that Emmalee didn't understand.

"Sorry, Emmalee," Gretchen sneered, rolling her eyes.

"By the way, Chase is looking for you, Gretchen. Should I let him know you're too busy for him?" Britney raised an eyebrow, and Gretchen shook her head.

"I'll go find him."

"Let's get back to having fun, Em, come on." Britney took Emmalee's hand and rescued her, leading her back to a night full of fun and dancing, and more than a few drinks.

CHAPTER 9

"Emmalee, this story is awesome! How'd you get it done so fast?" Mekayla snapped her laptop shut.

They were in the newsroom after school for another staff meeting. Emmalee had been assigned to write a feature on the new school counselor. She'd written the best questions she could come up with, then arrived at school early and caught Ms. Greene just as she was getting to her office. The rest of the day, she'd written the story in every pocket of time she could find, which wasn't too hard since most of her classes were easy.

"I just did it." Emmalee shrugged.

"Well, you did a good job." Wideman looked up from his computer screen. "I like the angle, turning her own life experiences into a way to help students. Good work."

Emmalee smiled, feeling a flush rise to her cheeks. "Thanks."

"And the writing is so good. You've been holding out on us in Creative Writing." Mekayla raised her eyebrows at Emmalee.

"That's different," Emmalee replied. She could feel her heartbeat picking up.

"No way. If you could do this with an article about a staff member of all things—" Mekayla was interrupted.

"Watch the ageism, Mekayla," Wideman cut in, giving Mekayla a sidelong glance. "Us old folks can be interesting, too."

"Sure, sure," Mekayla retorted, smiling. "Anyway, you're hiding some real talent, Em. You should be proud of it."

Emmalee felt a rush of warmth course through her body, part anxiety, but part something else. That old feeling was awakening, the feeling she'd stuffed down for two years. The feeling she'd chased at all costs. The feeling of being alive, of belonging, of being part of the world instead of hiding inside her own mind and room. The feeling that had resulted in tragedy.

She stood up abruptly. "Well, I need to get going. I have lots of homework." She started shoving her laptop and notebook in her bag.

"Okay, well, don't forget your history homework," said Wideman.

"Yeah, and you can start working on another story." Mekayla gave her a meaningful look and Emmalee's stomach clinched. She knew what she meant. Audrey.

"Oh, yeah," said Wideman. "How about a book review? You like to read, right?"

"Yes! I'd love that!" Emmalee was relieved that the focus shifted to something safe. But Mekayla caught her eyes and held them, communicating silently a reminder that Audrey's story couldn't tell itself.

She'd told Mekayla at lunch what she'd overheard at the party.

"Gretchen? I don't really see her as the bad guy here." Mekayla had looked thoughtful.

Emmalee had shrugged. "I'm just relaying what I heard. Besides, Britney was way nicer than Gretchen. She even stopped Gretchen from killing me when she found me outside the bedroom door."

"You got caught eavesdropping?" Mekayla rolled her eyes dramatically. "Em, you have a lot to learn about undercover investigating." Mekayla had grinned at her, and Emmalee had tossed her napkin across the table. It landed in Marshall's mushy-looking broccoli, and the girls had dissolved into laughter while he'd huffed.

Now, as she hurried out of the building, she was frowning to herself, wondering what she should do next. She was meeting Britney and the other girls that afternoon, and her stomach was churning with worry.

"Are you hard of hearing, Bitch?" Britney laughed and gave Emmalee a playful shrug.

"No. I just, I don't know."

Britney was talking really slowly, like she would to a small child. "Don't know what? Bodycount? It's a number that represents—"

"I know what the word means," Emmalee interrupted, laughing a little. She wasn't sure how she felt about being called a bitch, but all of these girls seemed to do that, and Britney was clearly just joking. The three of them were sprawled on Kristina's family room floor drinking Diet Cokes and watching *The Summer I Turned Pretty*.

"Well, if you know what it means, then answer." Britney stared at Emmalee, waiting for a reply.

"I just don't normally share that kind of thing." Emmalee could feel her face turning red.

"I see. We have a shy one, Kristina, and you know what that means." Britney raised her eyebrows conspiratorially.

"Total virgin," Kristina jeered. "I knew it!"

The two girls cackled, and Emmalee started to get up, but Britney grabbed her arm to keep her from moving.

"No, no, don't go, Em. We're just messing with you. It's sweet. Kristina's just jealous because she's such a whore."

"Hey! I'll bet my count's lower than yours!" Kristina laughed, but Britney's eyes narrowed.

"Anyway, when will the food be here?" Emmalee tried to change the subject.

They had ordered Chinese food and were planning to just hang out and have a girls' night since the guys all had a team dinner to attend.

"Should be any minute. I'm going to go get a glass of water. Anyone want anything?" Kristina stood up and collected the empty cans.

"No, thanks." Emmalee smiled at Kristina.

"Maybe a better friend." Britney grinned as Kristina flipped her off.

"So, Em, what teams did you sign up for?"

"Like, sports?"

"Yeah, like sports. What else?" Britney scoffed.

Emmalee shrugged. "I didn't sign up for any teams."

"Perfect. You can be on the tennis team, then." Britney smiled at her. "I'll let Gretchen know."

"Wait, I don't play tennis."

"You do now." Britney shrugged her shoulders, tapping out a text on her phone.

"Seriously, I don't even know how to play." Emmalee could feel her heart rate rising. She panicked at just the thought of sports. She'd never been good at any sports in gym class, and the one time her mom had forced her to play softball, her teammates had offered to pay her not to show up to games.

"No problem. You can learn." Britney put her phone down and looked up at Emmalee. "Gretchen needs someone to play doubles with, given Audrey's unfortunate situation." Britney paused, frowning briefly, before smiling again. "And there's no one else to ask – they're all busy. Everyone except you. Besides, you owe me."

"I owe you?" Emmalee wracked her brain, trying to figure out what exactly she could possibly owe Britney.

"Yes. For one thing, you owe me for the most excellent tennis racket I'm going to give you." Britney grinned. "And for another thing, I rescued you the other night when Gretchen found you snooping." She tucked her short blonde hair behind her ears and stared at Emmalee.

"I wasn't snooping." Emmalee's voice was so weak, she didn't even believe her own lie.

Britney snorted. "Please, you don't have to lie to me. I'm on your side."

"No, really." Emmalee's brain was racing to try and come up with a good excuse for being upstairs that night.

"Seriously, it's no big deal. Her house is incredible. Everyone wants to go poking around in all the rooms."

Just then, the doorbell rang, and Emmalee breathed a sigh of relief when Britney jumped up to get it. She returned a moment later with Gretchen, who looked amazing in a sapphire blue mini-dress and matching high heels.

"Hi," Emmalee said, smiling.

Gretchen looked at her briefly, muttering a quick, "Hi," before slipping her shoes off and taking a seat on one of the plush white couches, feet tucked under her.

Emmalee's heart rate picked up a little when she remembered she had an investigation to be doing. Part of her really wanted to just focus on being friends with these girls. But another part of her knew she really needed to stay focused on finding out what happened to Audrey.

She took a deep breath. "So, Bryce mentioned that benefit for your friend, Audrey. When is that?" Emmalee pretended to examine her nails very closely, trying to seem nonchalant.

"It's in October," Britney said brightly. "We're looking forward to it."

Emmalee looked up in time to see Gretchen roll her eyes. "Right. So excited." She sounded anything but.

"It must be so hard having one of your best friends in critical condition." Emmalee hoped her concern sounded real, not like she was pressing for details.

"Yeah." Gretchen's voice was like acid. "Now, what movie are we going to watch next?" She followed that up with a pointed smile.

Really? A movie was more important than one of her best friends in a coma?

Britney just laughed. "Gretchen, you're going to scare Emmalee away. Of course it's hard, Em, but there's really nothing we can do about it. Audrey was always drinking too much. We tried to warn her."

Gretchen huffed. "Right, alcohol was the problem."

Britney exchanged a look with Gretchen that Emmalee couldn't quite decipher.

There was definitely something more to Audrey's story. And Emmalee wanted more than ever to find out what. She needed to find a way to get herself invited to that benefit.

CHAPTER 10

"So, you need workout clothes for practice, Em." Britney was unpacking her usual lunch of calorie-free vegetables onto the lunch table.

Emmalee really wanted to stop this train of discussion. "Like I told you before, I'm not really into sports."

"Tough shit." Britney popped a baby carrot into her mouth and grinned. "Sometimes you have to take one for the team."

"Yeah, Em, we need you." Kristina took a long pull from a bottle of sparkling water. "Gretchen won't be able to play doubles if you don't play."

Gretchen's eyes rested on Emmalee, scanning her unkempt hair and baggy clothes. "Really, it's no big deal. I can just skip the doubles tournaments this year."

"No way!" Britney whined. "We can't be the three amigas without our Gretchy-poo." Britney stuck out her lips in a mock baby face.

Gretchen rolled her eyes. "Em, really, don't stress yourself out."

"Hold on," interrupted Chase. "I thought Samantha was

going to play with you?" He turned a quizzical stare at Gretchen as he stuffed half a cheeseburger in his mouth.

Gretchen sighed, her mouth opening to speak, but Britney piped up first. "Samantha's being a little bitch. She's all butt-hurt that Gretchen snatched you off the market after Audrey's incident."

Chase's eyes narrowed as he stared at Britney.

"As if you would ever consider touching Samantha," Britney continued, staring right back at him. "You'd probably end up diseased." Britney rolled her eyes theatrically.

Emmalee was confused. "Who's Samantha?"

"Samantha is that little bitch over there." Britney pointed at a dark-haired girl sitting with a few boys Emmalee recognized from other classes, but no one she really knew. "She's had the hots for Chase for years."

"You didn't tell me about Samantha, Gretchen?" He looked genuinely hurt, and Emmalee felt for him.

Gretchen shrugged her shoulders. "There was nothing to tell really. She just doesn't want to play, and Britney's just assuming it's about you, but that's ridiculous." Now Gretchen was staring at Britney, clearly willing her to shut up.

Emmalee's face must have shown her confusion, because Kristina chimed in. "We basically live in a soap opera, Em." She grinned at Emmalee and then popped an olive in her mouth.

Emmalee nodded. "I can see that." She laughed to cover her confusion about the complicated web of relationships that bound this group of kids.

"Back to the most important issue, though," Britney cut in. "You are playing tennis, Em. And that's final. We'll help you, so don't worry your pretty little head about it." Britney reached over and tousled Emmalee's hair. "You will definitely want to put that hair in a pony tail, though. And you can borrow some workout clothes from one of the other girls on the team for today."

Kristina nodded somberly, but Gretchen's eyes were still shooting daggers at Britney. Emmalee felt in the middle of something much bigger and more confusing. She didn't know what, but she didn't like it at all. She pushed that feeling aside and focused on what really mattered. Sure, she hated sports, but tennis could be a way in even closer to these girls. A way to find out what really happened to Audrey.

She flinched as a ball whizzed past her head. Gretchen was serving up balls in an attempt to see if Emmalee could hit any. So far, she hadn't.

"You have to try, Emmalee. If you just stand there and get hit, you're worthless to me."

I'll be worthless to you anyway, Emmalee thought. Her face was red from a mixture of exertion, embarrassment, and anger. Another ball came whizzing past her.

"God damn it, Britney! I told you this was a shit idea!" Gretchen screamed.

At the next court over, Britney called back, "Do I have to do everything for you?" Britney tossed her racket onto a bench near the fence and headed toward Emmalee. "I got you a partner for God's sake. You'd think the least you could do was show her how to play. Jesus Christ, Gretchen." Britney stuck out her hand toward Emmalee. "Give me the racket."

Emmalee handed over the racket Britney had given her before practice. Britney showed her how to stand — legs shoulder-width apart, knees bent, torso leaning forward. "Stay light on your feet, shifting your weight, don't get lazy. You want to be ready to move whichever way the ball goes." She handed the racket back. "Serve, Gretchen, and not a fucking ace. This is not the time to show off."

Emmalee could feel the heat of anger radiating off of

Gretchen from across the court, but Gretchen tossed the ball up and stretched her arm high, bringing it down and sending the ball across the court toward Emmalee again.

"Stay light, stay light!" Britney yelled. Emmalee watched the ball, lunging right toward it and swinging her racket, just missing it.

"Okay, that sucked. But it sucked less. Again!" Britney stood back, arms crossed, watching closely.

Emmalee got back into position again. And again. And again. Gretchen must have hit twenty balls, Britney constantly calling orders and corrections, until finally, Emmalee's racket made contact with the ball. It careened straight into the net, but Emmalee couldn't help herself from jumping up and down, screaming, "Yes! Yes! Yes!"

Britney grinned. "Relax, bitch. That was still terrible, but at least we're getting somewhere."

Emmalee still bristled at being called a bitch, but admittedly less. She was starting to get used to this term of endearment Britney used with her friends. Her heart skipped a beat at the thought of having popular friends again, the kind everyone looked up to, the kind everyone wanted to be.

Britney's voice brought her back to the present moment. "Again, let's go. We're not done here."

The sun beat down on them, and Emmalee could feel sweat soaking through the shorts and tee shirt that Britney had told a freshman to loan to her. The girl was about Emmalee's size but looked terrified when she handed the clothes over.

"Beat it, freshman." Britney had ordered, and the girl had sprinted away to meet the other girls on the freshman team outside.

Now, Emmalee worried she'd never be able to get the stench of her sweat out of these clothes before she returned them. But, by the end of the practice, she was reliably returning Gretchen's serve, which was slowly getting harder at Britney's command. It was exhausting and a little embarrassing, but it also felt good to be moving, to be using her body, to be in her body instead of in her head as she usually was.

"Alright, ladies, head on inside." Coach Ezzell was writing on a clip board outside the fence, calling orders to the freshmen. She hadn't said more than a hello to Emmalee during practice.

Emmalee leaned over to pick up a tennis ball, when Britney stopped her. "The freshmen can do that. Come on."

Emmalee made eye contact with Coach Ezzell, who just stared at her, saying nothing.

"Why isn't the coach more involved?"

Britney scoffed. "Ezell doesn't know anything about tennis. She just works with the freshmen."

"So, you're basically the varsity coach?"

"Yeah. Well, since Audrey fell out of the running for captain." Britney shrugged.

Emmalee stopped walking. "Wow."

"What?" Britney stopped, too, staring back at her.

"Fell out? That seems a little, I don't know–" Cruel.

Britney laughed. "Oh, shit. Sorry. I didn't mean it that way. Let's go get cleaned up before the freshmen steal the showers."

In the locker room, she grabbed her clothes and bag, planning to go home and shower, but again, Britney had other plans. "Go get in the shower. We're going shopping."

Emmalee hesitated. "I need to get home."

"And you will, after shopping." Kristina and Gretchen exchanged a look Emmalee couldn't quite decipher.

"Brit," Kristina broke in. "I'm supposed to meet Bryce—"

"You can meet Bryce later," Britney replied, grinning. "Shower, babes." She walked toward the back of the locker room, stripping her sports bra off as she walked.

"We're shopping for you, Em," Britney shouted ten minutes later, struggling to be heard over the roar of several hair dryers going at once. "If you're going to be on the team, you need some workout clothes."

"I have some shorts," Emmalee countered.

"No. If you're on the team with us, you deserve the best. Plus, we can gossip and eat tons of junk food." Britney smiled at her, catching her eye in the mirror.

Emmalee wanted to say something, but she knew her voice would shake, and she was pretty sure she'd start crying. One of them? It was like being in the middle of the best dream of your life, and then realizing it was also your worst nightmare, too. She wanted to be popular, to fit in, to have friends. Well, more than just one or two of the other outcasts at school. She'd never had this. Even though it felt kind of shitty, she had to admit, it was also kind of freaking fabulous. And anyway, she told herself, it would give her a chance to do some investigating.

In the end, she relented and smiled back at Britney. "Okay."

"Damn right it is," Britney smirked, arms crossed and hip cocked out to the side.

Shopping turned into more of an event than Emmalee realized. They'd all loaded into Kristina's Lexus and headed into Portland. The hour-long drive was not what Emmalee had anticipated. She'd assumed they'd head to the little strip mall near downtown Ravensville. They had an Old Navy, a Target, and a TJ Maxx.

On the drive, Emmalee mentally planned how she would handle the whole affair. Money would be a big issue. She had about 25 dollars in cash and her mom's credit card, but the cash was meant for food and other daily necessities, and the card was meant for emergencies only. Maybe this counted as an emergency? It certainly felt like it.

In the city, Kristina sped her way to a huge mall and parked outside a Nordstrom's. Inside, Emmalee cringed. She hated shopping malls — the stale air, the crowds, the bright lights and loud children.

"Come on," Britney ordered, leading them to LuLu Lemon. Emmalee simultaneously wanted to throw up and buy everything. Sure, the form-fitting shorts, leggings, bras, and tanks weren't her style, but they also represented everything she'd always wished she could be.

She felt the fabric of a black tee hanging on the first rack she came to. It felt buttery soft, and she thought that she could at least feel comfortable in it if not exactly hidden by it.

"Em, over here." Emmalee let the fabric drop from her fingers, making her way to where Kristina, Britney, and Gretchen were sorting through racks of white, pale pink, and cream-colored sports bras.

"What size? Large?" Britney asked, scrutinizing Emmalee's chest.

"Medium?" Emmalee replied, annoyed at herself for saying it as a question. She wanted Britney's confidence so badly.

Britney looked skeptical, but pulled a blush-colored bra from the rack. "Here, go try this on. We'll bring you some other stuff."

In the dressing room, Emmalee quickly pulled off her shirt and bra, not wanting to be half naked when the other girls arrived. When she slipped the sports bra on, it felt glorious. It was so smooth, soft, and supple. She'd never had anything this luxurious. She examined herself in the mirror. She looked good in it. Even though she was a little fuller than the other girls, the bra smoothed her curves and provided support that even made her look kind of attractive. She pulled the tag up from the band and her heart skipped a beat. Fifty-eight dollars! There was no way she could afford that! She was used to spending twelve dollars on a Hanes bra off the rack at Wal-Mart. She started to panic, but heard the other girls shuffling in. "Em! Open up!"

Her hand shook as she slid the lock and opened the door a crack. Britney shoved her way in.

"Nice rack, Bitch." Britney grinned and dropped a pile of clothes still on hangers on the small bench in the corner, then turned around and grabbed Emmalee's breasts with both hands, giving them a rough squeeze. "And all natural, too. Aren't you lucky?" Britney smiled, but a shadow of something flickered through her eyes. Emmalee pulled away, leaning down to grab a tank top and slip it on quickly. The cream-colored tank slid on perfectly over the bra.

"Nice, nice. Shorts now." Britney handed Emmalee a pair of matching cream-colored shorts.

"Ummm—"

"Don't be shy. We're not in kindergarten anymore."

Emmalee took a deep breath and tugged her pants down, leaning over in an attempt at some kind of modesty, and tried to quickly slip the shorts on, though her leg got stuck once or twice and she had to tug.

"Oh my God!" Britney laughed, bringing her hand to her mouth and swiveling her head between Kristina and Gretchen.

Kristina and Gretchen laughed as well, and Emmalee could have died at that moment. She hurriedly turned to the mirror to see what they were laughing at. When she saw, her face turned an even darker shade of crimson. She could see the outline of her underwear through her shorts, the darker material showing through, obviously, but also the fabric bunching, creating misshapen bulges through the sleek, buttery shorts.

"I can't believe you wear granny panties! What are you, eighty?" Britney shrieked. "This is too good."

Just as Emmalee turned around, Britney snapped a photo. "Hey, wait, no—" Emmalee stuttered.

Britney's eyes flashed with merriment. "This is just for us, babes." She started tapping on her phone, and then Emmalee heard her phone buzz. "I promise. Just between us! We have a group text with loads of pics like this. Here, look."

Britney turned her phone around, and Emmalee saw a picture of Kristina sleeping, her head on Tyler's chest, mouth hanging open, drool running down her cheek. "See? We all have our moments."

Emmalee nodded and forced a smile. She didn't know if she could really get on board with taking pictures of people who didn't know they were being photographed. That seemed a bit much. But, on the other hand, they all seemed okay with it.

Emmalee shrugged. "It's just laundry day." She quickly slipped off the shorts and pulled her pants back on, then set about changing back into her own bra and top, hoping that if she acted confident, her pounding heart would maybe start to believe it.

"We're just teasing you, Em. It's kind of cute." Britney grinned at her. "So, I recommend three of each – bra, shorts, tanks – so you have time to wash in between. And several pairs of undies. Let's go, Bitches." Britney sauntered out, her exit making it clear she expected everyone to follow. Which they did.

At the register a few minutes later, Emmalee's heart sank into her stomach. She watched the clerk ring up the three workout outfits, the total coming to over four hundred dollars. She pulled out her mom's credit card, the one she was only supposed to use for emergencies, and swiped it.

She had no idea what she was going to say when her mom found out, but she didn't know what else to do. It was so cliché, like she was caving to peer pressure in some teen angst movie. The reality, though, was that she was a teen, and she was definitely feeling a lot of angst. Saying she couldn't afford the same clothes as these girls just felt too embarrassing to admit. Like she didn't belong with them.

After another hour of shopping, during which she threw caution to the wind and splurged on a few more outfits – jeans, sweaters, blouses, and yes – underwear – she went to meet the other girls in the food court, where they were all sipping sodas.

"Here. I got you a Diet Coke." Gretchen smiled at Emmalee.

"Thanks!" Emmalee took a seat, tucking her bags under her chair, and took a long drink. Heaven. Her phone pinged.

MEKAYLA

Anything yet?

Her heart raced.

"So, whose house are we going to before the game?" Britney asked. "I'd offer mine, but my mom has her book club meeting tonight." The way she said *book club* made it sound like anything but.

"Ah, yes, the wine and whine club." Kristina nodded. "Getting old must be such a bitch."

"I don't know," Gretchen added. "My parents seem to be having the time of their lives, always off on trips together, making out with each other every time I walk into a room. It's pretty disgusting." She grimaced. "But, I hope I'm like that with my hubby one day."

Emmalee hadn't really seen this side of Gretchen before. There was something she liked about the girl's ability to see her parents as human and not just old.

"Your hubby? Do you mean Chase?" Britney batted her eyelashes at Gretchen. "Or is it your mystery man?"

Gretchen's face turned red. This is new, Emmalee thought. She hadn't seen one of these girls get embarrassed.

"Stop it. There is no mystery man." Gretchen was fidgeting with her straw wrapper, looking down at it. Emmalee felt bad for her, but she wasn't sure what to say. She had no idea what they were talking about.

"Then who were you on the phone with all night at your party the other night?"

"Brit, not that I have to defend myself to you, or anyone for that matter, it's just a friend."

"Since when do *friends* spend all night on the phone while

one of them has a boyfriend outside all alone?" Britney looked at Kristina for support.

"Yeah, Gretch," Kristina joined in. "Chase looked pretty down that night while you were off having phone relations with your – friend." Kristina and Britney stuck their tongues out toward each other, waggling them and making moaning noises at each other. An older couple nearby looked over, huffed, and stood up to leave.

"Stop it, you two." Gretchen reddened even more. "I'm with Chase."

"And also your mystery man." Britney pushed the matter.

"Enough. There is no mystery man. You don't understand everything, okay." Gretchen's voice had an edge to it, and Emmalee looked quickly to Britney to see her reaction. She didn't think Britney would like the challenge. She was right.

Britney's eyes were slits. "Oh? What don't we understand? Please, do explain it to us clueless morons."

"Brit, don't. You know that's not what I meant."

"I'm waiting to be educated, Gretchen. Please explain to me the reason why it's okay for you to spend all night on the phone with some other guy while your boyfriend is standing alone on the dance floor at a party." Britney crossed her arms, her head pulled back, and stared at Gretchen. Her voice was so loud that everyone in the food court was staring now.

"Un-fucking-believable, Brit." Gretchen pushed her chair back and stood. "I'll be in the car."

CHAPTER 11

Emmalee sipped her vanilla latte and frowned. Doing homework at Café Vibes with Mekayla and Marshall had become an afternoon ritual, and this Friday was no different. She was trying to work on her latest story, puzzling through her female main character's motivations for moving to a house in the woods all alone. She couldn't very well blame a mother in the military, because her character was twenty-three years old. Maybe she was a writer?

Emmalee sighed. Why did she keep coming up with ideas that mimicked her own life? It was supposed to be fiction, but she was so used to writing poetry about her own feelings. She wasn't used to inventing new people with new problems. She had plenty of her own to sort through. Like what she would say when her mom inevitably asked about the credit card charges.

She slammed her notebook shut and stuffed it back in her bag.

"Problems?" Mekayla pulled an earbud out and raised her eyebrows.

"Just a little writer's block." Emmalee pulled out her phone and opened Instagram.

"No doomscrolling." Mekayla snagged Emmalee's phone and laid it facedown on the table. "Tell me what you're stuck on."

"I just can't figure out my main character's biggest problem. Everything I come up with is basically just my own crap." Emmalee signed and reached for her phone again.

Mekayla put her hand on Emmalee's arm and gave her a gentle squeeze. "I know you're new to writing fiction. But, writers mine their own lives for material all the time. So, if an idea seems like something you could write about, try it. You can always change it later."

Emmalee grinned. "You sound like a teacher."

"As if! Gross!" Mekayla screeched and threw a paper napkin at Emmalee, laughing.

Emmalee's phone buzzed, distracting them.

BRITNEY

Meet at Kris's in an hour - 7721 Parkwood Lane. Pregame time!

Below that was a photo of Britney and Kristina, their faces together, tongues poking out toward the camera. They both had red devil horns applied by a filter Emmalee despised, but she had to admit, they looked like they were having fun.

"Time to go." She showed the message to Mekayla.

"You're leaving?" Marshall looked up from his math homework.

"Duty calls." Emmalee stuffed the phone in her pocket and stood up. "Game time."

"I kind of hate that you're pretending to be friends with them," Mekayla said.

"You forced me to!" Emmalee laughed and rolled her eyes.

"I did not!" Mekayla was mock-offended.

"You so forced her to, Mekayla," Marshall chimed in.

"No one asked you, Marshall." Mekayla stuck her tongue out

at him. "But seriously, Em, I hope you get some good information. Just be careful."

"Okay, Mom." Emmalee rolled her eyes again.

"Seriously, Em. Be safe." Marshall said this with such sincerity that Emmalee had a moment of pause before she turned to go.

"See you tomorrow." She smiled and waved, but couldn't help wondering why they were so worried about her safety. Britney and Kristina were fun.

An hour later, she was parking in front of another gated home, this one all white and angular, with walls of glass everywhere. When she rang the bell, a woman in a maid's uniform opened the door and pointed up the staircase. "Take a right at the top of the stairs. It's the last door on the left, Miss." The woman, old enough to be a grandmother, didn't even bother asking Emmalee's name or introducing herself. Emmalee snuck quietly up the stairs, hoping not to run into anyone else she didn't know. The interior was full of color. The white tile floors were broken up by brightly-colored rugs in modern, geometric prints. Vases in reds, oranges, teals, and yellows dotted the corners of rooms, filled with green ferns spilling over their openings.

At the last door on the left, Emmalee took a deep breath and knocked. The door swung open and Kristina reached out, grabbing Emmalee's arm and dragging her inside.

"Wow! Look at you!" Kristina's gaze travelled up and down Emmalee's body.

"Who is that girl?" Britney squinted her eyes at her. "That can't be our Em?"

Emmalee smiled shyly and tugged at the hem of her shirt, a white crop top she'd found in one of the stores at the mall, paired with cut-off denim shorts and white sneakers. She'd stopped by the house to change, hoping she'd fit in a bit better and avoid another makeover. "Thanks. I think," she laughed.

"You better get used to us. Bitchy is our love language." Britney flipped Emmalee off, and then turned back to filing her fingernails.

"Here," Kristina handed Emmalee a shot glass. "Drink up. You have a lot of catching up to do."

Emmalee paused before drinking, and Britney immediately jumped in. "Kristina's the DD tonight, so no excuses."

Emmalee put the glass to her lips and sniffed briefly before taking a sip. It tasted like she imagined battery acid would.

"That's not how you take a shot. Jesus. Here's how it's done." Kristina knocked her shot back, swallowing, then smiling as though it had been only water.

Emmalee was shocked. "I thought you were the DD?"

"Pffft. One shot's nothing." Kristina waved her off.

Emmalee took a deep breath, then squinted her eyes and followed suit, trying not to let on to how much it burned her throat. She failed, coughing uncontrollably, and both girls laughed.

"Get her another, Kris," Britney said, wiping away tears of laughter.

Kristina obeyed, and Emmalee knocked it back, bracing herself and forcing herself to take it like a champ this time. She hoped at least.

"So, Em, wasn't Gretchen being a total bitch today?" Britney didn't look up from her nails when she asked this question, and Emmalee's heart raced.

She didn't know what to say. Neither girls had said a word to each other during lunch, and it had been clearly uncomfortable for everyone. She didn't want to come between Britney and Gretchen and get caught in the crossfire. But she also needed to find out something about Audrey or Mekayla would kill her. She had an idea.

"I mean, maybe she's just worried about Audrey." The words had the effect of a bomb dropped in the middle of the room.

Silence before explosion. Except Britney was perfectly calm when she responded.

"Maybe. But, honestly, Gretchen has never liked Audrey all that much." Britney poured another shot and handed it to Emmalee.

Interesting. Mekayla said they had been best friends before, but then again, Gretchen had been kind of weird about Audrey. Best to play dumb.

Emmalee reached out and took the shot from Britney, not drinking it right away. "Were they having problems with tennis?"

Britney laughed, and Kristina joined her. "Right. Tennis. Enough talk about losers. Drink up."

The rest of the evening was a blur. She recalled everyone piling into Kris's car and singing way too loudly all the way to the school. There were vague flashes of the girls huddled together under blankets in the stands, gossiping about Gretchen, wondering why she wasn't at the game, watching Chase play football. Wondering whether she was out with the mystery guy.

There were some hazy images of another house, she had no idea whose, bodies churning to loud music, more drinks, hands grabbing her hips, someone's mouth on her neck.

Beyond that, she was at a loss Saturday afternoon when she woke up. She was in her bed in just her underwear and bra. She staggered out into the living room and looked out the front window. Her car was in the driveway. She hoped she didn't drive home herself because there is no way she was sober enough for that. Her head was pounding and her mouth tasted like she'd been chewing on sand.

After brushing her teeth and pulling on a pair of sweats and a tee shirt, she poured a bowl of cereal and sat on the sofa looking at her phone. She nearly choked when a message popped up.

BRITNEY

How much to keep this to myself?

Below it was a picture was of Emmalee, splayed out in her bra and panties on her bed. Her mouth was hanging open. "Classy, Em," she muttered to herself.

Please delete that.

I will lol — or will I? 🤪 jk

What're you doing today?

Chores

That sucks. Meet me and Kris at Fitness World at 4:00?

Why?

To work out obvs

We work out every day at practice.

The last thing Emmalee felt like was another grueling workout.

We work out on the weekends too. You should come with us. It's fun. Plus if you do I'll delete that photo 😌

Ugh. She knew Britney was joking, but it still bugged her that she took a picture like that.

I'll see you there.

Good girl :P

Another messaged arrived immediately.

MEKAYLA

So, any news about Audrey?

Sort of. Found out she and Gretchen weren't exactly getting along.

Emmalee wasn't sure if it was entirely true, or if it even mattered.

Noted. Keep digging.

Emmalee sighed. She felt like she was treading on dangerous ground. She wanted to know what happened to Audrey, but she also hated feeling so dishonest. Part of her just wanted to see where her friendship with the popular kids went.

CHASE

Busy?

Emmalee panicked.

Kinda

Why could he possibly want to know whether she was busy?

Will you be free at 2?

What's up?

She could not commit to anything without knowing what he had in mind.

I want to take you to lunch. Give me your address.

Her heart raced. It was doing that a lot lately. She was getting used to it, and she kind of liked it. She felt more alive than she'd felt in a long time. Her fingers paused over her phone screen. She knew he had a girlfriend, but then Gretchen hadn't been at the game the night before. And there was definitely something going on between Gretchen and her new *friend*.

Ok

1311 Pine

She leapt into action.

After doing a few chores, she took a shower, making sure she shaved her legs and underarms, and slathered on lotion. She blow-dried her hair and smoothed it back into a ponytail, then slipped into the LuLu Lemon workout clothes, choosing the pale blush-colored set and pairing it with white sneakers.

She added one of the cropped hoodies she'd found at the mall as well as a bit of concealer and mascara to bring some much-needed life to her hungover eyes, and was out front at the bottom of the driveway well before Chase pulled up at 2:00.

He insisted on opening her door for her, and paused before starting the car. "You look – different," he said, grinning.

"Ah, sorry. I'm meeting Britney and Kristina at the gym later. I just wanted to make sure I'm ready."

"Nothing to be sorry about." He smiled again. "You look great.

Her face reddened. She was not used to wearing such tight clothing. "Thanks."

He took them to the next town over, about a fifteen minute drive, where they were seated at a tiny table near the window of a diner. It looked kind of like one of those cute diners in television shows like Gilmore Girls. She loved it.

"They have great burgers," Chase commented as they waited for the waitress to take their order.

She considered it, but then settled on a grilled chicken salad and water with lemon. She didn't want to be over-full for her workout. The last thing she needed was to throw up at the gym in front of everyone.

While they waited for the food, Chase made small talk. "So, how are you liking Ravensville so far?"

"Fine, I guess."

"You guess?" He scrunched his eyebrows in confusion.

"Yeah. It's different. I'm used to a much bigger school."

"Ah. I see. Ravensville is definitely not a big school."

"True. But, the people are great," she added quickly.

He chuckled. "Sometimes, some of them are, yes."

She smiled and nodded, relieved he understood that it wasn't necessarily easy being a student at Ravensville.

"So, you must have a boyfriend back in Georgia?" Chase didn't look at Emmalee. Instead, he watched his french fry as he stirred it in a pile of ketchup.

Emmalee couldn't stop herself from laughing. "Ha! No. No boyfriend back in Georgia. Redneck cowboy is really not my type."

He looked up at her with a shy smile. "So what is your type, then? Blonde, blue-eyed athlete?" He chuckled at his own joke and popped another fry in his mouth.

Emmalee blushed and smiled. "Something like that, yeah."

His eyes flitted up to hers, and she could swear his cheeks reddened a little.

She couldn't believe she was actually flirting, and with Chase of all people. She knew she should feel guilty about Gretchen, but if she was honest, right now she didn't.

"Em, I asked you here under false pretenses." He stared at her, and Emmalee wondered what he could mean. Did he want her to do his English homework? Surely not. Mrs. Smith never gave her a grade higher than a C- on any of her work.

She stared into his eyes for a beat. "So, why am I here, Chase?" She was shocked again at how confident she sounded. Maybe it was the new clothes. Or the new friends.

"Well, I was wondering if you would go to Homecoming with me?" He looked so serious, his blue eyes took on a worried cast, and her heart leapt into her throat.

"Me? What about Gretchen?" Okay, that did not sound so confident.

He frowned. "Gretchen won't be at Homecoming. She has a, um, prior commitment." He said the last bit with a touch of sarcasm.

Emmalee wondered what Gretchen could possibly have going on that was more important than dancing in Chase's arms all night. "What trumps Homecoming?"

He was staring at a french fry again, this time nervously picking it apart.

"She's got this thing – um, she's going–" He stopped and sighed, deflated, his ears turning an adorable shade of red. "To be honest, I don't know. She just said she can't go."

"Well, I don't generally go on dates with other people's boyfriends." She kept silent about the fact that she didn't generally go on dates ever.

"I mean, Gretchen is fine with it, if that's what you're worried about. I told her I would ask you to go." When she raised an eyebrow, he quickly added, "as friends of course. I just thought it would be more fun if we had an even number in the group?" He smiled at her. "So, what do you think?"

"I'll think about it." She wasn't sure she wanted to stand in for someone else, even if it did mean spending the night up close and personal with Chase. He definitely wasn't her usual type. But then again, she'd never really had a boyfriend. Not a real one anyway.

"Please? Do you have someone else in mind? If so, tell me who I'm contending with. I'll break his knee caps." He smiled at her, and it was so warm and sweet that her heart melted.

"Okay. I guess I can handle that."

"Great! I think we're all going to this Italian restaurant in

Seattle for an early dinner, so I'll pick you up at 3:00 that afternoon. Let me know the color of your dress, and I'll make sure my tux matches."

"Will do." She was already panicking about finding a dress. "And, we're going dutch, obviously."

"I'm definitely picking up the tab for dinner. You're just going to have to live with that." He winked at her and went back to his burger and fries. She tucked into her salad again, spearing a chunk of tomato and popping it into her mouth with a smile.

The rest of lunch was great. They talked about music and books and movies. It turned out they both preferred indie films to Hollywood, and he was more of a classics reader than, well, a non-reader like most high school boys she knew.

After they ate, he insisted on paying the bill, then took her on a quick driving tour of Ravensville, showing her the gothic-looking library building, the cemetery where kids liked to drink and play hide and seek at night, and a couple other popular hangout spots.

At 3:30, he pulled up to her driveway and put the car in park, unclipping his seatbelt and turning to look at her.

"Thanks for coming with me today," he said, smiling.

"You're welcome." She started for the door handle, but he grabbed her arm.

"Hang on. I also wanted to thank you for agreeing to go to Homecoming with me. It means a lot." He squeezed her arm and leaned forward, planting a kiss on her forehead. He pulled back a little, just inches from her face. "See you later."

She got out and nearly stumbled her way up the driveway, she was swooning so hard. Chase had kissed her! Granted, it was only a peck on the forehead, but still. A kiss! She'd never been kissed before, not really. Relatives didn't count. She relived the sweetness of Chase's smile and that kiss on the forehead and melted as she climbed into her car and searched for Fitness World in her maps app.

It was certainly a whirlwind of a weekend. She'd been so used to hiding in her room for the last two years that she barely recognized herself. Flipping down the visor to check her hair in the mirror, she wondered. Who was this girl staring back at her? It certainly wasn't the Emmalee she thought she was. She just hoped this version would be one she liked.

CHAPTER 12

"Look at you, girl!" Britney shouted from across the parking lot at Fitness World. "This is the second time in a row you've shown up looking super cute. I think we're rubbing off on you!"

Emmalee laughed and shook her head, approaching Britney and Kristina. "So, the rest of the time, I look...?" She trailed off, letting Britney finish the sentence. Even though she still bristled at Britney's comments sometimes, she really was seeing that it was just her way. She didn't mean anything by it. At least, Emmalee thought she didn't.

"Just teasing, Em." Britney slung her arm around Emmalee's shoulder. "You need to take a joke. Remember, bitchy is my love language."

Emmalee let it go. "So, I don't have a membership here." She assumed like most gyms, you needed to join, and she wasn't sure she could make that happen. Not on her measly allowance anyway.

"Yeah, well, we're allowed to bring a guest, so you can always come with us. Plus, they give student discounts, so you can join later, right?" Britney pulled open the door.

Emmalee followed Britney and Kristina inside. "Yeah, I guess, and where's Gretchen?"

Britney scowled. "I have no idea where that raging bitch is."

Kristina bit her lip and remained silent.

Emmalee grimaced, and Britney jumped on it immediately. "What? You're Gretchen's best friend now? You know she talks shit on you constantly, don't you?"

"About me?" Emmalee was shocked. She'd barely spoken to Gretchen.

"Yep. She's just jealous because Chase is asking you to Homecoming. Right, Kris?" Britney's eyes narrowed in Kristina's direction.

They knew about that?

Kristina hesitated, then slowly nodded. "Yeah. She said you're trying to get in Chase's pants."

Both girls giggled and headed toward a room full of treadmills.

"What!? We're just going as friends. Because Gretchen can't be there." She hated how high her voice was, how guilty it made her sound.

"Relax. It's all good. Like I said, Gretchen's just a raging bitch." Britney hopped up on a treadmill and started pushing buttons. "Hey, wouldn't it be awesome if you and Chase got together instead? Then we could just cut Gretchen out of the picture." She made a cutting motion with her hand.

Emmalee did not like where they were headed with this conversation. As much as she liked Chase, she didn't feel good about coming between another couple. "Well, I don't think –"

Britney cut her off. "Just wishful thinking. Calm down."

Kristina rolled her eyes and hopped on the treadmill next to Britney. Both girls popped in AirPods and started running.

Emmalee looked around the room. There was one open treadmill left on the other side of the room.

Fifteen minutes later, after fighting with buttons and settings for seven of them, Emmalee wanted to collapse in a vat of ice cream instead of doing a single other exercise.

No such luck.

"Now we lift." Britney trotted away with Kristina close behind her. Emmalee groaned and followed.

After using a variety of machines designed to torture her legs, arms, and abs, just when she thought she would actually die, Britney called it quits for the day.

They agreed to stop at a local bar and grill for dinner. When Emmalee tried to order a burger, Britney cut her off.

"No." She looked up at the waitress. "She'll have a grilled chicken salad, no dressing."

"But—"

"Trust me," Britney interrupted.

"Okay." Weird. Maybe this restaurant had horrible burgers? When the waitress left, Emmalee asked, "What was up with that?"

"What do you mean?" Britney stared at Emmalee in disbelief. "We just spent an hour working calories off. You don't want to pile them all back on, do you?"

She wasn't sure how to respond to that. She was generally okay with her body. But, she also knew she could stand to lose a few pounds.

"That's what I thought," Britney said when Emmalee didn't answer. "You're welcome, bitch." She grinned and took a long drink of her Diet Coke.

After choking down more rabbit food, Emmalee was feeling ready to get home and dig around in the cabinets for something with fat. And sugar.

"You can meet us over at Kris's to shower and change before the guys come over."

Another night out? Emmalee didn't think she could handle another one.

"Don't even think about copping out." Britney smiled at Emmalee. "You're one of us now. You can't just ditch us."

One of us. Emmalee liked the sound of that. She hadn't been a "one of us" in a long time, let alone with the most popular people in the entire school. Even though she was tired and a little hangry, she couldn't deny it felt good to belong.

"That color looks amazing on you." Britney stood back and admired her handiwork on Emmalee's lips.

Emmalee turned to face the mirror. Wow. Britney was right. The dark red lipstick really brought out her eyes and paired nicely with her creamy skin. Emmalee couldn't help but smile.

"Now. You need something to wear." Britney stood back, finger on her chin, thinking.

Emmalee cringed. There was no way she'd fit into anything of theirs. They were model thin, and Emmalee was most certainly not. She wasn't fat, but she definitely had meat on her bones.

Britney broke the awkward silence. "Kris, go get one of your brother's jerseys."

"Um, a jersey?" What in the world?

"Just trust me, Em. I know what I'm doing."

Kristina came back with a huge Southern Oregon jersey. Emmalee wasn't sure how this was supposed to work, but she slipped it on over a pair of black spandex shorts Kristina loaned her. "They're too big on me," Kristina had said, and Emmalee tried not to take offense. There was nothing inherently wrong with being a little larger than someone else. Right?

Britney cinched the waist of the jersey with a gold belt, and then let Emmalee borrow black, heeled ankle boots.

"Hot." Britney looked Emmalee up and down, and Kristina nodded.

Then, they all set about working on their hair and makeup. As Emmalee scanned herself in the mirror, she admired her new skills with a flat iron, but she had to admit it was exhausting, too.

She already missed the days of taking a five-minute shower, running a brush through her hair, and slipping into comfy pants and a flannel shirt.

However, there was definitely something to be said for looking like this, she thought, as she turned and admired her curves.

"Before we head to the party, there's something we want to talk to you about, Em." Britney looked serious, and her tone matched.

"What's up?" Emmalee asked, no idea where this was going.

Britney took a deep breath and looked at Kris before beginning. "Look, we're worried about Chase. With Gretchen has been MIA lately, he's seemed pretty bummed, right Kris?"

Kris nodded seriously. "Audrey cheated on him, and with Gretchen looking like she's about to dip, too, we just don't want him to fall into a depression like he did last year." She looked over at Britney for confirmation.

"Yeah. It was bad. We were worried he wouldn't make it, if you know what I mean." Britney raised her eyebrows.

"That's horrible. I had no idea." Emmalee couldn't imagine how crushed Chase must feel.

Britney sighed. "Well, obviously Chase doesn't go around acting emo or anything. He keeps it in, you know?"

"Okay, yeah, that's awful." Emmalee felt terrible for him. She'd spent the last two years feeling extremely depressed and trying to keep it from showing. She knew how lonely that was.

"So, Em, we were hoping you'd kind of help him feel better?" Britney smiled suggestively at Emmalee.

Emmalee was confused, and looked between the two girls. "Feel better how?"

"Well, just, you know, hang with him, dance, flirt a little."

"Um, I'm not sure –" She didn't even know how to flirt. She thought back to lunch earlier that day. Okay, maybe she did know how to flirt a little.

"We're not asking you to get in bed with him." Britney laughed. "Just pay a little attention to him? Can you handle that?"

Kristina broke in. "Oh, and don't say anything to Chase. He would die if he knew we told you."

"Of course. I'd never –"

Britney interrupted again. "Good. Now that we've cleared that up, let's get going."

Emmalee hung back for a moment and texted the new information to Mekayla.

> So the rumors about Audrey cheating on Chase aren't just rumors.

She tucked her phone into the waistband of her shorts and hurried downstairs before the other girls wondered where she was.

Emmalee was definitely buzzed when they walked into Chase's house. The other girls disappeared, so she just wandered. The house was a little smaller than Kristina's and Gretchen's, but it was even more sophisticated. Everything was dark wood antiques, heavy fabrics, oriental rugs, old leather, and books. Emmalee loved it.

She particularly loved the thought of climbing into one of the well-worn leather arm chairs in the den they passed on the way to the kitchen. Maybe spending an afternoon in front of the fireplace, reading a good book, writing, napping.

She sucked in a breath when she realized it reminded her of her dad's study, of spending lazy Sunday afternoons in the big, cozy armchair, doing just those things — reading a book or writing a story until she dozed off.

"Here, Em!"

Britney's voice broke her out of the memory, and suddenly, she was starting on her second drink of the evening. She'd gotten out of Kristina's with just one shot of Tequila, and now she was having something that was bright blue and very, very strong. She planned to just sip it slowly, but then Chase walked in the room, and Britney gave her another meaningful glance, so she chugged it and pushed the empty glass toward Bryce for a refill.

"She's ready to party, bro." Bryce elbowed Chase and pointed to Emmalee. Chase just met her eyes and gave her a half-smile. She really liked his smile. And she really needed to get a grip. He wasn't her boyfriend.

"Hey, guys, let's go dance. I want to move." Britney started swiveling her hips, moving toward the French doors in the back. Emmalee took a nice long drink of her mystery drink and followed her outside, Kristina on her heels.

"You heard the ladies, let's take this outside!" Bryce called.

Out on the stone patio, Britney and Kristina pulled Emmalee close to them. "Come on, Em, let's get them warmed up." Britney held her drink up high in her left hand, and wrapped her other arm around Emmalee's waist. Kristina did the opposite, so that Emmalee was held between the two, and all three of them started moving to the music.

Emmalee wanted to run. Unlike the other parties, this was just the six of them, and she couldn't hide. Britney let her hand trail down Emmalee's waist. Is her hand on my ass? Emmalee could feel herself blushing, but she didn't want them to think she was homophobic or something. They were just dancing.

"Oh, ladies, ladies, I like it. Here, let me get those." Bryce collected their drinks, and the other girls turned so they sandwiched Emmalee, Britney behind her, Kristina in front, and the three of them moved their hips together, gyrating to the thumping bass of whatever Drake song was playing. Emmalee closed her eyes and let herself move, trying to ignore Britney's hands sliding up her hips, over her abdomen, then higher.

Chase's eyes caught hers when she opened them, and she saw a flash of anger. "Okay, ladies. Let me cut in there for a minute." Chase grabbed Emmalee's hand and pulled her to him.

Britney winked at Emmalee as she let Bryce pull her close, and Tyler switched the music to a slower song before wrapping his arms around Kristina.

Chase leaned down and whispered in Emmalee's ear. "Sorry about them."

"It's okay." It wasn't, not really, but she didn't want to seem like a prude.

"They just never know when enough is enough."

"It's okay, really."

He pulled back and looked her in the eye, troubled. "Really? You looked uncomfortable."

"Well, I guess, yeah, a little." She smiled up at him sheepishly.

He looked relieved. "Yeah, that's what I thought." He slid his arms tighter around her waist. She leaned her head back a little. She didn't want it to seem like she was hanging on him. But, it really did feel nice being in his arms.

"Hey," he murmured. "Want to see something?"

"Sure." She didn't really want to move, but she couldn't very well tell him that his arms were the only place she wanted to be right now.

He pulled away, taking her hand, and they quietly slipped out the back gate. When she saw the view, she gasped. They were about 100 meters from a cliff that overlooked the sound.

"Oh my god! It's gorgeous." She could see white caps churning around rocky outcroppings, the moon lighting the surface of the water as though it was touched with silver from an artist's paintbrush.

"I love it out here." He led her across the expanse of grass toward the rocky ledge. He sat down, then offered her his hand. She slipped her boots off and carefully sat beside him, swinging her legs over the edge, noticing him notice them. Her face flushed.

"That dress, jersey, whatever – it looks nice." He smiled.

"Thanks."

"I'd rather it was my jersey, though." His voice was low, and it made her blush.

She started to laugh, but he turned to her, putting his hand on her arm. "I'm not joking, Em."

Her cheeks were really red now, she could tell from the heat, so she stared out at the water. "I wonder where that boat is headed."

He looked out where her eyes were tracking a sail boat. "Hard to say."

"I love inventing stories about strangers. You know, the girl at the restaurant sitting alone with a book. The guy in the park feeding birds. I imagine what their lives are like, who they're meeting. Or missing."

"So you're a writer?" His voice was soft, quiet.

"I like to write, yeah."

"So, tell me this story. Who's on that boat?"

"I don't know. Maybe an old man whose wife died?"

He shook his head. "No. I think it's a young couple, maybe twenty five. It's their third date, and he's taking her out on his sailboat to spend the night under the stars and the moon, letting the waves rock them to sleep."

She swallowed a lump in her throat. "That's beautiful."

"You're beautiful." He turned and stared into her eyes with an intensity that made her blush even redder. She was glad for the darkness.

Then, his eyes wandered down to her mouth for just a moment before he leaned in, brought his free hand to her jaw, and kissed her. It was a soft kiss, sweet and gentle. A perfect first real kiss. She could feel warmth spreading through her body.

When he pulled away, he looked sheepish. "I'm sorry. I shouldn't have done that."

"No, I'm sorry. I should probably go."

She started to get up, but he touched her arm. "No, you shouldn't go. You didn't do anything wrong. I did. I'm sorry."

Her heart was about to beat out of her chest, and he was so close she could feel heat radiating off of him. She looked up at him. "I'll admit, It wasn't a terrible kiss, but –"

She couldn't finish her sentence because he leaned in and pressed his lips to hers again, curling his fingers behind her neck and pulling her in closer. This time, his kiss was harder, needier. He slid his handis up into her hair, his fingers tangling in it. He clasped his other arm around her waist.

Heat was pooling low in her abdomen. She knew she should stop it, but she really, really didn't want to.

All too soon, he pulled away again. "Oh, God, Em, I'm so sorry." His voice was ragged, rough.

She swallowed hard. "You keep saying you're sorry for kissing me. I'm starting to feel like I'm a bad kisser."

She meant it as a joke, but he ran his thumb over her smile, shaking his head slowly, then leaned in and took her mouth again. His tongue probed her lips, and she opened them for him, letting him explore her mouth.

She'd always worried she wouldn't know what to do when she was kissed, but her body told her. She let her tongue explore his as well, lifted her hands to his shoulders, let him press her against him.

His hands skimmed down her back, to her waist, back up her sides, drifting higher. That was when she tensed, and he stopped, pressing his forehead to hers, breathless, fingers clenching the fabric of her dress.

"I'm sorry, Chase, I just, I'm not –"

He put a finger to her lips. "Shhhh." He moved to kiss her again, but she didn't respond, and he pulled his head back, questioning her with his eyes.

Shit. This was not who she was. "You have a girlfriend," she whispered.

His eyes were dark. He sighed and hung his head. "Em, there are things you don't understand."

"Then tell me, Chase." He lifted his face, looking at her again. "Just tell me."

He sighed and rubbed the back of his neck. "Well, you know my dad." He said it almost like a question.

"Um, nope. Never met him."

He chuckled. "My dad is Adam Kessler."

She shrugged again. Clueless.

"HorizonTech's Adam Kessler? CEO of one of the biggest tech companies in the world?" When she shook her head, he laughed.

"What can that possibly have to do with Gretchen. With us?"

"Do you never watch the news?" He laughed again, in disbelief. "Gretchen's dad is Lyle Thomas."

Holy shit. That name she did know. "*The* Lyle Thomas?" She felt so small suddenly. Chase and Gretchen's families were crazy rich. She knew they were rich, but now she knew they were like *rich* rich. She couldn't believe he was sitting here with her — kissing her — on a Friday night.

"Yep. Clearsky CEO. The green technology hero of the world. When Gretchen and I hooked up at the end of the summer, my dad was so excited, I swear he almost kissed me." He pretend-shivered. "I think he could just see all the good press Horizon would get if he could somehow be associated with Clearsky —

especially considering all of the controversy about Horizon in the media lately."

Emmalee had no idea what he was talking about, but she did note that the timing of him and Gretchen getting together was extremely questionable. Hadn't Audrey just fallen down the stairs by the end of the summer? She needed to keep that question to herself, though.

"Okay. So even more reason not to be kissing me. Right?" Part of her hoped he'd disagree.

He started nervously playing with his watch band. "We haven't gotten to the second reason." He took a deep breath. "Gretchen and I were cool for a few weeks. But, to make a long story short, I'm just really not that into Gretchen."

"What?" She was even more confused. She'd seen him with his arm around her, whispering in her ear. Sticking his tongue down her throat. Emmalee was feeling guiltier by the minute.

"I mean, she's been weird lately. Just not the person I thought she was. But when I try to talk to her about it, she says everything's fine, like she doesn't want to break up. And I don't want to start a bunch of drama."

"I don't understand. If you're not into each other, just break up." It was still not clicking for her.

"It's not that easy. My dad would be pissed. I'd never hear the end of him screaming and yelling about the optics and PR nightmares."

She really was trying to make this make sense. But he lived in a world so much bigger, so much more, than hers. "But there have to be other ways than using you for publicity?"

He sighed. "First of all, you clearly don't understand how politics and business work." When she narrowed her eyes at him, he was quick to add, "No offense. Most people don't have a reason to know that much about it. But trust me, it matters. A lot."

She nodded, pretending she understood now. If she was

honest, though, she couldn't imagine being in a relationship for any reason other than wanting to be with that person. Especially in high school.

"I just wish you could be with someone you love, umm, I mean, really like." Her cheeks were on fire again. Love? Get a grip, Emmalee.

He chuckled darkly. "Well, in my world, that's what relationships are for – all kinds of reasons that don't have much to do with love. Or even like most of the time."

She would never understand. She didn't know what to say, so she said nothing.

"I know it seems crazy, Em, but it's my reality. I have responsibilities that are beyond what most teenagers are used to. Can't you just accept that?" He looked at her, his eyes pleading.

"Yeah, I guess so." No. Not really.

He stared out at the water now. Steely-eyed. "I know this is a really fucked-up situation, and I promise you, there's nothing I can really do about it."

She thought for a moment. "Chase, it's your life. I won't pretend to understand all the pressure you're under. But Gretchen's my tennis partner, and part of this group of friends, and she'd be upset if she saw you here with me right now."

He laughed bitterly. "Yeah. But not because she loves me so much. I promise you that. The way she's been acting lately, I think there's something else going on. Someone else. In fact, I know it."

"I see." She wondered if he was referring to her mystery caller from the night of the party. She looked back toward the house, suddenly worried someone had seen them kissing, but she didn't see anyone, and she could still hear the music thumping, even over the roar of the ocean below them.

"So." He looked at her, his face so adorable with worry. Her heart melted. "Do you hate me now?"

"I don't hate you, Chase." She smiled, and he took that as an invitation, leaning in for one more kiss, this time another soft, sweet one on her forehead.

"Good. I couldn't take it if you hated me, Em. You're the most real friend I've had in a long time," he whispered before he pulled away.

CHAPTER 13

The next morning, she was floating when she woke up. She'd dreamt all night of Chase's kisses, his hand on hers. The way he'd held her close while they danced. The way he'd pulled her next to him and let her head rest on his shoulder when they all went inside to make more drinks and talk.

The only dark spot was what had happened when Chase's phone dinged, and he stared at it for a moment, then looked up.

"What the fuck, Brit?" His voice was sharp, angry.

"What?" She smiled sweetly at him, eyes wide.

Emmalee peeked over his shoulder and her heart sank. It was a picture of Chase kissing her out on the ledge, his hand in her hair, his lips pressed hard to hers. She looked up at Britney, then back to Chase.

He was clenching his jaw, clearly upset. "If Gretchen sees this, she'll be pissed."

She could hear the anger seething under his voice. It bothered her a little. He said he wasn't that into Gretchen. But, he had said he didn't want drama. She would try to understand that.

"Right..." Britney stretched out the word. "Gretchen would be pissed." Britney and Chase stared at each other, something clearly being communicated between them. "That's why I'd never show it to her. Obviously. I just thought it was sweet." She grinned again.

"Right. Delete it, please." Chase's voice had softened, clearly backing down from his initial anger.

The conversation had gone back to normal, Britney refusing to show it to Bryce, who'd wanted to know if it had any naked girls in it.

Chase had walked Emmalee to her car, and given her a hug and a chaste kiss on the top of her head. "Drive safe," he'd whispered as he'd closed the car door softly when she got in.

Now, she stretched out, enjoying the morning sunshine and even the soreness in her muscles. It felt good to know she was getting stronger. She'd even woken up at a reasonable hour. Nine o'clock in the morning wasn't exactly Colonel Sloane time, but it was pretty good for a high school kid.

She spent the rest of the morning catching up on chores and her English and Spanish homework, reading a few chapters of her book, and even finishing up a rough draft of her story for her creative writing class.

While she snacked on carrots, she took a few minutes to read and respond to Mekayla's texts from last night and this morning. Mekayla had said it was interesting that they'd confirmed Audrey had actually cheated on Chase. "Kind of a coincidence that his cheating girlfriend gets in a coma and within days he's dating someone his dad just loves."

"I really don't think Chase had anything to do with it. He's really a nice guy, and he doesn't seem to be all that into Gretchen anyway."

"Hmmm. Just don't forget you're investigating."

"Lol."

"Seriously. Don't let them suck you in."

"I won't. MOM!"

Emmalee laughed uneasily. She wondered if Mekayla was just jealous that the popular kids liked her. She shook her head, clearing her mind, and tossed the phone aside.

By two o'clock, she was dressed in a fresh workout outfit and at the gym. It was a grueling session, given her sore muscles from her time at the gym the day before, but she pushed through and didn't even collapse at the end. Britney and Kristina even seemed somewhat impressed.

Afterward, they went back to Kristina's to shower — Emmalee had remembered to pack her own clothes – and then headed into the city to find Homecoming dresses. Emmalee barely even flinched at the $500 price tag on the silver dress they'd insisted she buy. She just swiped her mom's credit card and filed the whole experience under things she could – would – deal with later.

Since it was a Sunday night, they dropped her back at her car, and she went home, planning to make a simple meal of soup and grilled cheese, but was surprised instead by the sight of a shiny black Elantra in the driveway, her Uncle Dan leaning back against it, arms crossed.

Shit.

She took a deep breath and got out of the car, grabbing her shopping bag. "Uncle Dan!" she yelled, running to him and flinging her arms around his neck. Inside, her heart was hammering. Why was he here? Her globe-trotting, photojour-nalist uncle never just dropped in. It was always phone calls and the occasional FaceTime.

"Hey, Emma Bee." He pulled back, holding her at arm's length, examining her with his kind brown eyes. "Look at you. You get more beautiful every time I see you."

She blushed. "Right."

"Can't argue with the truth. Just look at you."

She had to admit, she did look pretty good. She had on new

jeans and a cropped sweater. Her hair was pulled back in a ponytail. Not the typical Emmalee.

"So, what brings you here?" Emmalee's heart still thrummed in her chest.

"Well, I heard from a little birdie that you and Nikki were here." He pushed his floppy brown hair out of his face.

She laughed. "Yeah, I was on FaceTime when Mom told you about her orders."

He grinned. "So, the truth then?"

Her heart hammered again. "Always." Please don't let it be about me, she thought.

"Your incredibly talented uncle won the bid on a Nat Geo book featuring state parks in Washington." He huffed on his nails, polishing them on his collar. Typical Dan move.

"That's awesome!" It really was.

"And, even better, I'll be putting down some roots for once. I'll be staying in the Seattle area for at least a year. It's going to take a long time to shoot all the parks in every season, at different times of day."

Emmalee nodded. "That's even better!" Not really. If Dan was one thing, it was passionate. About his work. About his family. Nicky and Dan's mother had been an alcoholic, her way of coping with their father's pain killer addiction after a Vietnam injury. They managed to work during the day, but nights were spent dead to the world, often screaming and slamming doors before the substances claimed them.

Nikki had raised Dan practically on her own, ensuring that both of them made it out of there and into better lives. And now, there was nothing Dan wouldn't do for Nikki. And that included keeping an eye on Emmalee when Nikki was away. The last thing she needed right now was another set of eyes watching her every move.

"Well, I have a lot of homework to do." She headed for the front door.

"No worries," he said, following her. "I know, you're eighteen. You have school, activities, friends. I won't bug you. But, how about I cook up something fabulous for dinner?"

She tossed her keys on the coffee table, still holding her shopping bag, and turned to him. His eyes sparkled and he grinned at her again.

"Yeah, okay. That sounds good." She smiled and leaned in for another hug. "I could use some real food."

"Okay, then. I'll scope out the kitchen, then head into town to pick up some groceries. You unpack your shopping bags and get started on that homework."

He began rifling through the refrigerator and cabinets. A few minutes later, she heard the front door close.

She sighed with relief. She needed to figure out her next steps. In her room, she hung up the new dress and gathered her dirty workout clothes. After tossing those in the washer, she checked the house over to make sure there was nothing embarrassing around, like the box of tampons she found sitting on the bathroom counter. Not that he didn't know about such things. But still. She didn't want him staring at it while he did his business.

Time to tackle homework. She'd somehow managed to keep her grades fairly decent in spite of all the time she'd been spending with Britney, Chase, Mekayla, everyone. She chalked that up to it being the beginning of the school year. Right now, however, she was staring at a set of Trig problems she had no idea how to solve. She was in the middle of watching a YouTube tutorial when she heard a knock at the front door.

"Wow! Need some help?" She reached out to take one of the bags in his arms, but he turned away.

"I've got it, Em. You just hit the books."

"Seriously, I can help bring the groceries in and do my homework. It's only 8:00."

"Nope. Get to work, soldier." His voice was stern, almost

parental, and Emmalee rolled her eyes, once she'd turned away and headed back down the hall. She had to admit, though, it was kind of nice listening to the clatter of pots and pans in the kitchen, Uncle Dan's 90s rap playing from his phone. She smiled the whole time she finished up her math and history assignments.

Dinner was delicious. He'd roasted fresh salmon with herbs. After cleaning her plate, she drained her glass of iced tea. "That was amazing, Uncle Dan. Thanks for cooking."

He smiled at her. "Just a little something to keep your belly full." He winked.

"Right. That was incredible. Where'd you learn to cook like that?"

"Being a bachelor, I've learned that if I want good home cooked meals, I'm going to have to do it myself." He shrugged and grinned. "It helps with the ladies, too."

"Gross!"

He laughed. "Speaking of, are there any boys or girls on your radar?"

"You can't just ask a question like that!" She stood up, cheeks turning red, and picked up their plates. She was scraping and rinsing them when he entered the kitchen behind her.

"I'll take that as a yes." He began putting away the leftovers. "So tell me all about them."

She could feel her anger flaring, so she turned on the tap and filled her glass with water and drank it down, buying herself time.

"I'd rather not talk about this."

"Okay, fair, I guess. I just like to know what's going on in your life."

She turned around. "School. Tennis. Newspaper. Chores. Homework. You know the basics."

"What about friends? Who are you hanging out with?"

She sighed. She was so tired of her mom and Dan worrying about her. "I've made some friends, okay? Kids from school."

Her phone buzzed in her jeans pocket. She pulled it out and looked down. Shit. Britney wanted her to meet at Kris's.

"I'm going to go finish my homework, okay? I'll take care of the dishes before I go to bed."

He just stared at her, his head cocked sideways for a few seconds. "Okay, go do your homework. I'll take care of the cleanup, though. Not much else to do." She didn't argue with him. She just wanted to get away.

The next morning, she awoke to the smells of bacon and coffee. She was going to get spoiled by this, she thought.

"We don't normally eat breakfast," she mumbled as she joined Uncle Dan in the kitchen and poured herself a mug of coffee.

"Well, I'm not normal." He shot her a goofy grin, and she couldn't help but smile back.

He'd clearly already showered. His hair was drying, and he was flipping a pancake onto a plate piled with them. "Sit. Eat."

"Gladly." She sat at the table and dug into a plate loaded with scrambled eggs and bacon, trying not to think about how many calories she was consuming. She wasn't used to thinking like that, but Britney and Kris had reminded her that even a few extra pounds would make it harder to haul herself across the tennis court to chase down a ball.

"Hey, Em, I just want to apologize if I was too nosey last night. Give me the benefit of the doubt, okay? I'm not a parent, so I don't always know the best way to..." He trailed off.

"You're fine." She was sorry she'd made him feel bad, but she didn't want to get into some deep conversation.

"No. I mean it. I'm sorry. I'll respect your privacy, but I just want you to know you can talk to me if you have problems. Or not problems." He smiled at her.

She smiled back, feeling bad for making him want to apologize. "I know, Uncle Dan." She scarfed down two syrup-soaked pancakes, chased them with coffee, and then darted to her room to change.

He called down the hallway after her. "What time will you be home from practice?".

She groaned. "I'm not sure. It just depends on the day. I can text you when I know for sure?"

"That works. I'm planning an even better dinner tonight."

Great. "Will do! Love you!" Then she escaped.

It was clear that Gretchen and Chase were not speaking to each other when Gretchen came into English and asked Tyler to switch seats with her. As soon as she sat down next to Britney, she pulled out her notebook, tucked her AirPods in, and hunkered down over her phone. Emmalee wondered if that was about Homecoming.

Chase's eyes betrayed nothing. He merely flicked Gretchen a glance, and then turned to Emmalee. "Em, how was your weekend?" His grin told her they were sharing a secret. She instantly felt guilt, but also all warm and melty inside. So confusing.

"Good." She grinned back, shyly, feeling her face warm. God, she wished she could control that.

"Glad to hear it." He winked and turned back to the front of the room.

Later, on her way to lunch, Mekayla caught her at her locker.

"So, what else have you figured out about –" Mekayla looked around furtively. "You know?"

Emmalee sighed and rolled her eyes. "Don't be so dramatic, okay? I didn't learn anything else."

Mekayla looked startled. "No need to be rude. I'm just checking in."

"Sorry. I'm just in a bad mood." She felt a little bad about being rude to Mekayla. "My uncle showed up last night, so I was basically under house arrest."

"Ah. I see. Well, maybe you'll get some new info at lunch?" Mekayla shrugged and gave Emmalee a hopeful smile.

Emmalee tried to smile back, but she wasn't entirely sure how she felt about snooping anymore. Britney and Kristina and Chase had never been anything but nice to her so far.

After tennis practice, Emmalee walked to the showers with Britney and Kris. Gretchen had sped ahead of them, not speaking a word more than necessary during practice.

Gretchen really was kind of a bitch, Emmalee had to admit. She'd always been rude to her, even though Emmalee had done nothing to deserve it. Well, she had done one thing, but she was sure Gretchen didn't know about that kiss. Besides, she'd put a stop to that Saturday night, no matter how much she really didn't want to.

"Hello! Em!" Britney shouted, breaking her out of her thoughts.

"Yeah, what?" Emmalee's cheeks pinked.

"We're hanging out at Kris's tonight, so we're just going to shower over there. The guys are coming over again, too." Britney raised her eyebrows suggestively.

"Oh, I can't tonight."

"Bitch, you already blew us off last night. No way you're doing it again tonight."

"No really, sorry. My uncle just showed up at my house last night and is staying for God knows how long. I'm in prison after practice, basically. I couldn't even get on my phone last night." It was a lie, but she wasn't sure how to get out of Britney's request the night before, so she'd simply shut her phone off and ignored it. She'd really needed to focus on her homework and process everything that had happened with Chase, anyway.

"Hmmm. How long is this uncle staying?" Britney's voice had a bitter edge to it.

"I'm not really sure." Emmalee shrugged and smiled apologetically. That was the truth, at least. "Probably not too long."

"Well, let's hope. I'd hate to have to kidnap you." Britney grinned at Emmalee. "Come on, Kris. Let's go have some fun."

Emmalee breathed a sigh of relief as the two left together. She was glad Britney had let her off the hook. Part of her was angry she was missing what would no doubt be a much more interesting evening, but she also felt like it would be rude to ditch Uncle Dan so soon after he got here.

She'd also have missed out on another amazing dinner. This time it was real fried chicken, from home instead of a bucket.

"You're going to make me gain fifty pounds with all this food," she groaned as she leaned back in her chair, trying to ease her overfull stomach.

"Yeah, well, between school and tennis practice, I'm sure you're starving by the time you get home at night." He gave her a pointed look. "You need fuel to get you through all the homework."

She laughed. "Fair." She didn't want to tell him that she was worried about gaining weight and earning the disapproval of Britney and Kristina. And maybe causing Chase to lose his attraction to her.

"You know, the cabinets were nearly bare when I unpacked the groceries the other day." His eyes were worried, and she felt bad for him.

She shrugged. "I just hadn't gone shopping yet, and like I told you, Mom and I don't usually eat breakfast. Plus, I'm busy, so I just pick something up when I'm out."

"Okay, okay. I get it. Just promise me you'll take care of yourself, kid."

"Of course I will." She raised her eyes to meet his.

"Also," he took a deep breath. "I saw a bottle of Crown Royal in the cabinet. You've not taken up a whiskey habit, have you?"

He said it lightly, but she could feel the tension and worry underneath.

"No, I haven't." She sighed. "It's Mom's." She knew how he felt about substances of any kind, given their parents' history.

He nodded, a sad smile on his face. "I'm leaving early in the morning. I've got a meeting with my publisher in Seattle, and then I'm going to start scoping out apartments. I'll probably stay in the city a few days at least, but if you need me, call me."

"Okay. I'll miss you." She only kind of meant it. She loved him, but she wanted to get back to her own life.

"Uh huh." He grinned at her. "It'll be so sad to have Uncle Dan quit nosing around in your life."

"So sad." She laughed, and he tossed his napkin across the table at her.

"Well, how about you help me with the dishes tonight so we can have a little more quality time together." He raised his eyebrows in invitation.

"Deal." She smiled and began clearing dishes from the table.

The next morning she found some cash beside a note on the counter:

Fridge is stocked. Left some cash for whatever. Call or text if you need anything. Love you, Emma Bee.

She smiled and set out for school, breakfast-free and, better yet, adult-free.

CHAPTER 14

The freedom meant that when Britney wanted everyone to meet at Kris's again after practice, she could say yes without having to ask or worry. She was free to gossip while sipping on flavored vodka, letting the warm buzz wash over her. And later, when the boys arrived, she was free to slip out back with Chase and let him hold her hand as they walked the extensive grounds together.

They'd stopped at a koi pond and stood watching the fish slipping through the dark water.

"I hope you don't think I'm an asshole, Em." He looked at her with worried eyes.

"I don't think that. Why would I think that?"

"You know." He rubbed the back of his neck. "Gretchen."

Her heart squeezed. "Yeah, but that's just a bad situation you're caught in. You can't really help it."

"I know, I just. I can't help but feel bad about it, you know?"

He looked so sad that she couldn't help feeling bad for him.

"I know. It's because you're a good guy." A small part of her wondered how true that was, but the way he looked, how bad he felt, made her push that thought to the back of her mind. She chose to take him at his word and squeeze his hand instead. "Don't worry. It will be okay."

Later that week, she wondered how true that was.

"I'm not sure that's such a good plan," Emmalee said. She was in Kristina's bedroom, sitting in the fuzzy chair in front of the vanity. Britney was sprawled on Kristina's bed, and Kristina was sitting cross-legged next to her, scrolling on her phone.

"Well, I'm not sure your opinion really matters here." Britney looked annoyed.

"Brit, be nice." Kristina sounded annoyed as well. At Emmalee? Britney? She really didn't want them to be mad at her.

"I'm always nice." Britney grinned.

Kris rolled her eyes.

"Anyway, I just mean that you don't know Gretchen like we do. She'll be more willing to listen if we're all on the same side."

"I know you've known her longer. But–" Emmalee hesitated.

"But what?" Britney's voice was controlled, but her eyes squinted, a challenge in them.

"Won't she just feel like we're ganging up on her?" Emmalee leaned back in the cushy chair.

Britney sighed. "No. Like I said, we've known her a lot longer, and we know how to get through to her."

"But you guys aren't even speaking to each other right now, are you?" Emmalee wondered where all her newfound confidence was coming from. She'd never been one to speak up and argue, and she definitely never would have to someone like Britney. But something about this just felt wrong somehow.

"Oh my god, Em, Jesus! No offense, but we've all known each other forever. Yeah, we're all pissed off at her right now, and she's maybe a little pissed at us, but it's not like we're never going to speak again. Get a grip. You know how it is with friends."

Emmalee stared at her, not sure what to say.

Britney raised her eyebrows in shock. "You have had friends? Right?"

That stung. Emmalee blinked back the hot tears that leapt to her eyes. How could she tell them that yes, she had had friends, a long time ago. And that it had ended badly. Very badly. And since then, she hadn't really allowed herself to make any. Until now.

She nodded. "Of course," she said, barely above a whisper, eyes focused on her nails.

"God, Brit, you're being harsh." Kristina shot Emmalee an apologetic look before turning back to Britney.

Britney sighed. "I'm sorry, Em. I guess I'm just stressed out about all this drama."

Kristina snickered.

"Shut it, bitch." She swatted Kristina on the leg playfully. "*Anyway.*" She gave Emmalee a look that dared her to interrupt again. "Gretchen's supposed to be back in town on the Sunday morning after Homecoming. She still won't even tell us where she's going. But, her parents will still be out of town, too, so we'll just have a private little surprise Homecoming party at her place. Then, once we're all there, we can have our intervention."

"How can you have a party at her house if she's not home?"

Britney looked at her like was stupid. "We know the garage code obvs."

Emmalee felt sick. She would be willing to bet that confrontation would be ugly, and she wanted no part of it. Plus, she couldn't help thinking how much it was like the incident with Audrey. They'd all been together at that end of summer party, right after Chase found out Audrey had cheated on him.

She took a deep breath. "Ummm, since I haven't been around as long, like you said, I can just stay home that night. I don't want to butt in."

"You have to be there, Em." Britney looked at her with wide eyes. "Chase needs all the support he can get. Plus, she knows you're going to Homecoming with Chase, and with you there, you'll be a reminder that she can't just expect Chase to watch her screw around with some other guy and him not do the same."

Emmalee shook her head. Screw around? Was that what Chase was doing with her — he'd seemed so sincere? Or, was that just Britney being Britney? She'd like to ask Chase, but there was no way she could already start the "what am I to you" conversation after just a few close encounters. She didn't get to dwell on it long because Britney continued.

"We'll force her to see things our way. She can keep her side piece if she wants, but she has to let Chase have his own fun, or she can suffer the consequences.

Emmalee shot Britney a look. "Consequences?" Like Audrey? She shoved that thought to the back of her mind. She really felt like Mekayla had poisoned her against Britney.

Britney grinned.

Emmalee looked to Kristina, hoping for clarification.

"Nobody wants Britney's consequences. Trust me." Kristina smirked, but held Emmalee's stare a beat too long for comfort.

"Well, then they shouldn't do stupid shit," Britney retorted lightly.

"Seriously, what kind of consequences?" Emmalee looked from Britney to Kristina.

Britney sighed. "Don't worry your pretty little head, Em. It's just that real friends stick together. If she wants to be in our group, she has to treat everyone well. Including her boyfriend."

Kristina rolled her eyes and got up from the bed. "Time to go, ladies. I'm going out with Tyler tonight."

"Time to freak it!" Britney, making moaning sounds and thrusting her pelvis in Kristina's direction.

"Shut up, Brit." Kristina laughed and headed for the bathroom. "See yourselves out, please."

Emmalee left, feeling nauseous. On the drive home, she brainstormed ways to get out of Britney's planned attack on

Gretchen. Short of having a massive heart attack or car wreck, she wasn't sure what to do.

She thought about Audrey lying somewhere in a coma. Being there when they confronted Gretchen would be a great opportunity to get more information and see if Britney really was the monster Mekayla made her out to be.

CHAPTER 15

Homecoming week arrived, and along with it came lots of headaches. Between classes, practices, dress-up days, hallway decorating, and the Homecoming King and Queen competition, Emmalee felt her nerves stretched thin.

Britney insisted that Emmalee and Kristina join her for each dress-up day, and their outfits just *had* to coordinate. That meant shopping for matching pajamas and Mean Girl outfits, for starters. Britney was also running for Homecoming Queen – and Gretchen was one of her competitors – so she insisted that they send out an endless string of messages and TikToks encouraging students to vote for Britney. The reward for doing so would be a rager hosted by Britney herself.

Every night was spent planning and prepping – and drinking – at Kristina's house. Emmalee wondered briefly why they'd never been to Britney's house, but thought it better not to ask.

By the time Saturday morning rolled around, she was exhausted – not to mention terrified. It was the first actual tennis match she'd be playing in, and she was nervous about letting Gretchen down. If there was one saving grace, it was that she didn't have to play singles. There was no way she was ready for that.

They were matched up with a pair of athletes from a nearby town, two tall, muscular girls who looked intimidating. Gretchen didn't seem intimidated, though. She'd walked on the court looking as sleek and put together as ever.

"Try not to get in my way." Gretchen shot an annoyed look at Emmalee. "I'll serve first."

Thankfully, Gretchen's first three serves were aces, so Emmalee didn't even have to move or attempt to hit the ball. They were up 40-love, and Emmalee was hoping for a quick win in this first set. But, one of the other girls managed to catch the ball with the edge of her racket and just get it over the net. Emmalee lunged forward, nearly toppling over, and missed the ball entirely. She did manage to hit the net, though, which was awesome. Just fantastic.

Gretchen rolled her eyes as Emmalee got back in position. She served again, and thankfully, that was another ace. Game one over. Only a bajillion more to play.

By noon, they were done. Emmalee was drenched in sweat and even a little proud of herself. She and Gretchen had won their match, mostly due to Gretchen's insane athletic ability, but Emmalee had even managed to hit two balls over the net. The hits themselves didn't result in any actual points, but it was an improvement.

"Emmalee, what color are you and Chase wearing tonight?" Britney called out across the court as the girls were all packing up and heading to their bus.

Emmalee's cheeks flushed even more than the exertion had already caused. "Um, my dress is silver." Britney, of course, already knew that and probably just wanted to rub it in for Gretchen's benefit. Emmalee felt conflicted – partly excited to go to the dance with Chase, and partly bad for Gretchen.

Gretchen said nothing. Didn't even look up from the bag she

was zipping. She just hefted it onto her shoulder and turned toward the bus.

Britney leaned over and whispered to Emmalee, "Operation Gretchen has begun."

Emmalee gave a weak nod, wanting to throw up, partly from the tennis, but mostly because the rest of the weekend was going to be tense at best. She was extremely nervous about the dance, a good nervous, but still. And downright terrified about their planned intervention with Gretchen Sunday night.

She coped with the anxiety the only way she knew how. She reverted to AirPods and folded into herself during the long bus ride home, ignoring Mekayla's texts asking for updates.

As she got dressed that night at Kristina's, she was almost trembling with anticipation. There were butterflies in her stomach – it was a cliché for a reason, she was realizing – as she thought about being in Chase's arms again, maybe possibly sharing another kiss, even just a sweet kiss on the forehead.

Britney and Kris helped with her hair and makeup, and as always, poured shots, this time Fireball to warm them up for the evening. Emmalee nearly choked to death after the first one burned down her throat and up into her nostrils. Britney and Kris laughed so hard, they'd had to fix their makeup.

"Oh my God, Em, don't die on us!" Britney doubled over.

"I'm sorry, I just–" Emmalee stuttered.

"No, no. Don't be sorry. You are just hilarious!" Britney dabbed at tears of laughter.

Emmalee bristled. "Yeah, I'm a regular comedian." There was a little acid in her voice, probably because the alcohol had loosened her up.

Britney's eyes snapped up and met Emmalee's, but she didn't say anything.

After a few finishing touches, she slipped her shoes on, and they headed downstairs where the guys were waiting. As she came around the landing, Chase's eyes met hers, and she could see a definite reaction, his cheeks flushing.

"Damn! Look at these hot bitches!" Bryce shouted up the stairs, hooting and hollering. Chase just held her eyes, watching her descend.

At the bottom of the stairs, Chase held his arm out and tucked her in close to his side to escort her to the car. "You look amazing," he whispered.

She blushed. "Thanks." She really did, though. The dress accentuated and clung to her curves in all the right places, and it was starting to feel a little less awkward.

They all piled into Bryce's Humvee and headed into the city for an incredible seafood dinner, and then back to Ravensville for the dance. On the ride back to town, they passed the bottle of Fireball around, each taking long pulls. The guys talked about the game the night before, reliving all the major plays that led up to the Ravens' crushing win over Smithton, their biggest rival.

Chase had his arm around her, and his fingers gently grazed her bare shoulder. She felt like she was in another world, a world she'd always imagined but thought she'd never be permitted into. She felt like a magical fairy princess sitting next to the most handsome prince in the land.

CHAPTER 16

The dance was indeed like her very own magical, fairy princess ball. When she walked into the gymnasium on Chase's arm, she could feel all eyes on her, and for the most part, they seemed appreciative. Mekayla's weren't – hers looked worried. Marshall was next to her, but he just gave her a half smile, looking a bit disappointed. She let it slide right off her, though, and let Chase lead her to the table where their friends were staking a claim.

As soon as they'd dropped off their phones and purses, the guys led the girls onto the dance floor. Britney and Kristina immediately started jumping up and down to the beat of a pop song Emmalee hated, but after a second, she just started jumping, too. It felt awkward at first, but then good to just let herself go. She glanced over and saw Chase staring at her, his mouth crooked in an appreciative grin. She closed her eyes and just let the music take over.

When the song ended and a slower one started, Chase moved in and took her hand. "Come here," he said, his voice soft and throaty.

He pulled her in close, and she looked up at him, grinning.

"Having fun?"

"I am." She was still grinning like a fool.

He tightened his arms around her waist and pulled her in closer. "Me, too."

He rested his cheek on the top of her head, and she could feel goosebumps rising on her arms. She felt like she could stay there all night, in spite of the nagging thought that people would start wondering about them. And about Gretchen. But he didn't seem to mind, so she just followed his lead.

Eventually, though, she had to let him go. The principal was announcing the Homecoming King and Queen, and Chase had to go on stage with the rest of the candidates. Emmalee waited anxiously, hoping Chase would win. And Britney.

"This year's Homecoming King is—" The principal paused for dramatic effect. "Chase Kessler." Emmalee's heart clenched, and she cheered as loudly as everyone else in the room when Chase walked out on stage to be crowned.

"Now, ladies and gentlemen, the moment we've all been waiting for. Please welcome to the stage your Homecoming Queen, Miss Gretchen Thomas."

The crowd cheered, but Emmalee stood there, not sure what to do. The principal waited a moment before Chase walked over and whispered something to him.

"It appears Miss Thomas was not able to attend tonight. We will make sure she gets her crown on Monday." He looked irritated, but Emmalee doubted he'd say anything considering how wealthy her parents were. He shoved the crown into Mrs. Jenkins' hand and scrambled off the stage.

Mrs. Jenkins' eyes were huge. "Oh, okay," she said, approaching the microphone. "Now it's time for the King and Queen to dance. Chase, since Gretchen isn't here, you'll have the honor of dancing with this year's Runner-Up, Miss Britney Whitfield." Britney walked on stage, smiling, but Emmalee knew she had to feel crushed. She'd worked so hard to win this. And ended up losing to a friend who wasn't so much a friend anymore.

There were cheers for Britney, too, but not as enthusiastic. Emmalee cheered as loud as she could to try to make up for the relative quiet response of everyone else.

Chase held his arm out to Britney, who looked up at him, smiling, and the two shared a look for a few moments — long enough to make Emmalee feel a twinge of jealousy pinching her heart. Then Britney took his arm , and he led his stand-in Queen to the dance floor.

The first strains of a Bruno Mars song filled the gym as Chase pulled Britney close to him, and the crowd drew back, forming a circle around the two. Emmalee watched as Britney looked up at Chase. Her eyes were a little shiny, like maybe she'd been crying, but Chase was apparently doing a good job of taking her mind off the loss because she was also smiling and laughing, and it looked genuine.

Jealousy tugged at Emmalee's heart again, but she forced herself to smile. She didn't want anyone to see her true feelings. When the song finally ended, Chase planted a kiss on Britney's forehead – that really stung – and led her off the floor to noticeably louder cheers from the crowd.

They all met back at their table, and before anyone could congratulate Chase, Britney loudly proclaimed, "I should have won over that bitch."

"Jealousy doesn't look good on you, Brit," Chase admonished.

Britney shrugged. "I don't get jealous. I get even." Her eyes glittered as she smiled at all of them. The others just laughed, but Emmalee thought she saw a worrying gleam in Britney's eyes. But then, the look vanished and Britney was dragging Bryce back out on the dance floor when an Ariana Grande song came on.

Emmalee snuck away to the bathroom, wanting a moment to catch her breath and collect her thoughts. She ran into

Mekayla, who was at the sinks, touching up her dark purple lipstick.

"Hey." Emmalee stepped up to the sink next to her.

Mekayla looked at her in the mirror. "Hey. I texted you."

"I know. I'm sorry. I was just really busy." It wasn't a complete lie. She *was* busy.

"Okay." Mekayla smiled kindly. "Listen, Emmalee, I'm worried you're getting in way too deep with them. I saw the way you were with Chase out there, and–"

"There you are!" Britney's shrill voice startled both of them. "You ran away from us." Britney looked Mekayla up and down, her brows knitted in confusion, as though trying to figure out who Mekayla was. But they'd gone to school together forever. Weird. "Come on, Em, we need to go."

"Hang on. I was talking."

"No, it's okay. I was done." Mekayla snapped the cap on her lipstick and walked out.

"What were you two talking about?" Britney asked.

"Nothing really. Just catching up."

"You should probably stay away from her. She sticks her nose into everyone's business and it's going to bite her one day. And you really don't want it to bite you, too. Now, let's go." Britney walked out, not waiting for Emmalee to reply.

Emmalee quickly texted Mekayla.

> Sorry - Café Vibes after school Monday?

Mekayla thumbs-upped the message, then followed up with two words.

> MEKAYLA
>
> Be careful.

CHAPTER 17

After the dance, Bryce drove them back to Kristina's house. Her parents were out at some charity event in Seattle and were spending the night in the city, so Kristina had spread the word that there would be a party at her house.

It didn't take long for people to show up and start inhabiting every empty space in the house. Emmalee walked through the crowd, searching for Chase. She found him in the kitchen, pouring drinks.

"What'll it be, princess?" He smiled, his eyes twinkling at her.

"Whatever you're making, your majesty." She smiled back.

He smirked and poured something red and slushy into a tall glass and handed it to her. She took it and drank a long gulp without hesitation, barely even flinching at the burn. She was getting used to this.

"Come on." He set the pitcher down, reached for her hand, and headed toward the stairway in the back of the kitchen.

She followed, excited about where the night might lead.

Upstairs, he peeked into one room after another as they made their way down the hallway. Most of them had couples tangled up together in various states of undress. At the last room, he slipped inside, waiting for her to enter before he shut the door and dimmed the light.

"God, it's nice to be away from everyone." He sat on the bed, back against the headboard, and stretched his legs out. She hesitated, but he patted the bed, so she took a deep breath and sat beside him, pulling a pillow up in front of her stomach, clutching it to her. She'd never been in a bed with a guy before. Clearly, he sensed her anxiety.

"Don't worry. I'm not trying to be a creep." He chuckled. "Sometimes, I just get so sick of all the people around all the time. You know?" He laid his head back and closed his eyes.

"Yeah, I get it." She did, truly. Until the last few weeks, she'd spent two years working hard to avoid most people. "Why don't you just go home?" She hated how much she really hoped he'd say he wanted to stay with her. She knew they were just friends, but every time she was with him, she wanted it to be more than that.

He sighed and opened his eyes again. "Everyone would want to know why I'm being lame."

"Yeah, but you're not hanging out with them anyway." She gestured to the closed door.

"It's okay. They saw me come in. And we'll go back down in a few minutes. I just need a little break."

She nodded, her insides warming that she wasn't one of the *people* he wanted to be away from.

He closed his eyes and laid his head back. "C'mere." He extended his arm, eyes still closed. She paused for a moment, then leaned into him, resting her head on his chest. He wrapped his arm around her and pulled her in, kissed the top of her head. "This is nice."

"Yeah," she said. It was more than nice.

"Chase, can I ask you something?" Her heartbeat picked up.

"Shoot." He kept his eyes closed.

"Well, I was just wondering about what happened with Audrey?" She rested her palm on his chest, fidgeting with the buttons on his shirt.

His voice was tight. "What about it?" She could feel his chest tighten as well.

"I've just heard that something happened with her, but I don't know exactly what?" Not entirely the truth, but not entirely a lie either.

He sighed. "We were at a party last summer. She was drunk and somehow fell down the stairs. She was always getting way too drunk." He sounded annoyed, not exactly like someone whose girlfriend suffered a horrific, life-altering accident. "I kept telling her to chill on the drinking, but she never listened."

She just waited quietly, her finger playing with a button on his shirt.

"Now she's in a coma and will likely be that way forever." His voice was quieter now, sadder.

"You two were..."

His fingers gripped her shoulder. "Yeah, we dated for a while, but it was no big deal. We weren't that serious."

She nodded. "How long is a while?"

He sighed. "A couple years." She could feel his breathing stop. "But it turns out she was cheating on me."

She raised her head up and looked at him. "Oh, my God, Chase. I'm so sorry. Are you sure?"

He laughed, grimly. "Yeah. I saw it with my own eyes."

Emmalee's jaw dropped. "You walked in on it, um, I mean, them?"

He shook his head. "A friend of mine walked in on them in the act and took a photo so Audrey couldn't deny it later. Thank God I have at least one real friend."

She couldn't imagine taking a picture of people having literal sex. And then showing it to their boyfriend or whatever. But then again, she would want to know if her partner was cheating.

"Who told you?"

"I promised I wouldn't say anything. It's not exactly legal to have that kind of photo on your phone."

She nodded. Gretchen maybe? She'd started dating Chase really quickly after that. Maybe she was trying to find a way to break them up.

"Audrey was friends with all of you, right?" She held her breath, worried she was pushing too much.

"She was, but then she started pissing people off with all of her drinking and drama. Why are you asking all these questions about Audrey?" He turned his head, eyes wide open now, looking at her.

"I just want to know more about you." She smiled at him, hoping he'd believe these were all innocent questions.

He stared for a moment, then nodded and settled back on the pillow, closing his eyes.

She had so many more questions, but decided now wasn't the time. Her phone pinged.

A text from Mekayla.

Any news?

She silenced it and snuggled into Chase's warmth and closed her eyes, too.

Then suddenly, a flash of light startled them awake, and both she and Chase leapt off the bed.

"Having fun up here?" Britney's tone was loaded with innuendo.

"Whatever, Brit. Delete that." Chase was pissed.

"Fine. God. Calm down. Pretty much everyone is gone now. I just wanted to remind you two to be at Gretchen's house tomorrow – well, tonight at 8:00."

"Wait, Gretchen's?" Chase looked confused, and Emmalee's stomach clenched.

"Yes. I talked to her this morning after the meet."

It was Emmalee's turn to look confused, but Britney shot her a *don't you dare* look. So Emmalee chose not to dare point out that Britney and Gretchen hadn't exchanged a single word before, during, or after the meet. Maybe Britney had texted her?

"Anyway, 8:00. Don't be late." With that, Britney left the room.

Emmalee glanced at her phone. It was 4:27 in the morning. She couldn't believe they'd slept for hours together like that.

"Well, I'd better get going. You okay to get home?" Chase gently smoothed some of her hair that must have gotten mussed while they slept.

"Yeah." She smiled, and he leaned close, pecked her on the cheek, and left. She followed, a little disappointed the kiss wasn't a little more — just more.

CHAPTER 18

At 7:58 that evening, she was sitting in Gretchen's driveway, watching rain run down the windshield. She didn't see any other cars outside, so she assumed everyone was running late.

She'd spent the day unable to focus. She'd tried to work on homework and chores, but she kept obsessing over how the night would unfold. She hated confrontation so much. She didn't want to be there for the group's *intervention* with Gretchen, and she really didn't want to be there when Gretchen reacted.

But, here she was. Waiting. She'd hinted to Mekayla that something was going to happen tonight, and Mekayla had insisted that Emmalee had to be there. And she was right. However nervous she was, it was possible that Audrey's name would come up.

Her phone beeped. Britney. "Where are you?"

She was so confused. "Where are you? I'm in the driveway."

"Come in, biatch!"

"Gretchen's house, right?"

"Obviously."

Oh. They were inside already. She took a deep breath, then

went inside, a very bad feeling about the night ahead still roiling in her stomach.

Inside, Emmalee was surprised to find everyone but Gretchen. Kristina had opened the door and led her into the living room where Britney was perched on Bryce's lap and Chase was arm wrestling with Tyler on the polished coffee table.

"About time," Britney remarked. She seemed more anxious than usual.

"Sorry, I didn't see any cars, so, I thought–"

"Ah, well, we just teleported in." Britney grinned at Kristina, who just rolled her eyes.

Weird. "Okay."

"Gretchen should be here soon. She texted me an hour ago that she was leaving the city." Chase slammed Bryce's arm to the table as he gritted out the words.

"What the hell was she doing last night?" Britney's voice was razor sharp.

Chase shot Britney a look. "You do know that not everything is your business, right?"

"Oh, like the fact that you're freaking it with Em here?" Britney batted her eyelashes, grinning.

"Whatever, Brit." Chase shook his head and stood up, and walked out of the room.

"You should leave him alone, Brit."

"Shut the fuck up, Bryce. Just sit there and be cute. I don't pay you to talk."

Bryce pinched her butt. Britney squealed and fell back against him. "Ouch! You bitch!" She dissolved in giggles, and the two of them started wrestling.

Everyone in the room seemed relieved that the tension had been broken.

Emmalee just shook her head and walked in the direction Chase had gone.

In the kitchen, she found him standing in front of an open refrigerator.

"Hey." Her voice came out as a whisper.

He turned around and stared at her. "Hey. Sorry about that."

"It's okay. She's just worried about you."

He frowned. "Don't make excuses for her. She says the stupidest shit sometimes."

She did not want to get started badmouthing Britney, especially not with her in the other room. Plus, friends were supposed to have each other's backs. "Well, I just came in to see if you're okay?"

"Yeah, I'm fine. Just tired." He ran his hands through his hair, mussing it adorably. Emmalee wanted to run her fingers through it.

She nodded, looking at the floor. "Yeah. Me, too."

"You want a drink?"

"Sure." She'd started to enjoy the way the alcohol calmed her nerves.

Just as he turned back to the refrigerator, the sound of a garage door startled them. Chase turned back around, and their eyes met. He popped the top off a bottle of beer and handed it to her. Then he popped his own open. "Here's to shit shows," he said. He tilted his bottle toward hers, and they clinked together.

Emmalee sucked in a deep breath as Gretchen appeared in a doorway at the side of the kitchen, startled when she saw them.

"What the fuck, Chase! You scared the shit out of me." She turned her eyes to Emmalee. "What are you two doing here? Looking for a threesome?" Her eyes shot daggers at Chase.

"Let's chat out in the living room." Chase moved toward Emmalee, pushing past her. Emmalee cast a weak smile at Gretchen, whose face looked confused, and still a little murderous, then followed Chase.

"Give me a sec." Emmalee could hear Gretchen disappearing up the back stairs.

They all sat in the living room, waiting. Britney was still lounging on Bryce's lap, but Kristina, Tyler, Chase, and Emmalee all sat separately, staring at their phones. They could hear Gretchen moving around upstairs, and then back down, the refrigerator door opening and shutting.

Finally, she entered the room, beer bottle in hand.

"So, what's all this?" There was a long pause. Emmalee dared not turn her head around, but she could see Britney smiling and waving.

"What the hell?" Gretchen sounded confused, even a little amused now. "Are we having a party I didn't know about?"

"You could say that." Britney pointed to an empty chair. "Have a seat."

"Don't tell me what to—"

"Sit the fuck down, Gretchen." Britney's voice was deadly.

Emmalee's heart leapt into her throat. She'd never heard that tone from Britney.

There was a long pause. Emmalee could see Britney's eyes darken, and she assumed they made an impression because the sound of footsteps followed. Gretchen plopped into the open chair and sighed.

"What do you want?" She looked from one person to the next, casually skipping over Emmalee, ignoring her presence.

Emmalee folded in on herself, wrapping her arms around her waist, and leaning forward slightly. She really wished she'd been able to find a way out of this.

"Look, Gretchen, we all know you're cheating on Chase," Britney began.

"What the—"

"Shut up. I'm not done." Britney paused long enough to make sure her order was being followed. "Don't try to deny it. You've been disappearing a lot lately. You skipped the Homecoming game and the dance."

"Jesus Christ! You don't know—"

"I said shut it!" Britney paused, waiting to be sure Gretchen complied. "You barely speak to any of us anymore. We're your fucking friends, or at least we used to be. We all know what's going on. And you've got rumors started about you, which also means everyone's laughing at Chase."

Emmalee could hear Chase suck in a breath, saw him twisting his class ring anxiously.

"Just let me explain!" Gretchen's face was bright red, and she looked ready to cry.

Emmalee felt bad for her. "Maybe we could all just–"

"Shut up, Em."

Emmalee felt like Britney had slapped her. She sat in stunned silence.

"We don't need your explanations, Gretchen." Chase's voice was calm, too calm. He was staring down at his hands folded together, elbows on his knees. "We need – I need – you to just admit it, okay?"

"Chase, wait, you don't–"

Chase jumped up and stared down at Gretchen. His face was tight with rage. "Shut the fuck up! I said I don't need you to explain! Just tell the truth. Admit you've been fucking someone else, and then this can all be over with." His voice sounded strangled on the last words, and then he turned and walked out of the room, slamming his fist into the wall as he went. Emmalee heard the back door open and slam.

Gretchen was crying now. Emmalee's own heart was pounding.

"He's right, Gretchen." Britney smirked. She looked happy, gloating.

"He is," Kristina chimed in.

Tyler added his two cents. "You have to understand what it's like for a guy when his girl is screwing around on him."

"Tyler's right, Gretchen," Bryce jumped in. "The other guys

give him tons of shit about it at school, in the locker room, on the field."

Gretchen buried her face in her hands, still crying. "It's not like that. And even if it was, he's screwing around with her–" Gretchen pointed at Emmalee.

"Wait–"

Emmalee was interrupted by Britney again. "What the fuck do you care if he is, Gretchen? You've got someone else, too."

"He deserves to have some fun–it's not like you're keeping his balls empty." Bryce chuckled, but Gretchen just put her head in her hands.

Emmalee's face burned with shame. She could feel tears stinging her eyes. It wasn't like that. They had kissed that one night, yes, but Chase had never even tried to go there again, let alone farther.

"Hold on. Can we just–"

She was interrupted yet again, this time by Gretchen. "You guys are so fucked up. You don't understand anything." Gretchen had quit crying now. She was just shaking her head.

Britney stood up from the couch and stalked toward Gretchen, showing her something on her phone. "We understand this."

Gretchen's eyes went wide in confusion, and her hand flew to cover her open mouth.

"Yeah. Pictures don't lie, do they, Gretchen?" Britney smirked again. "And after what you did to poor Audrey? You're lucky we haven't made sure you're in prison by now."

Emmalee had no idea what was on the phone, but it must have been awful because Gretchen stood up, shaking. And Gretchen *was* the one who hurt Audrey. Emmalee wasn't all that surprised. She filed that nugget of information away to tell Mekayla, who would be shocked she'd been wrong about Britney this whole time.

Gretchen stood, horrified. "You are fucking sick! I fucking

hate all of you!" She lunged for the phone, but Britney hung on. "Give this to me, you psycho bitch!"

Britney and Gretchen were full-on fighting over the phone. When Britney pulled it away, Gretchen pulled her hand back, and Emmalee could feel the sting of the slap from across the room, see the palm print left on Britney's face.

Britney was silent for a moment, as if in shock, and then her eyes turned almost black. She turned and tossed the phone back to Tyler. "I know some people who would just love to get their hands on this photo. I think it's time to leave, guys. Em, go start your car."

"But—"

"Now." Britney shot her a threatening look.

Britney was right. It was time to leave. This was getting way too out of control. Emmalee stood up and headed for the door. She could just hear Britney's parting words as she walked out.

"Good luck explaining when this is in everyone's feed tomorrow."

"No!" Gretchen's scream sent shivers down Emmalee's spine. "Give me that, you bitch!"

Then there were footsteps behind her as the others caught up to her, trailed by Gretchen's animal wail.

CHAPTER 19

The rain was falling in heavy sheets as they piled into her car and slammed the doors. "Go," Britney ordered.

Emmalee froze, remembering that cold, icy night two years before.

"I said go!"

Britney's scream shocked her into action. Emmalee turned the car around, catching a glimpse of Gretchen's car pulling out of the garage, and then sped down the driveway.

"Where am I going?" Her heart was pounding. She had no idea what was happening.

"Turn right at the end of the driveway," Britney directed.

She turned right. "Now what?"

"Just drive. Not too fast. I don't want to end up in a ditch."

"What was the picture you showed her?" Emmalee asked, not sure what could have caused Gretchen to get so angry, so desperate so fast.

Britney snorted, tapping her phone, then held it in front of Emmalee.

Emmalee glanced over quickly, afraid of not paying attention to the road in the dark and the rain. What she saw was horrifying. Gretchen's face contorted, a man behind her, clearly having sex with her. And that man was definitely not Chase. He was heavier, not as muscular. Emmalee wanted to throw up.

"Watch out!" Britney yelled.

Emmalee jerked the car automatically, sending the car swerving on the wet pavement.

Then she looked in the rearview mirror and could just make out headlights behind them. Gretchen?

"Where are we going?"

"You do the driving. I'll do the thinking, okay?"

"She makes a fair point, Brit. What's the plan now? Send out the pic and then what?"

"Shut the fuck up, Bryce! Don't try to be the brains of the operation now."

"Stupid bitch," he shot back.

"Hey, guys, really, though, what's next?" Emmalee's hands were shaking on the wheel, her eyes continually glancing up to the rearview mirror, the headlights getting closer. Definitely Gretchen's car. "Maybe we can go somewhere neutral? A park? Somewhere we can all calm down and talk?"

"Jesus, shut up, Emmalee! Let me think for one fucking minute! Fuck!" Britney screamed, holding her head in her hands, contemplating.

Kristina chimed in. "Maybe we should go back, try to talk to her one more time? Maybe now that she knows you're going to send that pic out, she'll be more willing to listen?"

"Maybe." Britney's voice was quiet, thoughtful. "Maybe." There was a long pause, then, "Actually, turn left up here."

"Where do I–"

"Jesus Christ, Em, just turn!" Britney's voice sounded unhinged, her hand reaching to turn the wheel to the left.

Emmalee could feel the blood pulsing in her ears as she tried to correct the car. "Don't do that!" she yelled.

"Well you passed the fucking turn!" Britney's scream pierced Emmalee's skull.

She pulled over, leaving the dark two-lane road. When the car came to a stop, she took a deep breath and turned the wheel. It took a couple of attempts at turning, stopping, backing up, and turning the wheel again to line the car up with the small dirt logging road Britney had been pointing to. Fortunately, there was no one else in sight. Nothing but tall trees lining the road, somberly watching over them, and the heavy rain blurring everything.

After a few seconds, she could see Gretchen's headlights behind them again, mud splattering up the sides of her car.

"Pick up the pace, Em." Britney sounded a bit brighter now, which made Emmalee worry even more. Her foot shook as she stepped on the pedal.

"Keep going," Britney cycled her hand in the air in front of her. "Don't be such a grandma."

"I thought you didn't want to end up in a ditch?"

"Don't." Britney's voice was like a knife. "Don't argue. Go."

Emmalee sped up a little more and could feel the tires slipping in the mud, her fingers turning white as she gripped the wheel.

She was honestly going way too fast for the conditions. She needed to slow down, but Britney screamed again when the car slowed.

"Go, Em! What the fuck!"

She rounded a curve and slammed on the brakes, the car barely stopping before it hit a tree down in the middle of the road.

"Fuck!" Britney yelled.

Gretchen's car swerved up behind them, brakes squealing, eventually slamming into a huge pine tree on the side of the road.

Everything was eerily quiet for a moment. Then Gretchen

was out of the car, barreling toward Emmalee's passenger door, screeching incoherently, blood trickling from her hairline.

Britney tossed her phone to Kristina. "Hide this."

She opened her door and jumped out. "Hey, Gretch! What's up?"

"You made me wreck my fucking car!" Gretchen was screaming so loud her throat must have been raw. The icy rain-water was running down her face, dragging mascara and eyeliner – and blood – with it.

"You did that yourself." Britney smiled, and it was terrifying as Emmalee watched through the open car door. Who was this person?

"Fuck you! Give me the fucking phone!" Gretchen reached out toward Britney's hand, tucked in her pocket. Britney pulled her hand out first, though, and showed Gretchen it was empty, then grabbed Gretchen's car keys out of her hand.

"You better run, Gretchen." Britney smiled that psychotic smile again, her teeth showing, and jumped back in the car, slamming the door.

"Turn the car around. Go."

"Where?" Emmalee was shaking now. "I'm not sure I can drive."

"Drive now!" Britney screamed.

Emmalee's fingers shook as she turned the key in the ignition and started backing up, getting enough distance from the log to start the process of turning around.

Gretchen appeared again, beating her fists on the windows, her screams muffled by the glass and the rain.

Somehow Emmalee managed to turn the car around, tires spinning and slipping in the mud, then stopped, waiting, hoping Gretchen would move.

"Go." Britney was staring straight ahead, Gretchen right in front of them, staring through the windshield.

"But–" Emmalee's throat tightened.

"Hit the gas or get out!" Britney didn't even look at her. Just kept glaring at Gretchen through the rain-streaked windshield.

Emmalee gingerly hit the gas, inching the car forward. Gretchen started backing up, eyes wide, still yelling.

"Faster," Britney ordered.

Emmalee closed her eyes, took a deep breath, then opened them again and pushed harder on the gas pedal, nearly hitting Gretchen, who scrambled backward faster, then turned and ran.

"Keep going."

"Britney—"

"Do it."

She kept going.

"Faster."

She pushed the pedal harder.

Just as they were about to overtake Gretchen's rain-soaked, muddy form, scrambling to reach the side of the road, Britney yelled "Watch out!" and grabbed the wheel.

Emmalee would never know exactly who was to blame for what happened next. Was it Britney grabbing the wheel? Was it Emmalee herself that had made a mistake, a mistake that Britney was just trying to correct?

The horrifying truth was that it didn't really matter in the end, because in the end, no one would ever get the sickening thud of Gretchen's body against the front of the car out of Emmalee's head. Or the horrified face that impacted the windshield, terrified eyes looking in at her for just a second before Gretchen's body disappeared from view.

Emmalee slammed on the brakes, the car fishtailing a little in the mud before skidding to a stop.

Her ears were throbbing with the sound of her own heartbeat. A horrific, wailing scream pierced the otherwise silent car. After a moment, she realized it was her own scream, because Britney grabbed her by the arm and started shaking her.

"Shut the fuck up, Em! Drive!"

"We need to help her!" Emmalee's fingers scrabbled for the door handle, but Britney's hands wrenched hers away.

"If you get out of this car, I swear to God I will run you over like a dog in the street." Her eyes were unrecognizable, like a rabid animal. Emmalee knew she wasn't lying.

She started shaking so hard, she couldn't figure out how to even start moving the car. After a few seconds, she heard a door slam before hers opened. "Get out," Britney ordered.

Emmalee pulled herself out of her car, still shaking, and stumbled toward Gretchen's unmoving form. Rough hands grabbed her and dragged her back to the car, shoving her into Britney's vacated passenger seat.

Britney hit the gas hard, turning the car around in the middle of the muddy road. Fuck. Fuck. Fuck. This couldn't be real. Had to be a nightmare. There was a nauseating thump, thump as the car drove over Gretchen's body.

"What the fuck!" Emmalee screamed. "What the fuck are you doing?"

Britney said nothing. Emmalee looked around, frantic, as Britney maneuvered the car between trees and came back around toward the heap of darkness that was once Gretchen. No one was saying anything, no one was even looking at her. Their eyes were cast down at their hands, their laps, refusing to acknowledge the horror unfolding in front of them.

"No, no, no!" Emmalee pleaded, sobbing, but the engine revved up again and the tires snuffed any final remains of life out underneath them. Britney hit the gas again, and they were suddenly racing back in the direction of Gretchen's house.

Emmalee let out a low, keening sob. She thought about jumping from the moving car. She was afraid Britney would just run her over, too, but maybe she deserved that. Still, she was too much of a coward to do it.

She pulled out her phone, fingers shaking as she unlocked it and tried to dial 9-1-1. Britney reached over and wrenched the phone out of Emmalee's hands, tossing it to the back seat.

There was nothing left to do but sob.

CHAPTER 20

When the car passed Gretchen's house and kept going, Emmalee wondered what was happening. Why weren't they stopping? She couldn't bring herself to form words. Eventually, Britney pulled up to Kristina's house, where Tyler and Bryce got out as well.

"Take Em's phone, Kris." Kristina leaned in, grabbing it from the floorboard. Emmalee tried to get to it first, but Britney grabbed her arm, nails digging into her skin.

The three of them just walked away, not saying a word, not looking back, nothing. Emmalee heard the click of the car doors locking.

She jerked her arm away from Britney and tried to open the car door. She had to get away from here. The door wouldn't open, though. Britney must have engaged the child safety locks.

"Why are we here?" Emmalee sniffed, wiping tears and snot from her face.

Britney backed out and started driving again. "Well, we can't exactly go back to Gretchen's now, can we? That's why we had Chase drive us and left our cars at Kris's." Britney chuckled. "You really need to calm down, Em."

"What?" Emmalee was stunned.

"You're overreacting."

Britney was a psychopath, Emmalee realized. Emmalee had always thought Britney was just outgoing, a little abrasive sometimes, but now, now she realized she was in the car with a murderer who thought she was overreacting. She was afraid she'd never make it home, never see her own mother. She wondered if she'd end up dead on the side of the road somewhere like Gretchen, or if Britney would pull out a gun and shoot her, or a knife. Emmalee was shaking even harder now.

"Please, just let me go home." Emmalee could feel fresh tears scorching her cheeks. The image of Gretchen's crumpled body kept flashing in her mind.

"Seriously, Em. Relax. You're not going home until you help me clean this mess up. If you're going to be a big baby about this, you're going to get in so much trouble." Britney shook her head, a lopsided smile on her face, like she was amused.

Psychopath.

"What? What do you mean, trouble?" Emmalee's teeth were chattering so hard, she could barely get the question out.

"If you're acting all weird, people will know it was you."

The car slowed, and Emmalee realized they were back there. Back where the tall, shadowy trees were standing watch over Gretchen's body.

"What's happening?"

"Get out." Britney got out of the car and opened the trunk, rummaging. When Emmalee got out, worried Britney was looking for something to murder her with, she saw Britney holding a garden shovel and a tarp. What? She didn't keep a shovel and tarp in her car. She didn't even own a shovel. Britney grinned at the shock and fear on Emmalee's face.

"Christ, Em, I'm not going to murder you." Britney grinned, her small white teeth flashing when lightning cracked overhead.

"Here, carry this." Britney handed her the tarp and walked off between the trees.

Emmalee grabbed the tarp and followed. Maybe Gretchen would still be alive? A small spark of hope lit up in Emmalee's chest. But it was crushed when they arrived at the shadowy form lying in the middle of the muddy road.

There was no way Gretchen could be saved. Emmalee could see that from how disfigured her body was. It was no longer a human shape, but something very, very dark and twisted.

Britney dropped the shovel, then stood, looking down over the bloody, broken mess that had been one of her best friends.

"Stupid bitch." Britney kicked at Gretchen's limp body. "Here, start digging, over there in the trees, far enough from the road that you won't be seen. Use the tarp to wrap the body and drag it into the hole." Britney pointed into the dark woods.

She couldn't bury a body. Bury Gretchen. "But..."

"Now."

When Emmalee looked up at Britney, she was holding her phone up. "Or, I could call 9-1-1 and tell them you ran Gretchen down with your car after saying you'd kill her because you wanted her boyfriend. Tyler, Bryce, Kristina, even Chase, all heard you say that."

"I never said that!" Emmalee screamed, her heart racing.

"I promise you, Emmalee. That's what they will say they heard. And four of us witnessed you run her over."

Emmalee crumpled to the ground. "Why are you doing this?" She hated how weak her voice sounded.

Britney ignored her question. "I'm going to keep the car moving. When you're done, come stand by the side of the road."

She couldn't believe she was living this hellish nightmare. She wanted to argue, but Britney had already started walking away. She stared after her for a moment. She didn't know what to do. She couldn't call the police. It was too far to walk home.

Besides, Britney would find her, and she'd end up like–she forced herself to look at Gretchen's body.

Then she started digging.

The rain had slowed by the time she saw headlights appear again. The passenger window lowered, and Britney yelled, "Get in!"

Emmalee grabbed the shovel and headed to the car. Her shoes, hands, clothes were covered in mud. She was shaking, blistered, panting, crying, nose-running. A mess.

Britney looked her over and scowled, then stepped on the gas. "You look like shit."

Emmalee wanted to scream at her. Remind her that she had just spent hours digging a fucking grave in the middle of the fucking woods. Instead, she just wrapped her arms around herself, shivering from the cold and the disbelief. I'm a murderer, she thought. I murdered a human being. Did she? The whole thing was such a confused blur.

Her teeth were chattering when Britney pulled into Kristina's driveway again.

"Stay here." Britney opened the door and disappeared inside for a minute. When she returned, she tossed Emmalee's keys and phone into the driver's seat. Emmalee noticed Britney was wearing gloves. Was she wearing them earlier? She couldn't remember.

"Clean your car when you get home. Wipe the outside down. You don't want mud on it, or they'll know right away it was you."

"Me?"

"Yes. You. Did you lose your hearing?" Britney's eyes glittered in the streetlights.

"But, it was–we just–" Emmalee stammered.

"We? There's no *we*. *You* were driving. It's your car. Your fingerprints on the car and the shovel. You buried the body. Like I said. No *we*. But look at the bright side. Chase is free now." Britney winked at her.

With that, Britney slammed the door and was gone.

Emmalee sat shaking in the passenger seat for what felt like forever. Mekayla was right. Britney pushed Audrey down the stairs, planning to kill her, but somehow Audrey was still breathing.

Finally, she climbed into the driver's seat and somehow managed to fumble her keys into the ignition and start the drive home.

She drove slowly, heart pounding, hands shaking. Hoping not to attract any attention. She was too focused on her fear to see a stop sign. The tires squealed when she slammed on the brakes and the car fish-tailed into the intersection. She breathed deeply, looking around to see if anyone noticed. Fortunately, the intersection was empty at this late hour.

Later, parked as close to her house as she could get, she tried to calm her erratic breathing. "What the fuck am I doing," she whispered, fresh tears rolling down her filthy face.

She'd almost convinced herself to just drive to the police station and come clean, but her body was frozen. She could call the police, then. She picked up her phone and saw a lot of missed texts from Mekayla. She couldn't open her phone and face those.

Eventually, too afraid of what might happen if she turned herself in, she pried her stiff body out of the car and dipped rag after rag into a bucket of soapy water, scrubbing mud from the car, from the tires, from the undercarriage, from the pleather seats.

By the time she was done, her fingers were raw and shriveled, and gray morning light was beginning to filter through the clouds.

She wanted nothing more than to hide under the covers, inside the cocoon of sleep. But Britney had texted.

See you soon

To anyone else, it would seem friendly, but Emmalee knew it for what it was – a threat.

She stood under a scalding hot shower, letting the water sluice mud and blood from her body, scrubbing her finger nails, triple washing her hair. She focused on the soap, the act of washing, and refused to let her mind drift to images of the night before. Of that night two years ago. If she let herself go there, she'd fall apart.

CHAPTER 21

She got through the school day somehow, moving zombie-like from class to class, strategically avoiding Mekayla. Pretending to listen, take notes, fill out worksheets. Trying to ignore teachers' and other students' questions about Gretchen's absence. At lunch, she tried to hide out in Creative Writing, but the door was locked, so she slipped into a bathroom stall and sat on the closed toilet, distracting herself with mindless scrolling.

Then she saw it. An Instagram post. Gretchen's Instagram post. From the day before. In it, she was smiling at the camera, a serene college campus spreading out behind her. It was captioned. *Too bad I can't be in college now! #collegelife #highschoolsucks.*

Emmalee's heart started pounding. She scrolled through the comments. Her heart stopped. Britney had commented "Looks fun! Missed you this weekend!" at 7:30 in the morning. This morning.

When the bell rang, she had to force her legs not to give out on her as she exited the bathroom. She had to hang on to the wall for support when she passed the main office, though, and saw two uniformed police officers standing at the reception desk. One looked over at her, then flicked his eyes back to Mrs. Jenkins and Mr. Brown. The adults were all talking quietly, but Emmalee could tell by their posture and their expressions that it was something serious.

She contemplated slipping out a side door and going home, but just then Britney and Kristina came around the corner, nearly running into her.

"Watch out, bitch," Britney grinned, then paused, really looking at her. "You okay? You look like you've seen a ghost." Emmalee's eyes widened, but Britney unleashed another grin. "Meet us in the locker room immediately after school. Don't be late."

The two girls moved on to class, seemingly without a care in the world, and Emmalee resigned herself to see the day through. As shattered and worried and numb as she was, she should keep Britney's warnings in mind. It was smarter to play it safe, not draw attention to herself. Just the thought made her want to throw up.

In Creative Writing, she slipped in her AirPods and tried to focus on her notebook, but Mekayla leaned in and tapped her on the shoulder.

"Are you alright? I looked for you at lunch," she whispered.

Emmalee wanted to tell her everything, hear her say there's no way it was true, it was just a bad dream. Instead, she took a deep breath and nodded her head. "I'm just tired. And I wasn't hungry."

Mekayla tilted her head, examining her. "Okay. Well, how'd it go last night? You never responded to me. I was worried about you."

"Ladies, respect the sanctity of writing time," the teacher whispered.

"We ended up not doing it," Emmalee whispered, shrugging.

Mekayla didn't look convinced, but she bent her head back to her own work and left Emmalee alone.

After school, in the locker room, Emmalee walked in on a large group of girls talking worriedly.

"I haven't heard from her at all today," said a younger girl on the tennis team, one Emmalee had never spoken to.

A short brunette, also unknown to Emmalee, raised her eyebrows at the other girls."Me either. I heard she was seeing some guy in Seattle. An older guy."

"Maybe he's a creeper and he locked her up in his mom's basement." This time it was Britney speaking. She was laughing and grinning, then turned to Emmalee and just stared at her. After a moment, she added, "Have you seen her, Em?"

Emmalee's heart rate picked up. "Um, no. Not today."

"I heard she's actually a lesbian," another girl said, one Emmalee didn't recognize.

Everyone laughed, and Britney rolled her eyes. "Who knows. Gretchen's turned into a total loser. It wouldn't surprise me."

"Well, she's never missed a practice before." Emmalee's heart hammered in her chest when she realized the coach had been listening to them. "You ladies get outside and warm up. I'm going to give her mom a call."

The girls all headed for the door that led out to the courts. Emmalee grabbed Britney's elbow to stop her. "Hey, Britney, hang on. Did you hear–"

Britney ripped her arm away. "Don't touch me. Ever." Her eyes were black and angry. "Especially not here," she whispered. "Jeez, Emmalee. Get a fucking grip."

During practice, Emmalee was paired with a freshman, but she couldn't hit a ball no matter what. Every serve went way out of bounds. She tripped over her feet several times, and once she landed square on her butt and bruised her tailbone. Even the freshman was mocking her.

As she was finishing getting dressed to go home, Britney

called out, "Hey, Kris, would it be cool if Em and I come hang out at yours in a few?"

"Sure, babes." Kris grabbed her bag and smiled. "We can have a few after-practice refreshments."

"Cool." Kris turned to go.

Emmalee opened her mouth to object, but Britney shot her a look that struck fear in her heart. So she just shut her mouth and followed them outside.

At Kris's house, Emmalee was all too glad to take the tequila shot Britney handed her.

"That's right, drink up, bitch." Britney sounded sarcastic, but her face looked pissed.

Emmalee threw back the shot and relished the feel of it burning its way down her throat, scraping the scream out of it before it could get loose.

"Wow, Em, thirsty?" Kris laughed derisively.

"Another?" Britney challenged.

Emmalee nodded and Britney obliged.

As the second shot slipped down, Emmalee closed her eyes. This one didn't hurt as much. Her throat was still a bit numb from the first one. Now she just needed her mind to go numb.

"Em here is having a hard time today," Britney explained.

Kris shrugged and took the shot Britney handed her, but her eyes looked as haunted as Emmalee felt.

Britney nodded. "I get it. It must be hard knowing you ran someone over." Britney downed a shot this time and then poured another, holding it in front of Emmalee. "Drink up."

She wanted to argue, to say that she didn't do it. But maybe she did? Emmalee hesitated for just a moment. Fuck it. She needed it. This time, as the shot made its way down her gullet, there was no burn, just a pleasantly warm feeling expanding in her chest, soothing her.

"Calmer now?" Britney asked.

Emmalee nodded.

"Good. Now listen. If you keep acting like a dumbass, you're going to get yourself caught. Understand?"

"But–"

Britney's hand shot forward, fingers pressed against Emmalee's lips. "No buts. Let's try again. Understand?"

Emmalee did not understand. Not even a little bit. She was having a hard time grasping the fact that they were murderers. That she was a murderer? She stared at Britney's dark, angry eyes, then looked down and nodded. It would do no good to argue with Britney. She knew that much.

"Good girl. You remember that. Because if you open your mouth one more time about Gretchen outside of this group, or if you ever get that scared deer in headlights look again in public, I swear you will not live to regret it."

Emmalee eyed the tequila bottle again, knowing she shouldn't drink anymore, but needing to tamp down the shaking she could feel starting in her core.

Britney followed her eyes. "Yes, that's fine. Have another drink and get yourself together."

Kris poured another shot. Emmalee drank.

She woke later with no idea where she was. Her head was throbbing, her throat was dry. Her tongue felt like she'd been licking dog hair. With great difficulty, she pried her eyes open the tiniest fraction, seeing only a faint glimmer of moonlight through lacy curtains. Kris's room. She was still there. She couldn't quite remember anything after her fifth shot of tequila, and she barely remembered that. She could hear music thumping downstairs somewhere.

She must have passed out there on the floor. She sat up, careful not to move too quickly, and scanned the darkened room. She couldn't make out much but the outlines of furniture. Enough to see she was alone. She knew she should get up and drive home, but images of the mud, the rain, the broken thing that had been Gretchen kept flashing in her mind. Those images alternated and then mixed with visions of ice and broken glass and blood, the sound of screaming and sirens. She let sleep take her back into its hard, cold oblivion.

Hours later, she awoke to Britney's foot nudging her. "Time to go, bitch."

Emmalee groaned. Every time Britney's foot touched her, the shockwave sent tremors of pain through her head.

"You should learn to hold your liquor better. Now, let's go. Don't want you to be late for school. And for God's sake, wash your face and brush your hair."

After struggling to remind herself how to use soap and toothpaste and a hairbrush, Emmalee swallowed four ibuprofen from Kris's medicine cabinet and slipped into the short dress and sandals she'd packed in her workout bag. It was definitely not something she wanted to wear today. She'd rather get lost in old Emmalee's baggy clothes.

But old Emmalee was dead now.

CHAPTER 22

"Oh fuck," she whispered as she pulled into a parking space in front of the high school. There were two police cars in the circle drive. She tried to convince herself it likely had nothing to do with Gretchen. Maybe it was just a standard drug dog search or some kind of presentation on the dangers of drunk driving or smoking weed. She wasn't doing a very good job of convincing herself, though. Her heart was racing. She could hear Britney's threats in her head. She had no desire to be subjected to Britney's wrath. She shuddered as the image of Gretchen stumbling in the rain, barely illuminated by headlights, flickered in her mind.

Deep breaths. Deep breaths. She had to get it together. Once her breathing settled, she picked up her bag and shuffled her way to the front door, head down, staring at her phone screen like any normal teenager. Safely at her desk in first period, she breathed a sigh of relief.

It was short-lived, though. Chase scooted his chair closer to hers and leaned over, his lips brushing her ear as he whispered. "You okay?" Her spine tingled.

She nodded, barely.

"Really?" Again his soft breath rustled her hair against her ear. "Cause I'm not." She looked over at him, then, took in his bloodshot eyes, the dark circles under them. He looked like he hadn't slept in days.

"Mr. Kessler, please move your seat back where it belongs." Mrs. Smith sounded sharp, but she gave him a bemused look over her glasses. Unbelievable.

"Meet me after school," he whispered.

"I have practice."

"Skip it."

"Mr. Kessler!" Mrs. Smith gave him a withering look. Apparently her patience had limits, even for the handsome, popular quarterback of the football team.

He rolled his eyes and moved his chair back into position. "Sorry, Mrs. Smith. Emmalee needed help with one of the sentences." He looked over at her and winked. What the hell was she going to do?

When the last bell rang, Emmalee ducked out of class quickly and hurried for the door to the parking lot. Chase was waiting for her.

"I really want to talk to you, Em," his eyes pleaded with her. "I don't know who else to talk to." His voice cracked.

She stared at him, and he stared back, his face an open mask of pain.

"Please?"

She relented.

He led her to his car, despite her recommendation that they just meet at a restaurant or the park. He opened her door and helped tuck her inside the passenger seat, then took off out of the parking lot faster than he probably should have.

He snaked his way into the woods and rolled the windows

down. It was a cool fall day, and Emmalee let the wind blow her hair, let the loud music wash over her. Anything to help bleach her brain of the horror she'd been reliving. Her phone buzzed. A text from Mekayla. She shoved her phone into a cup holder and sat back, resting her eyes for a moment.

After a few minutes, Chase's hand snaked across the seat and took hers. Emmalee looked over. He was staring at her for a moment, then looked back at the road. His face was so pale. His eyes so dark from the circles under them. He looked like a zombie. Emmalee glanced at her reflection in the vanity mirror. He wasn't the only one.

He took an exit onto a small state road that wound even further into the woods. The leaves were changing color, the sky overhead was blue, sunshine filtering through the window. It felt so wrong for it to look so beautiful when this world was so ugly. She took a deep breath, then another. Then, suddenly, she was crying.

Chase pulled over to the side of the road, and pulled her to him. She buried her head in his neck and let him hold her. His fingers tangled in her hair as he whispered, "Shhhh," over and over again, rocking her, his other hand kneading her back.

Eventually, her tears were spent. She tipped her head back and looked up at him. His eyes searched hers for a moment, then suddenly his lips were on hers. She opened her mouth and let him inside, hating herself as she let his tongue slide over hers. She sighed into him, and he groaned, pulling her even closer.

A break in the kiss, then, "Em, God, come here." He pulled her into his lap, her legs on either side of his, his hands on her hips. He stared into her eyes, pushing her hair back from her face.

"We shouldn't be doing this," she shuddered. "Gretchen–"

He put his finger on her lips. "Shhhh. It's okay."

It wasn't okay. She didn't know how she would ever be okay again. She knew it was wrong, but she needed an escape.

She leaned down, the one to initiate the kiss this time, and lost herself in his lips and tongue and breath and touch. She shivered when his hands slid under her dress, skimming up her sides, and to her back, pressing her body to him.

She pulled back, trying to think, to slow things down. But his eyes were on fire, and he brought his hands around to her stomach, stared into her eyes as he traced up, over her ribs, under her bra. She gasped, then sank into his kiss again. She let herself get lost.

Later, after she'd let him keep touching her everywhere, after she'd let him inside her, after he'd panted and shuddered under her, after he'd kissed her long and slow, stroked her hair, held her close to him, let their breaths slow down. After all that, he'd whispered to her. "I love you, Em."

She wanted to believe he'd meant it. She wanted to believe she felt it, too, but she didn't know what was just horror or adrenaline or the fact it was her first time, so she said nothing in return.

She just climbed back into her seat, pulling her clothes back into place while he zipped his pants and buckled his belt, and they'd sped back to the school without talking. She felt empty inside. And it was somehow better than the crushing pain she'd felt before.

The lot was nearly empty when he pulled up next to her car, got out and walked her to it. This time it was her he backed up against the door, not Gretchen. Her hips that his hands gripped, dragging the hem of her dress up a little, possessing her mouth again. She clung to him, made him be the one to pull away, even though she thought the guilt would suffocate her.

"I'll call you later, Em," he murmured before climbing back into his car and speeding off.

At home, she went straight to her room, peeled off her clothes, and washed every trace of the day off of her before she climbed into bed. She tried to sort out her feelings about losing her virginity. About losing it to Chase.

She'd never subscribed to the idea that she had to wait for marriage. But she'd certainly never imagined it would be like this. Two people just crashing into each other, trying to escape the horror of what they'd been through together.

She waited for his call, worried maybe it would never come, that he really had just used her as an escape. Like she'd used him. Fuck. Why were her feelings such a tangled, humiliating mess?

He did call, though. When he did, they talked for hours. First he talked about when he was little. How he'd been thinking a lot lately about how his dad used to take him to work, told him the whole place would be his one day. That he'd never told anyone he wasn't even sure if he wanted that.

Then he told her about Gretchen. Admitted that he had thought he loved her before, had wanted to date her for years. About how when he'd found out she was cheating on him, he was crushed. How he'd wanted to end it, but she'd sobbed and threatened to kill herself if he did. How she'd called him a few days ago, screaming at him for cheating on her. With Emmalee.

"Wait. What!" Her heart thundered in her chest.

"I know. It's crazy. But she had that picture of us that Brit took. The one of us kissing."

Emmalee's heart raced. "Britney sent it to her."

"I talked to Brit about it already. She said Gretchen grabbed her phone from her, joking around. Then she said Gretchen threw the phone down and just walked out. She must have seen the photo and sent it to herself. That's the picture that was on the screen when Brit picked it back up."

Emmalee knew that wasn't true. She knew that pretty much everything Britney had ever said was a lie. She had to talk to him about it.

"Chase?"

"Yeah?" His voice was slow, sleepy.

"Last night?"

He was quiet so long she thought he'd hung up. Then finally, "I know. Britney told me Gretchen was chasing you guys, wrecked her car."

Her heart sank. "Chase, I need to tell you–"

"Em, it's okay. I know. She ran in front of you. I told you she threatened to kill herself. She was crazy. And I won't tell anyone." His voice was barely audible.

"No, Chase," she whispered.

"Just let it go, okay?" His voice was sharper now. "You don't get it, do you? Nothing good is going to come of it if you start trying to talk about it anymore. Just let it go."

Her heart felt like it was splitting in two. He had to know it was Britney. Always Britney.

"So, Audrey?"

"Don't, Em. Seriously. Don't."

She was silent.

"Tell me you understand, Em. Not a word. Tell me." His voice was hard. "I couldn't take it if something happened to you. I'm barely hanging on." His voice broke as he begged, "Please."

"Okay," she whispered.

"I'll see you tomorrow. I love you."

He waited a beat, probably hoping she'd return those words. But she didn't.

And then he was gone.

CHAPTER 23

In Creative Writing the next day, she sat down and got right to work again, hoping Mekayla and Marshall would just ignore her. Today, though, Mekayla dropped her things loudly on the table and sat down across from her.

"Have you heard?" Mekayla's eyes were piercing, making Emmalee squirm.

"Heard what?" Her heart thrummed in her chest. Please don't be about Gretchen.

Mekayla tilted her head to the side and stared at Emmalee for a moment, as if trying to figure her out. "Gretchen?"

Emmalee focused on keeping her breathing even. "What about her?"

"She's missing."

"What?"

"You heard me." Mekayla crossed her arms across her chest. "Are you seriously trying to tell me that you had no idea that one of your best friends was missing?"

"We weren't – aren't – friends really. I mean, I've noticed she hasn't been here, but I barely ever talked to her, so no, I didn't know. I assumed she was on a trip."

Mekayla squinted. "Right. Well, I was in the office earlier, and I overheard Mrs. Jenkins talking on the phone about it. She said the police are looking into some person of interest in Seattle, but Gretchen's parents want to keep things as quiet as possible. They don't want the media finding out."

Police? Seattle. Emmalee could feel her breaths come faster. Part guilt. Part relief. She really hated herself sometimes.

"You okay?" Mekayla's face was worried.

"Yeah, fine, just really tired."

Mekayla nodded. "Have you found out any more about Audrey?"

Emmalee shook her head.

"The benefit is soon, though. Maybe something will come up there?" Mekayla looked hopeful.

Emmalee shrugged. She really hoped not. She knew the answer to who hurt Audrey already. She didn't want to poke that bear. And she really wanted to keep Mekayla out of it, too.

"I'm glad you're going." Mekayla smiled encouragingly at her.

"Mekayla!" Mrs. Murray admonished. "Some of us are trying to write here."

"Sorry, Mrs. Murray. My bad." Mekayla winked at Emmalee as she opened her notebook and started writing.

Emmalee couldn't gather any mental energy to write, so she just doodled trees and rainy skies all over her blank notebook paper. Mekyala noticed and slid a piece of paper across the table.

"Coffee after school?" She was smiling at Emmalee when she looked up at her.

"Can't," Emmalee wrote. She was required to be under surveillance at Kristina's again.

Mekayla frowned, disappointed.

Me too, thought Emmalee. She'd give anything to be the girl who could just go get coffee, carefree.

Those days were over.

CHAPTER 24

Emmalee held Chase's elbow as they entered the ballroom. She gasped. She'd never been to anything so fancy and expensive-looking in her life. And she was beginning to wish she'd never agreed to come to this benefit.

Chase smiled down at her. "Over the top, huh?"

She nodded. Everywhere she looked, there were fresh flowers, fairy lights, sparkling crystal and crisp white linens on tables. She let him lead her to a table where a classy-looking older couple was seated.

"Mom, Dad, this is Emmalee." He pulled her chair out for her and pushed it in, holding her coat over his arm.

Emmalee's heart stopped. She'd known his parents would be there, she was just shocked to meet them so casually. He hadn't warned her. Then again, why would he? To him, they were just parents.

His father nodded at her across the table. His mother, a striking woman with blonde hair in an elegant updo, smiled.

"It's lovely to meet you, Emmalee. Tell me, how did you meet Chase?" Her mouth may have been smiling, but Emmalee detected a gleam in her eyes that wasn't entirely friendly.

"Mother." Chase paused, his tone more warning than greeting. "I told you, Emmalee is new this year. She just moved here." Chase's voice was tight.

"Tell you what, Em, let's go find the others." He held out his hand for her.

"Why didn't you warn me?" she whispered when they were far enough away to not be overheard.

"Warn you of what?" He sounded absentminded, his head swiveling. "Ah, there's Brit."

Emmalee cringed. She did not want to see Britney right now. "Never mind," she said, taking a deep breath and trying to keep her face neutral.

"Hello, Darlings," Britney gushed, smiling at them. "Isn't this just too scrumptious?" She was glancing between Emmalee and Chase.

Chase slipped his arm around Emmalee's waist, pulling her close. "Where are the grieving parents?"

Britney's eyes narrowed, anger glinting in them. "Over by the altar to their angelic Audrey." Her voice dripped with sarcasm.

Emmalee wanted to tell Britney that she was being rude, but that would be absurd considering Britney had done so much worse to Audrey. To Gretchen. Emmalee couldn't help laughing at herself, try as she might to hold it in.

"What's so funny, Em?" Britney's glare was directed at Emmalee now.

Emmalee shook her head. "Nothing. Sorry." She wanted to get away from Britney. Now. "I'm going to go find a drink."

"I'll come with you." Chase grabbed Emmalee's hand.

"God, Britney can be a lot sometimes." Chase fidgeted with his tie, clearly uncomfortable.

"Hmmm." Emmalee made sure her answer was noncommittal. She was scared about Britney's *a lot* being aimed at her.

Chase raised his hand to signal a passing server and grabbed two champagne flutes from the tray. He handed one to Emmalee, then raised his.

"Here's to making it through this alive."

They toasted and Emmalee hoped he was exaggerating. She tried to put that thought out of her mind, emptying her glass in one go.

"Easy, babe. This is not the place to get drunk. Trust me." His eyes were scanning the room again.

"Shit. Incoming." He put on a big smile. "Mrs. Thomas, you look stunning as always."

Gretchen's mother. Emmalee panicked, not sure how Chase could act like nothing had happened. But, to be honest, Gretchen's mom did look stunning. Her long black evening gown was cut very low, and a slit up to her hip revealed a perfectly toned, tanned leg. But, if you looked close, you could see the haunted look in her eyes.

"Chase," Mrs. Thomas responded curtly, examining Emmalee.

"Mrs. Thomas, I'd like you to meet Emmalee, a friend from school."

Friend?

Gretchen's mother did not say a word to Emmalee. Instead, she touched Chase's arm. "Chase, dear, can we speak privately?"

He hesitated a moment, then inclined his head toward the woman. "Of course. Lead the way. I'll be back in a few minutes, Emmalee."

As the two moved toward the entrance, Emmalee followed carefully, stopping to say hello to a few familiar faces from school.

In the entryway, she didn't see them at first. There were two long, dark hallways leading in either direction, curving around the exterior of the large ballroom. She picked the right one first. If she ran into them, she'd say she was looking for a restroom.

After passing the ladies' room and the coat check room, she heard whispers. She slowed her pace and proceeded carefully.

She stopped when she approached what appeared to be an alcove hidden to the left. She could see shadows on the floor and the whispers were louder now, clearly angry, and clearly Chase and Mrs. Thomas.

"I don't care what you say, I know that you have more information than you're telling us." Mrs. Thomas sniffled.

"I swear, Mrs. Thomas, I don't know what's going on with Gretchen." Emmalee's heart thrummed as she listened to the lie, guilt and relief flooded through her at the same time. "She hasn't been herself lately."

"Maybe that's because you're cheating on her with that trailer trash." Mrs. Thomas's whisper was furious. "I imagine my daughter is hiding out with her friends in Seattle, trying to avoid the humiliation of you hanging all over your little whore!" Mrs. Thomas's voice rose above a whisper now.

Emmalee could feel her cheeks flush, shame lighting her on fire.

"You have it all wrong, Mrs. Thomas." Chase must have reached out to calm her because Emmalee heard fabric rustling.

"Do not touch me, Chase Kessler. I know who you are. I never wanted Gretchen to be with you, but you fooled her into thinking you cared. Clearly you don't. As if any son of Adam Kessler's could ever care about anyone but himself. "

"Please, Mrs. Thomas, just listen."

"Enough, Chase. You will help us locate her, or I swear to God, you will pay, and we both know your family can't afford another scandal."

Emmalee backed away, nauseous. She hurried to the ladies' room and heaved the champagne into the toilet.

She stayed there until she felt reasonably sure she was alone. And in control of her emotions again. She knew Gretchen's mother was angry, but why wouldn't she be? Her daughter was missing.

No. Not missing.

Dead.

And it was Emmalee's fault.

"Dance with me." Chase took Emmalee's drink, set it on a nearby table, and tugged her to an open area of large tiles, pulling her close to him. After an hour or so at the benefit, Britney had insisted they all go to Bryce's house, knowing that all of their parents would be having a very late night schmoozing with all of the big wigs at Audrey's benefit.

Now, here on Bryce's patio, she was beginning to feel the buzz of alcohol and Chase's closeness. But she couldn't get Gretchen's mom out of her head. She pulled away.

"Ummm — I don't really feel like dancing."

"Shhhh." He pulled her back to him, sliding his arms around her waist, pressing her to his chest, moving his hips against hers, following the pulse of the music, kind of slow, kind of not, very suggestive.

He looked into her eyes. "In a dress like that, you have to dance."

"I don't really dance," she stammered, as she stepped on his foot. "I'm sorry."

"No apologies. Just let me lead." He held her tighter, and she let herself follow him, feeling her body relax as they moved. She knew this wasn't exactly dancing, but she had to admit, it felt good.

As the song continued, his hands drifted a little, just below her waist, not quite so low that she'd have to make an issue of it, but her cheeks reddened.

"May I cut in?" Britney's voice was unmistakable. Emmalee nearly jumped out of her skin, quickly pulling away from Chase.

"A little jumpy there?" Chase laughed. "Thanks for the dance, Em. Don't go too far."

Britney grinned. "Yeah, I won't keep him too long, and I promise to return him in perfect condition."

Chase slid his arms around Britney's waist this time. Emmalee could see Britney's face as they turned, her lips curling in a smile. It was hard to stifle the pang of jealousy that cut through her, hot like a knife.

Emmalee looked around and noticed at least thirty more people had filled the outdoor space, almost all of them coupled off, dancing or lounging at tables.

She stuck out like a sore thumb, standing there all alone, wondering how Britney, Chase, Kristina, all of them, could act like nothing had happened. Like one of their lifelong friends wasn't just murdered. By Emmalee. Like they weren't all trying to cover it up.

She had to get out of there. She made a quick exit through the French doors and back into the relative sanctuary of the kitchen.

Inside the kitchen, she saw Bryce facing away from her at the counter, opening beers, so she snuck past him through the hall and into the foyer of his McMansion. From there, she found a large living area off to the left of the main entrance. She was making her way around the perimeter, wondering at the lack of family pictures or any personal items in the room, when she could feel eyes on her, making the hair at the back of her neck stand on end.

"Get lost?"

She turned around and saw Bryce leaning against the arched opening into the living room, smirking.

"No, I just wanted to come inside and take a breather."

"It's a party. You're supposed to be where everyone else is." He started moving toward her.

"I know. I was just taking a quick break." She tried to move around him before he could get any closer, but he mirrored her movement and blocked her path.

"You don't have to go anywhere." He'd quit smiling and was

moving forward, backing her up against built-in shelves full of breakable – and surely expensive – decor.

"Sorry, I need to go." She tried to duck away, again wondering why the stupidest words sometimes came out of her mouth. She had nothing to apologize for.

He didn't move, though.

Instead his arms came up on either side of her shoulders, effectively pinning her against the shelves. If she moved, she'd surely knock something she couldn't afford to replace onto the floor.

"Shhhhhh." He leaned his head in, and she could feel his breath on her, but unlike with Chase, the feeling was not at all pleasurable. He smelled of beer and vape and sweat, and she definitely did not like the look in his eyes. Where Chase's sparkled, his eyes were full of dark shadows and danger.

"Excuse me." She timidly placed her hands on his chest and pushed, ever so gently, just a nudge.

His eyes flashed. "No need to get aggressive. I just wanted to let you know how hot you look in that dress." He peered down at her low neckline, practically salivating over her exposed cleavage. "Very hot indeed. I appreciate that in a woman."

"Thanks, but I need to go." Thanks? Was she serious? She pushed a bit harder, but this time his hand closed around her wrist. She could feel the strength in that hand and knew she wouldn't stand a chance of getting out of it if she tried. She wanted to scream, but no sound would come out. She felt frozen.

He leaned in even closer, his lips touching her ear as he whispered, "If you want to get handsy, two can play at that game." His fingers tightened on her wrist, squeezing hard enough that it hurt.

"Bryce?" Britney's voice felt like salvation at that moment. Bryce grinned at Emmalee and let go of her wrist, backing away slowly.

"Yeah, Babe?"

"I was looking for you." Her voice was sharp, and her eyes shot daggers at Emmalee.

"I was just helping our new friend here. She got a little lost, huh, Em?" His eyes dared her to correct him.

"Yeah. I was lost."

"Right, okay," said Britney. "Well, follow us, and next time, ask before you go snooping around someone else's house."

Emmalee swallowed a response, not wanting to start an argument with Britney.

Britney snagged Bryce's elbow and pulled him away. Emmalee wasn't sure what to do but follow.

Outside, she gasped. There were more people than she could count, and more were still arriving, coming from the sides of the house, directly into the back – what it was – yard was too ordinary a word. She found the table where Chase had set her drink when they started dancing, and picked it up, gulping the fiery concoction, hoping it would make the lingering fear and anxiety fade.

She tried to reason herself out of the impending panic attack. Bryce hadn't exactly done or said anything extremely criminal. He had put a hand on her, and even though her wrist was still a little sore, there were no marks. She knew she should quit making excuses, but she was afraid of what backfire a confrontation would bring.

"Want one?" A girl Emmalee didn't recognize shoved something small and white in her face. Emmalee focused, realizing it was a pill of some kind.

"No thanks." She smiled, hoping not to seem too rude. It was literally the first time she'd ever been offered drugs, other than the Tylenol or cough medicine her mother kept around for headaches and colds.

The girl giggled. "Suit yourself. More for me." She popped the pill in her own mouth and started dancing away. Emmalee watched her heels wobble across the patio tiles, her green silk romper shimmering under the fairy lights.

Again she wondered what she was doing here. How she'd wandered so far from who she'd been before moving here. Before getting involved with these people.

Her wondering was cut short, though, because a hand landed on her elbow, making her nearly jump out of her skin. She found herself wobbling, and the hand tightened, steadying her.

"Whoa. Are you okay?"

She looked up to see Chase staring down at her, his eyes assessing her face, full of concern, and maybe a little sad.

"Yeah, I'm fine." Was she imagining it, or did she just slur?

"Dance with me again?"

"Ummmm–"

"Come on. I'm lonely." He smiled out at her, and it was so friendly and sad and genuine all at once, so unlike Bryce's, that she couldn't say no.

"Okay, I guess. One song, but then I need to go."

"Sure thing." He took her hand in his and led her into the middle of a group of young people writhing to pounding music.

"Like I said, I don't really know how to dance," she warned him again.

"Shhhh. You're doing fine. Besides, I've got you." He slid his arms around her waist again, pulled her in, and they swayed together, far too slowly for the music. She looked around but no one else seemed to notice. They weren't the only two moving slowly. She felt so much safer here in his arms.

When they turned, her eyes landed on Britney and Bryce, sitting at a table on the edge of the patio. Their heads tilted together, and they were both looking at Britney's phone, apparently at something funny. There was no hint of Britney's anger from just a couple minutes ago. She and Bryce looked like a happy couple.

Maybe Emmalee and Chase looked like a happy couple, too.

Maybe. Probably not. Definitely not. She wasn't the kind of person Chase normally dated. She was nothing like Gretchen or Audrey. She was short, where they were tall. She had messy brown hair next to their flawless locks. In looks, style, mannerisms, they were complete opposites.

Then again. Lord Huron came on, and Chase was pulling her tighter against him, his right hand sliding up over her hip and side, taking her wrist and gently pulling her arm up around his neck. She moved her other arm to match, let her body fit to his, let his hand caress her lower back in slow circles, his cheek resting lightly against her hair. Let the horror of the past few days slip away from her for just a few moments.

She felt woozy, maybe from the drink, maybe from being this close to Chase. Something kept tugging at her mind, something she should be worried about, but all she knew was that in that moment, she didn't care what anyone thought or what she should be doing. She wanted to just lose herself in Chase, in the music. It was magic.

She didn't think she'd ever been this close to another human in her life. She'd imagined it, but in those imaginings, it had never felt so dizzyingly intoxicating. She laid her head against his chest, and his hand moved up into her hair, stroking the long strands. There were no words, but she felt they didn't need words. She'd swear she could feel his heart beating and that he could hear hers. It was thudding so loud.

Then it was over. She felt him tense, then gently extricate himself from her. "Thanks," he mumbled, before hurrying away. "I need a bathroom break." She watched his long, quick strides toward the house, watched him disappear inside, and felt the cold loss of him all the way from the top of her head to her toes.

Suddenly overcome with dizziness, she reached out to steady herself, her hand landing on an arm. She clung, and the arm turned into two, turned into too close, too warm, too everywhere, but she couldn't make her muscles work, couldn't make her mouth move. Her head sagged, and she just let it fall against the new chest. There was a sweater there, soft, probably cashmere. At least she'd always imagined this was what cashmere felt like.

Then the hands were too low, grabbing her butt. She said no. She was sure she did, but she must not have because the hands didn't stop. Instead, they slid up her body, kept moving, touching, groping her in places she didn't want. Alarm bells were going off in her head, and somehow she convinced her arms to work. She pushed, but it wasn't as strong as she intended, just enough for the hands to stop a moment, grab her hips, and twist her around, pull her back in.

She felt her hair sticking to her face, a groin pressed to her lower back. The cool evening air shocked her, made her realize that the top of her dress was too low. She tried to coordinate her hands to fix it, but his arms pinned hers at her side. She could feel a tongue in her ear, and wanted to throw up. Then a flash of light, and that was it.

Darkness.

CHAPTER 25

The first thing she noticed when her eyes opened was that her tongue felt like sandpaper. She tried to swallow, but there wasn't enough moisture. She reached for her phone, but there was nothing there, not even her nightstand. Then she noticed the light was all wrong, too bright. A glance to the right, and she realized where her little window with yellow curtains should be was a wall of bare windows looking out at a forest full of trees, the sunshine filling all of the spaces between the branches. She sat up in a panic. Where was she?

After a moment, she remembered the night before. Bryce's house. The party. Dancing with Chase. Then, the hands. She felt bile rising in her throat and jumped and ran, looking for a bathroom. She wasn't going to make it, so she grabbed a trash can next to a large desk in the room and emptied her stomach into it. Thankfully there wasn't much since she hadn't eaten dinner the night before.

"Classy."

Her heart stopped, but she forced herself to turn around. Britney stared at her, her eyes like black coal. But, when they flitted down from Emmalee's face, she smirked.

"Even classier."

Emma looked down and was mortified. Her dress top was pulled out of shape, showing too much. She tugged at the fabric in an attempt at modesty.

"Ummm — what time is it?"

"Time to go. Bryce's parents won't want you hanging around here all day. Especially like that." Britney curled her lip in disgust.

"But, my car." She tried to rub the blurriness from her eyes, finally remembering she'd ridden with Chase last night. "Where's Chase?"

"Not here. I told him I'd make sure you got home. We leave in five. Bryce's Hummer's out front."

With that, Britney turned and walked away, leaving Emmalee confused, disgusted, sick. What on earth happened the night before? Whatever it was would have to wait.

She tiptoed through the main floor of the house until she found a bathroom and some mouthwash to swish with, then ran her fingers through her hair in an attempt to tame it. She took a look in the mirror. Mascara was floating in black pools under her eyes. Shit. She pulled open cabinet doors looking for makeup remover, but had to make do with soap. After she'd gotten most of the mascara off, she dug through the sofa cushions in the living room until she located her phone. It was dead. Of course.

Outside, her stomach clenched at the thought of getting anywhere near Bryce again. But she had no other way to get home. No phone to call someone. Hesitantly, she opened the back door and collapsed into it just as he took off.

"You look like you've been rode hard and put away wet, as Gramps used to say."

The voice was like needles in her head. Bryce. He was driving, Britney in the front seat next to him, putting on makeup in the vanity mirror. Her eyes met Emmalee's in the mirror. Did they look angry? Bored? Wounded? She couldn't tell. She didn't know what to say, so she just kept her mouth shut, her heart a jackhammer in her chest being this close to Bryce and Britney.

Bryce seemed oblivious and just turned up his stereo, letting Kanye send earthquakes through her throbbing head all the way home. The second the car stopped, she was out the door. "Thanks for the ride," she mumbled, trying to ignore the laughter behind her.

She locked it, then turned around and leaned against it, closing her eyes and breathing a sigh of relief. She was alone. Finally. She didn't think she'd ever been that glad to be alone in her life.

She plugged her phone into a charger, then filled a glass full of water and emptied it, then filled it again and went to her room, where she collapsed. She closed her eyes and for once, sleep didn't evade her. Instead, it took her under.

When she woke later, the gray slant of light through her window told her it was early evening. The night before came rushing back again. Even though no one was there, she could feel her cheeks heat with shame that she couldn't remember exactly what had happened. Had she been that drunk? She could only recall having the one drink. But she was clearly wasted.

She'd missed a lot since her phone died, it seemed. All of her notifications were text messages from Mekayla. The message preview had Emmalee sighing.

MEKAYLA

We need to meet and talk about this.

She wasn't sure she could handle much more from Mekayla about the investigation. She clicked on her messages app anyway and tapped on her thread with Mekayla.

Almost every missed message was a picture. Each picture an arrow to her heart.

In the first, Emmalee was drinking from her glass on Bryce's patio tiles. From this vantage point – outside of her own head – she looked like a hooker. The split in her black dress was splayed wide open, showing a lot of thigh, and with a low cut top, far more skin was showing than she'd realized, or at least, it felt that way now, knowing Mekayla had seen it.

Her heart pounded as she opened the second picture. In this one, she was pressed up against Chase. There wasn't even enough space between them to slide a playing card. Her head on his chest, his mouth against her hair – it looked extremely inti-mate. She could explain, though. They were just dancing. She didn't really know how to dance. He was just helping her. She hadn't wanted to say no to him because he'd looked so lonely and sad. And, if she was honest, because she liked it, and he seemed to like it, too.

She swiped to the next picture, in which she was just standing alone, legs askew, tilted a little sideways, as if she was about to fall down. Her mascara had started to smudge, and her hair was damp and sticking to her face.

She remembered that moment. Chase had just left her abruptly, and she didn't know what to do. She remembered feeling weird, dizzy, like she might pass out. Then she remem-bered the drinks he picked up from the table, the girl who'd offered her a pill. The thought crossed her mind that maybe someone had put something in her drink. Surely not, right? These kids had rich, important parents. There was no way they would want to be in the news for drugging girls at parties. Right?

Her fingers trembled as she opened the final photo. When she saw it, she gasped and dropped her phone on the counter, shaking all over. "No, no, no, no, no," she cried, tears welling in her eyes.

Just then, her phone rang. Uncle Dan. She had to answer or he'd get worried, and the last thing she needed was him coming over right then.

She breathed in deeply, her shoulders shaking as she tried to control the urge to sob instead. Just breathe, she told herself. After the third ring, the call went to voicemail. Shit. She grabbed the phone and went to recents, clicked on the missed call. "Come on, pick up," she whispered as it rang.

"Em?"

Finally. "Uncle Dan! Hi! How are you?" She tried to make her voice as cheerful as possible. Nothing to worry about here.

"Are you okay?" His voice was slow, suspicious-sounding.

"Yeah, yes, sure. I'm fine." She tried to sound bright. "I'm sorry I missed your call just now. I was–"

"Em, honey, stop. Remember who you're talking to. What's wrong?" He was starting to get that parental tone he always got when her mom was away. She needed to fix this now.

"Really, I'm fine, Uncle D. I was just cooking dinner and dancing to some music, and I'm just a little out of breath."

"Hmmmm. Okay. For now." Whew. She breathed a sigh of relief. "What are you making?"

"Chicken." She quickly added, "And salad," before he could jump on her about not having vegetables.

"Good, good. How's school going?"

She closed her eyes and took a deep breath. "School's good." She really hoped he didn't hear the way her voice went just a little too high at the end, her tell that she was lying. She squeezed her eyes shut and bit her lip, waiting to see the verdict.

"Glad to hear it."

"Have you found a place yet?" She wanted to get him off the topic of her. Fast.

"Actually, that's what I was calling about. I rented a very cool downtown loft. I was going to see if you want to come check it out next weekend?"

No. "Maybe, yeah. Depends on if I have a tennis match." Whether there was or not, there would be one at least as far as Uncle Dan was concerned.

"Well, okay. Let me know. Also, have you heard from your mom?"

"No, why?" Emmalee was immediately on alert. "Did something happen?"

"No, no. Sorry. I was honestly just asking. I should quit doing that."

"It's okay." It wasn't. Ever since losing her dad, Emmalee worried nonstop about losing her mom.

"Well, kiddo, I better go get some dinner myself. Take care, and call if you need anything, okay?"

"Okay, Uncle Dan. Love you."

"Love you too, kiddo."

The call ended, and then there it was. That picture. Her head lying on a guy's shoulder, her eyes closed, his hands far too low. The guy was Bryce. Her skin wanted to crawl off as she remembered the way he'd backed her up against the shelves before that, grabbed her wrist, and made her feel like he was going to really hurt her.

In the picture, though, she looked like she was really into him. Which wasn't true at all. She remembered being dizzy, feeling like her brain was full of cotton and she couldn't think straight. She remembered being angry, scared, disgusted. But this picture said something else, and next to the one with Chase, it looked like she was willing to get what she wanted from any guy willing to put his hands on her. What the hell am I going to do? Think, think. First things first, text Mekayla back. Her fingers flew over the keyboard.

This is not what it looks like.

MEKAYLA

Obviously!

Where'd you get these?

SnapChat - some loser on an anonymous account sent them to the Ravensville High group chat.

Fuck. Fuck fuck fuck.

It's okay Em. Let's meet after school tomorrow and talk. We'll figure this out.

Emmalee just dropped her phone on the counter again and went back to her room. Under the covers, with the lights out, she felt hot tears slide down her cheeks, and she tried to ignore the glaring reality of how badly she had screwed up her existence in Ravensville, and so freaking fast.

Ironically, she wished more than ever for a do-over, for her mom to get new orders that would take them to another state, or maybe to a whole other country, so she could try again. Maybe this time, she'd be smart and not try at all.

CHAPTER 26

She woke up the next morning and immediately panicked about unfinished homework. She quit caring in half a second when she remembered the state of her life.

Gretchen.

Bryce.

The pictures.

She groaned and contemplated pulling the covers back over her head and hiding from the world, but if she did that, the school would contact her mom. If they didn't reach her, they'd call Dan, which would result in the same thing. She reluctantly shut off the alarm on her phone and hauled herself into the shower and somehow got herself to school.

By the time she pulled into a space and saw students talking, laughing, rushing into the building, she wished she'd stayed in bed. Even though she knew it probably wasn't true, she imagined all of the talking and laughing was about her and those pictures. But, she reminded herself, it was a little conceited to assume anyone really cared.

In English, a red-haired, freckled kid in jeans and steel-toed boots kept looking back at Emmalee and snickering, sticking his tongue out and waggling it at her. Once, he held his hands up to his chest and mimed lifting and squeezing make-believe boobs. Emmalee did her best to ignore it, but she could feel her face warming, the blood rushing in her ears again. She knew he was referencing her pictures – one in particular. She felt like she was going to throw up and contemplated raising her hand and asking to visit the bathroom, but suddenly, Britney's voice shot out like a dart.

"What's the matter, Landon? Horny? I guess you have to touch yourself since girls would rather die than do it for you."

The rest of the class laughed. Emmalee was sure most of them had no idea what the creep had been doing, but Britney's words, and the fact she was Britney, worked in her favor. Landon went red in the face. Emmalee could see a vein throbbing in his neck.

"That will be enough, Miss Whitfield. Leave the room this minute and report to the Principal's office."

Mrs. Smith stormed toward the door and pointed across the hall.

"I'm sorry, Mrs. Smith," Britney whined sweetly. "I just hate to see students bullying other students."

"Out. Now."

"But, Landon was—"

"I said out." Mrs. Smith was having none of Britney's excuses.

Britney walked down the row toward the door, letting her bag hit Landon in the shoulder as she passed. "Oops. My bad." The class giggled and watched her leave, hips swaying like a supermodel on a runway.

Emmalee noticed Landon's face was still beet red and his eyes bored into hers. There was a lot of anger there, but he looked away quickly.

She was so confused. Why was Britney helping her? She thought Britney was her enemy now. Nothing made sense anymore. Emmalee didn't even know who she was anymore, let alone Britney or anyone else in this psychotic group of kids.

Mid-pushup in gym that afternoon, she heard Coach Taylor call her name. "Sloane. Office."

She leapt up. "Me?" Her heart was in her throat.

"No, the other Sloane." He made a face at her and shook his head. "Yes, you. Go. Now." He hooked his thumb over his shoulder, pointing toward the door, and went back to counting pushups.

Her hands were shaking as she approached the main office. The door was closed. It had never been closed before, at least not in the weeks she'd been here. She considered making a run for it, but she knew she wouldn't make it far. She wasn't the criminal type. Except — an image of muddy ground in the woods flashed in her mind, her hands slick with mud and blood. Technically she was a criminal. Suddenly, the door opened and Mr. Brown was right there.

"Miss Sloane." He looked her over with disdain. She couldn't help that he'd called her here in her gym clothes. "I was about to come find you myself. These gentlemen are very busy. Let's go." He gestured toward his office, where she could see two men in suits sitting on the visitors' side of Brown's desk, both heads turned, eyes boring into her, assessing her. Cops.

Emmalee swallowed down the lump in her throat and followed the principal into his office. He pointed to a small classroom chair in the corner of the room behind his desk. One of the suited men reached over and shut the door. The click sounded ominous and everything in Emmalee's body warned her to run. Instead, she tucked her hands under her thighs, sitting on them, the pressure reminding her to stay seated and stay calm, or at least appear that way. She could hear Britney's voice threatening her. Emmalee shivered.

Brown cleared his throat. "Miss Sloane, these gentlemen have a few questions for you."

"I'm Detective Arnold." The man who'd shut the door smiled grimly, then gestured toward his partner, a burly, angry-looking man. "This is Detective Sutherland. We just have a few questions. You're free to go any time you want, and Principal Brown here has agreed to sit in as an interested adult. Can I get your full name, Miss Sloane?" The older man looked at her with eyes that showed no emotion.

She hesitated, looking between the three men in the room. "Shouldn't my mom be here?" She hated that her voice shook.

Sutherland frowned. "You're 18, so no, your mom doesn't have to be here." His voice was sarcastic, hard.

Arnold, clearly the good cop, smiled. "No need to worry. This isn't an interrogation. Just a few questions. Okay?"

Emmalee tried to control her breathing. "Okay."

"Now," Arnold sat up straighter. "Can we get your full name, then?"

"Emmalee Renee Sloane."

"Spelling, please?" His tone was dry, fingers moving his pen quickly over his notepad as she answered.

"So, Emmalee...can I call you Emmalee?" His eyes flicked up at her, pupils narrowing.

"Yeah," she whispered, kicking herself mentally. Everything about her was screaming that she was scared, lying. Guilty.

If Arnold felt that way, too, he gave no indication. Just smiled and carried on. "Emmalee, then. When was the last time you saw Gretchen Thomas?" He looked at her, still no hint of accusation on his face.

"Um, I don't know. The weekend, maybe?"

"Can you be a little more specific? Which day?"

"Saturday?"

"Is that a question or a statement, Emmalee?" Sutherland jumped in now, clearly the bad cop in this duo.

"It's a statement." Shit. She had to get it together.

"Okay." Arnold again. "What time on Saturday?"

"In the morning. We had a tennis match."

"You play tennis?"

"Yeah. Gretchen needed a doubles partner, so I agreed to help out and join the team."

"Why did she need a doubles partner?" He narrowed his eyes a little as he watched her.

"Well, I guess her usual partner wasn't able to play." She could feel her heart racing so fast. She swallowed to try and get herself under control.

"Let's see," he turned back to a previous page in his notepad and skimmed it quickly. "That was a girl named Audrey, yes? What happened that made her unable to play?"

She had a feeling he knew the answer. She cleared her throat and shifted in her chair.

"Ummm, I didn't know her, don't know her." Shit. "I never met her. Anyway, she had some kind of accident, I guess?"

"Mmhmm." He paused, looking at her, waiting for her to keep going. But she didn't. "Tell me about Saturday."

"Well, we — the whole team, I mean — we rode the bus to the match and then came back to school on the bus."

"What time did you get back here?"

"Noon, I think?"

"Question or statement?" Sutherland snapped.

Emmalee could feel her face flushing. "It was around noon. I didn't notice the exact time." Jeez, he was making her nervous. Her hands were sweating under her thighs.

"What did you talk to her about?"

"Not much, really. She gave me some directions when we played. She knows a lot more about tennis."

"What else?"

"Nothing else much."

"Nothing else much is not nothing else." He stared into her eyes, pen poised over the notepad. Her eyes flicked to Sutherland, who looked ready to eat someone for lunch. He was big, burly, and angry.

"Sorry, nothing else."

"Really? She's a friend of yours, right?"

"No." His eyes lit up at that. Fuck.

"No?"

"I mean, we were, are, friendly-ish. We didn't talk much."

"Why is that?"

She swallowed hard. How did she answer this? "Um, I'm new here, and I have been hanging out with her group of friends, but she hasn't really been around quite that much."

"But she played tennis with you?"

"Yes."

"How often are practices?"

"After school."

"Every day?"

"Yes."

"So, she wasn't around much, except every day after school, and at tennis matches?"

Fuck. "Yes, but she just didn't talk to me a whole lot."

"Didn't or doesn't?"

Fuck fuck fuck. "Doesn't. I just meant that she didn't Saturday." Fuck, she wanted out of here.

"But you two are partners?"

"Yes."

"How would you describe Gretchen's tennis abilities?"

"She was great," she stammered, quickly adding, "I mean, she was great on Saturday. We won."

He looked at her thoughtfully for several seconds, then nodded. "How'd she seem on Saturday, besides *great* at tennis?"

Emmalee took a deep breath, letting it out in a rush. "She was quiet."

"Any idea why?"

"She's quiet a lot. I think she's just like that."

"I see. Could you tell if she was upset with anyone, if anything was bothering her?"

"Um, no, not really."

"That sounds like maybe a little?"

Shit, this was exhausting. "Maybe a little."

"About what?"

She shrugged. "I'm not sure."

He paused for a few seconds again, waiting for her to keep going. It was all she could do to not start filling the void with chatter to break the tension.

"Really?" He looked at her in complete disbelief. "Listen, Emmalee. We need you to be honest here. You know, we've talked to some of Gretchen's other friends, so I'd like you to tell us about some of the issues between you and Gretchen."

What the hell? Who told him that she and Gretchen had problems?

"Emmalee?"

"Yes, sorry. Um, she was maybe a little annoyed that I was going to Homecoming with Chase. That's her boyfriend."

"Okay. So she was jealous of you two. Did you two fight about it Saturday?"

"No." She said that quickly, and firmly. That was the absolute truth. Gretchen never gave her the time of day. She'd never stoop to arguing with someone beneath her. Someone like Emmalee.

"Where'd she go after you returned to school Saturday?"

"I don't know."

"Arnold sat back, not taking notes now.

"Did you see her leave the school?"

"Not exactly. I just got in my car and went home."

"Straight from the bus?"

"Well, no. I put my gear in the locker room first?"

"Did she put hers in the locker room, too?"

Emmalee paused. She recalled seeing Gretchen and Britney whispering angrily, huddled near Britney's locker, and Gretchen's eyes flashing over to Emmalee more than once.

"Well?"

"Yeah. I think she dropped her stuff off, too."

"You think?"

Emmalee could feel heat rising in her cheeks. "Yes, I think. I didn't pay a lot of attention. I didn't realize I'd be interrogated about it." Immediately, she regretted the snappish tone in her voice.

He just stared at her for a bit, then leaned forward and scribbled a few lines on his notepad again.

"Last question, Emmalee. Have you seen or heard from Gretchen since Saturday?"

"No." She said it too quickly, and then swallowed too hard, shifted her hands under her legs too much.

"Well, if you see or hear from her, give me a call." He handed her a card, and she unstuck a hand from between her leg and the hard plastic chair. She could feel the sweat on her fingers dampening the card.

"Okay." Another lie.

"Thank you, Emmalee. You've been very helpful." He stood and opened the door, followed by Sutherland, who stared at her so hard she swore he could see into her soul. Was she the last person they were talking to today? Who else had they talked to?

"You can go back to class, Miss Sloane." Brown shooed her toward the door.

She left the office and headed back to the gym, checking the time. Class would be nearly over now. As she turned into the stairwell that led down to the girls' locker room, a shadow moved out from behind the door. Emmalee screamed, and the figure grabbed her arm and hissed.

"Shut up!"

Britney.

"You scared me," Emmalee breathed, clutching her chest.

"What did you say?"

"What? To the cops?"

"Obviously. Who the fuck else?" Britney's eyes were flashing darkly.

"I didn't say anything. Just that I saw her at tennis Saturday and that was it."

"That better be it."

"But he did find out Gretchen was mad at me about Chase. Did you tell him that?"

"Are you seriously fucking questioning me right now? I'm the one trying to help you, you little baby bitch. Keep your mouth shut and that scared little girl look under control. Seriously. Don't fucking be an idiot, or you'll bury yourself, Em." Britney's lip smirked, like she was joking, but her eyes said otherwise.

CHAPTER 27

Things only got worse after school. Mekayla was waiting at Emmalee's car, arms crossed over her chest. Marshall was standing awkwardly next to her, digging his toe into the concrete of the parking lot.

"Hey," Emmalee said, waiting for Mekayla to move.

"We need to talk." Mekayla's voice was stern, and Emmalee's heart raced again. She figured it wouldn't be too long before she had a heart attack from all this insanity.

"I have homework."

"I don't care. We need to talk. Now."

Emmalee sighed and her shoulders fell. "Where?"

"Coffee shop. You drive." Mekayla reached out for the passenger door and waited for Emmalee to unlock the car.

Marshall climbed in the back and remained quiet the entire time they drove to café Vibes. Inside, they were greeted by 90s grunge music and a barista with a nose ring and pink hair.

"Hey, Chloe." Mekayla practically skipped up to the counter, smiling. "What's good today?"

"Hey, yourself, KayKay. Everything's good today, now that

you're here." Chloe winked and put her hands on the counter in front of her. "What'll it be?"

Mekayla ordered three lattes and cinnamon rolls and stopped Emmalee when she reached for her wallet. "My treat," she said. The three of them tucked into a table in the back corner to wait for their orders.

"So, let's not waste any time." Mekayla pulled out a notebook and pen. "I'm working on a story about Gretchen's disappearance for the newspaper."

"No, Mekayla." Emmalee could feel her hands start shaking. She squeezed one in the other to try to keep them calm.

"Emmalee, one of our own students is missing. Like, gone. Like, no one has seen her in days. We can't just let this go."

"I don't want to be part of this."

"You are part of this." Mekayla's eyes narrowed, challenging Emmalee. "Tell me I'm wrong."

Emmalee could feel her face heating. "I don't know what you're talking about."

"Bullshit. You were interviewed by detectives today."

"What the hell, Mekayla?" Emmalee looked over at Marshall, who was staring at the table, drawing figure eights with his index finger.

"Here you go, gorgeous people." Chloe wielded a tray of massive coffee mugs and even bigger cinnamon rolls. When she left, Mekayla started up immediately.

"Em, I know for a fact that you were interviewed. What I don't know is why."

"I don't know why, either. Maybe because I'm on the tennis team, too?"

"Maybe. But three quarters of the team were not interviewed. Why is that?"

Emmalee shrugged, nervously rubbing the tops of her thighs through her jeans. "Maybe because I'm her doubles partner?"

Mekayla stared for a moment, then nodded. "Okay. Maybe."

She jotted something on her notepad. "What did they want to know?"

"Just stuff. When I saw her last, what she was like that day. You know, just general stuff." Emmalee desperately wanted this conversation to be over.

"You see, there's a problem here. Marshall heard something very — interesting." Mekayla elbowed Marshall, who looked up. Emmalee noticed his face was very, very pale. He looked like he might throw up.

"Um." He paused.

"Spit it out, Marshall. She needs to know."

"Um, I was in the library during lunch today. I like to eat lunch there when Mekayla's not eating lunch because–"

"Skip it, Marshall," Makyala interrupted. "Get to the point." She rolled her eyes at Emmalee and shook her head.

"Okay, okay. Jeez. Anyway, Kristina and Tyler came in. They didn't see me. They were kind of making out in the corner, but then Britney came in, and they were all whispering."

"Jesus Christ, Marshall, I swear to God I will pierce your brain with an ice pick if you don't get to the point."

Emmalee winced. Mekayla noticed.

"Just kidding." She smiled, taking a sip of her latte from her huge pink mug. "Mostly." Emmalee noticed that when Mekayla made these ridiculous threats it seemed so innocent. Her smile so genuine. So much different from Britney's.

Marshall sighed. "Britney told them to keep an eye on you."

"On me?" Emmalee tried to act confused. She knew, of course, that Britney wanted to make sure Emmalee didn't say something stupid or act weird. She was pretty sure she was failing on both counts.

Marshall nodded. "She said she didn't trust you."

Emmalee swallowed hard. "That's weird."

Mekayla watched her closely. Emmalee picked at her cinnamon roll and tried to look confused.

"I mean, trust me about what?"

"Well, they're your friends. You'd know better than us." Mekayla sat back, arms across her chest again, and waited for Emmalee to respond. Marshall began making those figure eights on the table again.

"I really don't know. And they're not my friends. I'm just investigating." Emmalee's mind raced to come up with something believable, but she couldn't think of a single plausible reason.

"Mhmm. Okay. Let's change gears. When did you last see Gretchen?"

"Come on, Mekayla. I already told the detectives everything I know."

"You come on, Emmalee. Gretchen is your friend–" Emmalee opened her mouth to say something, but Mekayla jumped in first. "Okay, okay. Maybe not a *friend* friend, but she's your tennis partner, and she's friends with your friends – and don't lie about them not being your friends. It's obvious they are. Anyway, I'd think you'd care a little more about what happened to her."

Shit. "I do care. Of course I care. Jeez, Mekayla." Emmalee's face had to be bright red at this point based on the heat she was feeling.

"Then why don't you want to help us? Help her?"

"I do. I mean, I would. If I knew anything."

"Well, leave that part to me. You just answer my questions."

Mekayla then started firing questions at Emmalee, all the same ones the detectives asked, and Emmalee tried to answer them all the same way. When they got to the part where Gretchen was upset about Emmalee going to the dance with Chase, Mekayla stopped, looking thoughtful.

"Yeah. Why did you go with Chase?"

"He asked me. Since Gretchen was out of town that night."

"Okay, but why did he need a date? Everyone knows he's dating Gretchen. He could have just gone on his own. Why cause a problem with his girlfriend?" Mekayla started scribbling furiously on her notebook.

Emmalee sat silent for a minute, deep in thought. Why had Chase asked her to the dance? She knew obviously that Chase liked her, but she couldn't very well tell Mekayla that. She needed to come up with something, though.

"I think he just didn't want to be a fifth wheel with the rest of the group, you know?"

Just then, Emmalee's phone pinged. A text from Britney:

911. Kris's now.

"I need to go." Emmalee stood to leave.

"Hang on a second. What's going on? You can't just leave us here. You're our ride."

"Let's go then."

"We're not finished, though. What is happening?"

"Britney sent a 9-1-1 text saying to meet at Kristina's now."

"Awesome!" Mekayla's eyes lit up as she jumped up from her seat. "Maybe you can get some more info. Call me as soon as you leave there."

"Yeah, sure." No way. "I need to go. Now." Emmalee could only wonder what the hell Britney's text meant, so she rushed outside to go find out.

Emmalee was dumbstruck. She was sitting in Kristina's living room, next to Britney and Kristina on the sofa, with no idea how she'd gotten to this point in her life.

Across from her sat a girl in her mid-20s, who seemed to be a stranger to everyone in the room. Camry.

"I just don't understand," she said, raking a nail bitten hand through her long, brown hair. The grimace, the confusion on her face spoke volumes. She was really worried about Gretchen. "How can she just be gone? She was headed home when I said goodbye to her in Seattle on Sunday evening."

Britney shrugged. "It's hard to say. What was she doing with you in Seattle? Maybe it has something to do with that."

Her eyes shot up and met Britney's. "Why does it matter?"

"Well, considering we've never heard of you, Camry, it's kind of weird she's hanging out with you in Seattle and then no one has seen her since? Right?" Britney's voice was hard, her eyes flicking to Emmalee's and Kristina's looking for confirmation. Emmalee nodded feebly.

"No. I mean, I know she was fine when she left."

"Awesome. You know she was fine. I guess we'll just have to take your word for it then." Britney's voice was dripping with sarcasm, "Maybe you two were secret lesbian lovers?"

"Britney," Kristina warned.

"No, it's okay." Camry squared her shoulders and looked at Britney straight on. "I'm not even going to answer that. Look, I can't tell you exactly what Gretchen was doing with me in Seattle."

Britney scoffed. "Right."

"Seriously. But I can promise you that she was fine when she left."

"No one is ever going to believe that. We know she's had someone secret on the side, always hiding away on the phone, disappearing to Seattle, skipping Homecoming and parties."

Camry rolled her eyes. "I know you're still teenagers into all that immature shit, but Gretchen was beyond that. We were friends."

"Friends." Britney put air quotes around the word. "Right. Look, Camry, we can't help you. You were the last person to see her, so you know better than us."

Emmalee's heart revolted at that blatant lie from Britney, but she worked hard to keep her face neutral.

"That's just it. The cops are asking me questions because they think I know something, but I don't. I need to find her."

"Sorry we can't be more help, but I think it's time you leave." Britney stood.

The front door opened just then, and a fifty-ish man in a gray suit stepped through the door and looked around.

"Daddy!" Kristina jumped up and crossed the room to give him a hug while Emmalee and Camry stared in confusion.

"Hi, Kristy. Britney. Who do we have here?" He smiled graciously at everyone gathered in the room.

"Daddy, this is Emmalee, she's new at school. And this is Camry." She pointed at an obviously distressed Camry, and her father frowned. "Camry is trying to find out where Gretchen is, but we've told her we have no idea." Kristina's voice was higher and sweeter than Emmalee had ever heard it.

"I see. Nice to meet you, Emmalee. Camry, it's awful about Gretchen, and I'm sorry we won't be able to help you. Maybe you should speak to the police." He held the door open and pointed. "I don't think I'm blocking your car."

Camry looked shocked. "Um, I was just–"

He interrupted her stammering. "I understand. Terrible thing, really. We hope for the best. Here, I'll walk you to your car."

Camry stood and shuffled helplessly to the door. Kristina's father closed the door behind them, and Britney immediately combusted.

"What the actual fuck! Who the fuck does she think she is?" Britney's face was red.

"No idea," Kristina offered dryly.

"The real question is what the fuck did Gretchen tell her? I mean, you saw how nasty looking she was. Definitely beneath us." Britney's eyes flickered over to Emmalee. "What could they possibly have been seeing each other for?" Britney stood up and peeked out a window.

"Maybe they really are just friends?" Emmalee barely squeaked out.

"Don't be an idiot, Emmalee. Something's wrong here. If Gretchen was just friends with Camry, she'd tell us more. What the fuck!"

Emmalee couldn't understand why Britney was so upset. "Well, she doesn't know what happened, obviously, so maybe we don't need to worry about it?"

"You are such a simp, Em. You have no idea what the fuck you're talking about."

Emmalee felt her anger rising. "Then enlighten me."

Britney whipped her head around and glared. "Don't give me orders. Ever. Tell you what. Get the fuck out of here. Go home and play with your baby dolls and let the grown-ups figure out what to do."

"But—"

"No buts. Go." Britney moved to the door and held it open. "And keep your fucking mouth shut. Or else. Don't forget that we all know what really happened."

Emmalee's eyes stung, her face red, like she'd been slapped. She grabbed her bag and ran for her car. At home, she texted Mekayla that there was no new info — yet another lie — then hid under covers, ear buds blasting, trying to drown out the voices in her head telling her that her life was over.

CHAPTER 28

She woke some time in the night to a loud thump, followed by a rustle. Someone was in the house. Emmalee bolted out of bed and went to her closet, pulling down the shoebox her mom had her keep there. She slipped the handgun out and made her way quietly toward the bedroom door. She listened for a moment, finding it hard to hear over the thumping of her heart.

There it was again — a definite rustling sound, coming from the living room. Her sleepy brain conjured images of Britney sneaking in to do — something — she didn't want to think about what.

Quietly, she twisted her bedroom doorknob, and peeked out, gun held down to her side. She couldn't see anything but the dark outline of furniture. She worked to calm her breathing and inched down the hallway, gun held in front of her now, both hands on it, ready to shoot if needed.

"Em?"

Nikki.

Emmalee's breath rushed out, and she put the gun down. "Mom? You scared the crap out of me!"

A light suddenly came on and Emmalee squinted.

"Sorry, Em. I was just trying to be—" Her mom stopped mid-sentence. "What the hell? You have the gun out?"

"Well, I thought someone broke in." Emmalee rubbed sleep from her eyes.

"Put that thing away, then get back out here. I was going to wait until morning, but we need to talk."

Shit. Nothing was ever easy. Emmalee headed to her room, cheerily asking, "What's up? How was the deployment?"

Only silence greeted her questions. This was not good.

Back in the living room, her mother was seated on one end of the couch, still in uniform.

"Sit." That was her officer tone. Great.

Emmalee sat.

"I'm going to let you start. Anything you'd like to tell me?"

Emmalee swallowed. "Umm, no, not really."

"No? How about we start with why the General told me I had to take emergency family leave?"

"I, I don't know," Emmalee stuttered. Her mind was whirling.

"Don't lie to me."

A lump too big to swallow formed in Emmalee's throat and before she knew it, she was crying. Sobbing actually.

"Em, what the hell is going on?"

There was no way she could respond. Her body was finally releasing all of the emotions she'd been carrying around all boxed up for days.

Her mother scooted over and pulled Emmalee into her arms, hugging her close, stroking her hair.

"Em, breathe. Talk to me."

She took several slow, ragged breaths. When she trusted herself to speak again, she choked out, "I don't know where to start."

Her mother pulled back, holding Emmalee's shoulders. "The beginning. Let's start there."

As the sobbing subsided, she realized she needed to tread carefully here. There was no way she could tell her mom everything.

"I made some friends." She could feel her eyes tearing up again, see the confusion on her mom's face.

"Yeah? That's good, right? I knew you would." Her mom was rubbing Emmalee's back in big circles.

"Yeah, it's good. I mean, I guess. Kind of. The girls play tennis, and they convinced me to partner with one of them whose normal doubles partner is, ummm, not able to play right now."

"You're playing tennis? That's great, Em!"

Emmalee slid her eyes over sideways to look at her mom, and her mom was staring back, nodding, encouraging her like one might a frightened toddler. It was so unlike Nikki that it scared her. Emmalee took a deep breath and sat up straight, scooted away a few inches.

"Anyway, this girl, Gretchen, she's missing."

"Missing? As in—"

"As in, she hasn't come back to school this week." Emmalee broke into sobs again.

"Well that's disturbing." Nikki frowned. "Do you know what happened?"

She swallowed hard, trying to put on her poker face. "No. We had a tennis match Saturday morning, but that's the last time I talked to her." That was kind of true, but she felt sick at the lie, the reality of what happened flashing in her mind over and over again.

"Okay. Keep going. How did this end up in me being called back?"

Emmalee sniffled, wiping her eyes. "Some detectives interviewed me since I was one of the last people to see her. Maybe that's why?"

Her mom's brows knit themselves together. "Maybe. They

interviewed you without me?" She could sense an angry edge to her mom's voice.

Emmalee nodded. "They said since I was eighteen, they could, and that I was free to go anytime."

Nikki nodded. "But you're okay?" She looked deeply concerned.

Emmalee nodded. "Yeah, I'm okay." The lies just kept stacking up.

"Good. Now, you need some rest. There's more to talk about, but we can do that tomorrow."

"Wait, what else?"

"Tomorrow. Go to bed, soldier." Her mom ruffled her hair, then pointed down the hall. "That's an order."

Emmalee had never felt such dread in her life since, well since two years ago.

She slipped out of bed and out the door before Nikki woke up. She didn't want to face any more questions at the moment, and she'd breathed a sigh of relief when she saw Nikki snoring on the couch with an open bottle of Crown Royal on the coffee table.

She sat in the parking lot in front of the school for a long time, watching the janitor arrive and open the building, followed by the cooks and then teachers, one by one. Taylor was in first. Shocking. She assumed he'd get here at the last minute like most of the coaches she'd had as teachers over the years. Then she saw a group of football boys show up in one truck, Jay-Z blaring from the speakers.

When Chase's car pulled into the lot, she jumped out and waited outside the driver's side door.

"Hey, Em," he said as he got out, eyes scanning the lot.

"Hey." She leaned in for a hug, but he backed up a bit, putting a hand on her shoulder. "Is everything okay?" she asked, confused.

"Yeah. Em, Listen." He looked over his shoulder again, then straight into her eyes. "We need to be careful, okay? With everything going on, I can't, I mean, we can't be seen *together*, you know? I don't need people asking too many questions, or getting any ideas."

"Ideas? What ideas? You mean like the truth?" Heat was crawling up her spine.

He grabbed her shoulder and pulled her closer to the car, head swiveling to see if anyone heard her. "The truth? I don't even know anymore what the truth is, but I know I don't need any more drama right now."

"Wait. What?" She couldn't make sense of the words he was saying. "Are you worried about your reputation? Are you afraid to be seen with me? Is that why we haven't spoken in the last two days?"

"God, Em. No." His eyes softened. "You know how I feel about you. Let's just keep things under wraps for a while. Let things settle down, okay?" After a quick look around the lot, he leaned in for a quick peck on her cheek. "Meet me at our spot out on the highway after school today, okay? I'll be waiting for you." Then he gave her that smile that undid her every time before he darted to the main door.

She watched him go, feeling lonelier than she'd ever felt. She wanted to be angry, but he was right. The two of them together right now would look all kinds of bad. He needed to play the part of the worried boyfriend. Hanging on another girl would be insane. Hanging on to Emmalee could be especially disastrous, since the detectives were already acting suspicious of her.

She took a deep breath and steeled herself for the day ahead. Inside, she found a quiet table in the library and tried to get some homework done. Her grades were atrocious. She hadn't done much homework of any kind since she was trying to just survive and stay out of prison.

Not long into a particularly nasty math problem, she heard the library door squeak, footsteps shuffle in behind her. The hair on the back of her neck stood up. She should have sat facing the door. She looked over her shoulder and made eye contact with the red-headed kid who'd stuck his tongue out at her after those pictures had been sent out. Landon.

His face flushed now, anger painting it red, but there was something else there, too. Fear? Yeah. He was afraid of her. She wasn't sure how to feel about that.

She didn't have time to decide, though, because there was suddenly an announcement over the intercom.

"All staff and students, please report to the auditorium for an important announcement. All students and staff to the auditorium immediately."

The redhead just stared at her for a second, eyes wide, deer in headlights, then backed toward the library doors, turning to push them open and leave only after his back hit them.

She took a deep breath, packed up her books, and headed for the auditorium. She wondered what the announcement was. Things surely can't get any worse, she thought.

CHAPTER 29

"We are very sorry to announce that one of our own, Senior Gretchen Thomas, has passed away. Her body was found early this morning. Authorities are conducting an investigation. That is all the information I have at this time." Mr. Brown paused, for dramatic effect it seemed. He scanned the student faces staring up at him, almost as if accusing each and every one. There was no response. Just a long, long hush. "The office is open if anyone needs to talk, or perhaps share any information that might help the investigation."

There was a long silence. Time stood still for a few moments. No one knew what to say, until they did. Then the voices began swarming around her head like bees, threatening to attack. Every word, every line, every whisper, felt like a sting on her skin. On her soul.

She'd tucked herself into a corner of the auditorium, hiding out in the shadows at the back, hoping to make a quick escape and get to first period before everyone else.

Instead, she stood there in shock as students began rising and filing out, talking in hushed, excited tones about the body.

Body. Gretchen was just a body now. And Emmalee was responsible for that. At least partly. Her heart thrummed in her chest, and it felt like each beat would send blood exploding out of her head. She didn't know how her body held together. She felt frayed, ragged, threadbare. She turned, melted into the crowd, and then toward the doors to the parking lot.

"Miss Sloane!" She heard Mr. Brown behind her. She picked up her pace. "Miss Sloane! Come to the office with me immediately. We need to—"

She heard nothing else. She just shoved the doors open and ran to her car. After fumbling to start it, heart pounding, watching Mr. Brown speed walk toward her, she slammed it into drive and sped over a parking block toward freedom. She needed to get as far away as possible. She needed to think.

She traced back roads south of town, west, east, anywhere but north. Anywhere but that horrible road through the forest. That dark, wet, muddy slash of road that had ruined her entire life. At some point, she pulled over to shut her phone off and shove it in the glovebox, not even checking to see who all the missed calls and texts were from. She wanted to just disappear.

Eventually, she came to a small town she hadn't been to before. It looked shabby and sad. Like a good place for her right now. She parked behind a little strip of storefronts, carefully keeping her car off the main road.

She paced the streets for what felt like hours, counting sidewalk buckles, weeds growing through split concrete, letting images wash over her. Terrified eyes through a rain-soaked windshield. Hands muddy from a freshly-dug grave. Headlights through the fog and trees. The bone-deep cold of losing her very soul.

She needed warmth. She ducked inside a small diner, cringing at the bell that jangled over the door. She took a seat at a booth where she could have her back to the wall and keep an eye on the road in front of the shop. On the door every time it opened.

"What'll it be today?" An older woman with curly gray hair and a grease-stained apron had appeared out of nowhere, making Emmalee jump.

The woman just stared, unmoved.

"Um. Coffee, please."

"Cream and sugar?" No expression still.

"No thanks. Black."

The woman shoved her notepad in the apron's pocket, tucked a pencil in her hair, and sighed loudly.

A minute later, Emmalee's hands were clinging to a steaming porcelain mug of coffee. She watched the road, counted the very few cars that drove by – a whole seven of them in an entire hour – and let her coffee grow cold, her stomach too nauseous to even take a sip.

She kept trying to come up with a plan that would make this all go away, but every pathway seemed to end with her in trouble. Or dead, a little voice whispered in the back of her mind.

"You gonna eat something?" The waitress had arrived without Emmalee even noticing.

Emmalee jumped again, looking around. "No, thanks. I'm not hungry."

The woman's eyes narrowed. "Shouldn't you be in school?" She crossed her arms over her chest, eyes watching Emmalee's shaking hands, clearly suspicious.

"Teacher work day." Emmalee tried to plaster a fake smile on her face, but she could feel it was more like a grimace.

She left a five dollar bill on the table and dragged herself back outside. She guessed she needed to face real life anyway. In her car, she checked the glove box to make sure her phone was still there. She didn't pull it out, didn't check it. She couldn't handle it. Not yet. She slammed the glove box shut and headed toward home. Time to face the music.

CHAPTER 30

Emmalee was sitting in the driveway at home, just getting up the nerve to go in, when a dark sedan pulled in behind her. As soon as she saw the suited men emerge, she knew they were the detectives.

She took a deep breath and opened the car door, stepping out into the unknown. The front door opened and her mother emerged, arms across her chest, looking from Emmalee to the men.

"Em, where have you been? School called hours ago."

"We were wondering the same thing, Miss Sloane. We were just at the school." The older detective who had interrogated her at school looked annoyed.

Emmalee said nothing. She ducked back into her car to get her phone out of the glove box, and all of the adults leapt into action.

"Keep your hands where I can see them!" the older detective yelled as the big, burly guy lunged for her through the open door.

"Emmalee Sloane! Don't you even think about going anywhere!" her mother yelled at the same moment.

She dropped her phone and held her hands up. "I was just grabbing my phone! I swear!"

They let her pick up the phone and her bag and then led her inside.

"Gentlemen, can I ask who you are and why you're here?" Nikki's voice was firm, authoritative. Emmalee wished more than anything right now that she could have her mother's confidence.

"Yes, Ms. Sloane. I'm Detective Arnold, and this is my partner, Detective Sutherland. I'm not sure if you're aware, but a classmate of Emmalee's has been murdered."

Nikki's eyes flared wide, the only sign she was caught off guard. "No. I knew her classmate was missing, but I haven't had the news on. How can we help you?"

"Could we come in and visit with Emmalee for a few minutes, Ms. Sloane?"

Nikki's eyes slid over to Emmalee's, a silent question in them. "What would you like to speak with her about?"

Detective Arnold smiled, an attempt to be personable, friendly, safe. "We just wanted to ask a few questions, gather some information so we can find whoever did this."

"Didn't you already question her at school?" Nikki was using her Colonel Sloane voice. Emmalee just stood there watching, hoping Nikki would win this battle.

"She did, in fact, agree to answer some questions. We just have a few more. I promise we won't take much of your time. We know Emmalee's surely anxious to see justice done for her friend." He glanced over at Emmalee, waiting for her to respond, daring her to disagree.

"It's okay, Mom." It was not okay, but Emmalee could only hear Britney's deadly voice reminding her that there would be hell to pay if she did anything to draw attention to herself. "I don't mind."

Arnold smiled again and nodded his head. "Thank you,

Emmalee. I know it means a lot to Gretchen's family that she has so many friends willing to help find her killer."

He held her gaze a little too long, so Emmalee tore her eyes away and led the way inside, willing herself to act normally, pretend her heart was not going a hundred miles an hour, that her palms weren't sweating, that she wasn't seeing Gretchen's lifeless body every time she closed her eyes.

After they'd left, Nikki just stared at Emmalee, assessing her. They were sitting at the kitchen table. Her mom had made coffee for the detectives while Arnold asked Emmalee the same questions he'd asked her at school, just in different ways, like he was trying to trip her up.

Now that they'd left, she and Nikki were seated at the table sharing a second pot of coffee. Her mom was quiet, too quiet. That meant she was thinking, analyzing. Rarely a good thing if Emmalee was the subject of the analysis.

"Em, you need to talk to me. We can't fix this if you don't tell me what's happening."

"You know everything. You heard all that." Emmalee looked into her coffee cup, swirling it slowly.

"Don't bullshit me. I know when you're lying. You know more than you said, and I guarantee you Arnold knows that as well."

Nikki got up and started opening and shutting cabinet doors, pulling out bread and peanut butter.

Emmalee swallowed hard, trying to slow her heart rate. "I'm not lying." Even she didn't think her voice sounded convincing.

Nikki slammed a cabinet door. "You're playing a very dangerous game, Emmalee Renee. This isn't like coming in after curfew. A girl is dead. *Dead*, Em."

"I'm not playing a game!"

Nikki's eyes flashed. "Do not raise your voice at me. Ever."

"I'm sorry, but I'm not lying." Emmalee could feel her face burning.

Nikki shook her head and ran her fingers through her short hair, her tell that she was about to explode. She sighed. "Look, I have to go in and fill out some paperwork for family leave. You stay here, and that's a direct order. I was disappointed you left without us talking this morning."

"You were – asleep." She made sure to emphasize the word asleep, fully aware that Nikki would know she was thinking of that open bottle of Crown.

Nikki lowered her eyes to the floor. "Right. Well, I don't want you to go anywhere. Give me your keys." Nikki held her hand out. Emmalee grudgingly placed the keys in her outstretched palm. "Lock the door. Have some lunch. Clean your room. Wash your laundry. Do your homework. We'll talk when I get back." Without waiting for a response, she headed for the front door., then turned back. "Oh, and Em? Don't think we won't talk about the credit cards at some point."

Emmalee's heart leapt into her throat, but Nikki just stepped outside. When she heard the Tahoe's engine start and tires crunching on the driveway, she put her head down in her arms on the table and screamed.

She was just switching her laundry to the dryer when the doorbell rang, making her heart leap into her throat. Her mom would have just come in. She crept to the front window in the living room and peeked out, worried the detectives had returned to arrest her. It was just Mekayla and Marshall, though. She opened the door, shocked.

"How'd you find my house?"

"Hello to you, too." Mekayla's tone was dry. "Going to invite us in or make us stand here in the rain?"

"Sorry. Come on in." She was pretty sure her mom would have wanted her to leave them in the rain, but Emmalee was really creeped out being home alone.

Marshall stood awkwardly in the doorway while Mekayla wandered the room, inspecting walls, furniture, everything.

"I assume you're not here for a social visit," Emmalee snapped.

"You assume correctly," Mekayla snapped back.

Emmalee softened. She had no desire to fight with Mekayla. "Sorry, I'm just in a bad mood."

"I would assume so, considering you were interrogated again."

"What? How do you know that?"

"We came looking for you. Marshall's an office aid right before lunch, and I forced him to get your address when we realized you'd left."

Marshall shrugged his shoulders and grimaced apologetically in Emmalee's direction.

"Then, we cut school, came here, saw three cars out front. So, we parked a ways back and surveilled the place until we saw the detectives leave, then your mom we presume, and then we waited a while to make sure the coast was clear." Mekayla smiled. "And here we are."

Emmalee rolled her eyes. "You *surveilled* the place? What are you, the FBI?"

"Better." Mekayla smiled again. "Seriously, though, we're here to investigate."

"Mekayla–" She was cut off immediately.

"Don't Mekayla me. It's pretty clear you need our help."

Emmalee definitely needed help, but she also needed to keep Britney from turning her in to the police. Or worse. She shivered and wrapped her arms around herself. So as far as she was concerned, keeping her mouth shut was the most important thing at the moment.

"I don't know what you want from me, Mekayla. The detectives were just here because I was Gretchen's tennis partner. I already told you all this." Emmalee was starting to sweat, the kind of sweat brought on by anxiety. She could feel a bead of it running down the center of her back.

"Em. The detectives interviewed you twice. They came to your house. They must have a reason to keep interrogating you."

"I told you–"

"Don't give me that bullshit, Em! Audrey's in a coma. And now Gretchen is dead. *Dead!* Don't you even give a damn about that?"

Emmalee's face flushed, heating her cheeks. "Of course I do!" Her voice cracked. No, no, no. She did not want to cry.

"Then talk to us. We know you know more than you're saying. That much is obvious. You've been walking around like a zombie most of the time. You look like you're not sleeping. You're jumpy. You're skipping classes, not doing your work. It's clear there's something haunting you, Em."

Now the tears came anyway. Mekayla's tone had softened, opening the floodgates. Emmalee swiped at her eyes quickly and turned away.

"You're wrong. I'm not a zombie. I've just been busy lately."

"With what? Playing doubles?" Mekayla's tone was like acid again.

Emmalee turned to face her. "You don't understand, Mekayla."

"You're right. I don't. So enlighten me."

"It's not that simple."

"Oh, Em," Mekayla shook her head. "It is. Just talk to us."

Emmalee crossed to the couch and collapsed on it, letting the tears flow freely now. Mekayla and Marshall perched on the arms, one on each side of Emmalee. Mekayla reached down and rubbed Emmalee's back in reassuring circles, just like Nikki had the night before.

"Just talk to us, Em. We can't help you if you don't talk." Mekayla's voice was gentler now.

"I can't. Britney will kill me." Emmalee buried her face in a pillow and sobbed harder. She'd already said too much.

"Why would Britney kill you, Em?" Mekayla's tone was soft

and soothing, the circles she was rubbing on her back lulling Emmalee into a feeling of security.

Emmalee groaned. "She's just–"

"A crazy, psychotic bitch?" Mekayla finished Emmalee's sentence.

Emmalee laughed a half-hearted laugh.

Mekayla grinned. "She is. I know it. And I know *you* know it. I've known Britney since preschool, Em. Long enough to know she's involved in this somehow."

How could she know that? "What do you mean?"

"Em, any time anything terrible has happened in Ravensville, Britney has been lurking at the center of it."

"That sounds a little over the top." Not really.

"Yeah, okay, she had nothing to do with Bob Miller's DUI last year, I'll give you that."

"Who's Bob Miller?"

"Focus, Emmalee. Britney's always been circling when something bad happens. She's evil."

Emmalee stilled. She didn't want to argue, but she also didn't feel entirely safe to agree.

Marshall joined in. "In 4th grade, someone pantsed me on the playground. When I looked around, Bryce and Tyler were standing there laughing and pointing. But Britney was sitting on a swing, grinning evilly at me." Marshall closed his eyes and shivered. "Later, Mekayla told me she'd overheard Britney offering them her best Pokemon cards if they did it."

"You're still on about that, Marsh?" Mekayla rolled her eyes. "Don't worry. No one remembers your Lightning McQueen underwear. Oops." Mekayla grinned, and Emmalee couldn't help but smile. She dragged herself up to a sitting position, pulling the pillow onto her lap and hugging it close to her.

"And yeah, pantsing doesn't seem like such a huge deal. But as she's gotten older, it's gotten worse. Now, talk to us, Em. We want to help you."

"You want to get a scoop for your story."

"I think you know me better than that." Mekayla sounded genuinely hurt. "We want to uncover the truth to expose Britney for who she is. But, we also want to help you." Mekayla paused. "I guess I do owe you an apology. I've been on your back all the time about investigating Audrey's accident. I can see why you didn't feel like you could trust me enough to tell me everything."

Emmalee sighed. "It's not that, Mekayla." Then she told them everything.

CHAPTER 31

"Just go in, Em. She's not going to bite."

"I'm going," Emmalee huffed. "I'm just preparing myself."

"Well, prepare less and go, before she decides you're not coming and leaves."

Emmalee was sitting in Mekayla's car outside a coffee shop in downtown Seattle. She was supposed to be meeting Camry to talk about Gretchen, but the butterflies in Emmalee's stomach were more like elephants stomping around, threatening to send her lunch back up.

"Em. You have to go." Mekayla clicked the unlock button. Again. "Go."

"But it's packed in there. What if someone overhears us?" Emmalee took a deep breath and opened the door.

Mekayla just gave her a look and sighed. "Out. Now."

Emmalee gave in and opened the door.

Inside the café, she saw Camry tucked into a back corner table. She looked just as nervous as Emmalee felt.

After a half-hearted wave, she sat across from Camry. She looked pretty terrible. Dark circles ringed her eyes. Her hair hadn't been washed in a few days at least, and her clothes looked slept in. She was nervously tap-tapping her fingers on the table in front of her.

"Hi, Camry. How are you doing?"

"Cut the crap. What did you want to talk to me about?"

Emmalee took a deep breath. "Well, I'm just hoping you can shed a little light on what was going on with Gretchen?"

Camry stared at her, scrutinizing her a little too closely for Emmalee's comfort.

"Tell me, why do you want to know anything about this? You and your friends were less than helpful the other day." Camry glared at her from across the table.

"I just, she was my tennis partner." Mekayla had warned her not to give away too much, especially not about the detectives interrogating her twice. Since Camry was also being targeted by the police, she might decide to help them go after Emmalee to get them off her back.

Camry sat back in her chair and folded her arms across her chest. "Gretchen mentioned you."

Emmalee wasn't sure what to say to that. She was sure it wasn't anything good. She began tracing graffiti words on the table in front of her.

"Don't worry. She didn't say you were planning to murder her."

Emmalee's eyes darted up to Camry's, but she just grinned sadly.

"What she did say was that she was having a hard time. Do you know anything about that, Emmalee?"

"I, I don't, I'm not sure."

"Not sure?" Camry stared at her, daring her to speak.

"I just, I mean, she wasn't super happy to have me as a tennis partner. I suck at sports."

"Nope. Tennis wasn't her biggest problem. Try again."

"I guess she wasn't super happy about the Homecoming dance."

"And why would that be?"

She squirmed in her seat, suddenly even more interested in the signatures on the table. "Well, Chase, her boyfriend, asked me to go to the dance with him because she was out of town that night." She looked up.

She nodded. "You're warmer."

"I think she was with you, though, right? Chase said she was seeing someone else."

"She was with me, yes. But seeing me? No. I told you that the other day."

"I know what you said. I'm just telling you what Chase said."

"Chase says a lot."

"So you know him?"

Camry paused, considering. "I know of him. I know he's not the nicest guy."

Emmalee felt a little defensive. "I think he and Gretchen were just in a bad situation."

Camry sighed and shook her head. "Emmalee, tell me, why are you here? You don't seem to know all that much, and forgive me if this seems mean, but you and your friends sure as hell don't seem like the type to care about anyone else."

She bristled a little. "Well, I did play tennis with Gretchen, and I do care about people. A lot." Visions of Gretchen's scared eyes and crumpled body made Emmalee's eyes water.

Camry shook her head. "I don't know why you're here or what you really want, but I will give you a word of warning. Gretchen was trying to cope with some pretty bad shit that happened to her. And you and your friends," Camry's eyes narrowed, "were largely responsible for making her life even more miserable."

They were interrupted by a waitress. "Can I get you anything?"

Camry looked annoyed. "Yeah, just a couple coffees, whatever."

The waitress blinked. "Okay. Do you want creamer? Sugar?"

"Just bring the coffee," Camry snapped.

The waitress looked at Emmalee, and she smiled. "Actually, I'll have a latte. Sorry."

When the waitress left, she looked at Camry. "What the hell? You don't need to snap at her. She's just doing her job."

Camry put her head on her hands, burying her face. "Shit. I know. I'm sorry. I'm just so freaked out."

"Yeah, we all are."

Camry's head snapped up, eyes meeting hers.

"You're freaked out? Why?"

Shit. "I mean, Gretchen died." She was stammering a bit. "That's horrible, right?" Right? Did she really just ask that?

"Obviously. Shit. Not to be rude, but you're kind of weird. I can kind of see where Gretchen was coming from."

Emmalee felt her pulse quicken. Camry was not making this easy. "Yeah, well, thanks for confirming what I already know. Anyway, what was Gretchen going through? I'd really like to know. I'd like to help."

"Right. Help with what? She's dead." Camry was looking at her like she was a moron.

At that moment, the waitress quickly put two cups of coffee down on the table, letting the hot liquid slosh over the edge. Emmalee reflexively put her hands around the cup, the scorching heat a comforting distraction from her internal feelings.

"I mean, I'd like to help find out what happened to her." Her stomach did flip flops as she said that, remembering the mud on her hands, on her car.

Camry stared, then relented. "Okay. But, first, how close are you with her other friends? Are you going to go running to them the second you leave here to report everything I say?"

"God, no!" She mentally kicked herself as soon as she said it.

She'd clearly sparked Camry's curiosity. The older girl leaned forward at the table, staring at Emmalee earnestly. "I thought you hung with them?"

"I do. I mean, I don't just go around spreading other people's business. I'm not like that."

"Well, I hope not. Look, Gretchen and I met a few months ago at a support group session for trauma survivors. I'm not going to tell you exactly what happened to her. It's not my story. But I can tell you, it's the kind that makes you want to go kill someone."

Emmalee flinched.

"Believe me. It's that bad. Anyway, we met and talked, connected. My dad was really abusive when he was still alive. He was an alcoholic."

"I'm sorry."

Camry crossed her arms. "Don't be. You don't even know me."

"That doesn't matter. I'm sorry it happened to you, you're a human being." What was the chip on Camry's shoulder about?

"So, anyway," Camry shifted nervously, clearly uncomfortable with Emmalee's attention. "She was still having some problems with the person involved, and some other people. Some of your friends, specifically. She was trying to get out of Ravensville. She wanted to graduate early, at semester, and enroll in college in January. She needed a fresh start."

So many things were making sense now, at least the connection to Camry, the being out of town, the college tour post on SnapChat.

"Other than that, there's not much I can help you with." Camry glanced at her watch, then fished a $5.00 bill out of her purse and laid it on the table by her untouched coffee. "I've wasted all the time here I can. Good luck to you."

"Hang on. Camry?"

She stopped mid-stride and turned to look back at Emmalee. "What?"

"For what it's worth." She swallowed, knowing she shouldn't be saying this, but she had to. "I don't think you had anything to do with – you know."

Camry nodded. "Awesome. Too bad you're not the cops." She frowned, and then she was gone.

––––––––

At school the next morning, Emmalee met Mekayla and Marshall in Mrs. Murray's room before the first bell. She'd been lucky to get home from her meeting with Camry before Nikki made it home. And she made it out today while Nikki was still asleep on the couch, empty whiskey glass on the coffee table.

"Shut the door," Mekayla ordered as Emmalee entered.

Emmalee closed the classroom door and took a seat at the table where Mekayla and Marshall were huddled. "Where's Mrs. Murray?"

"No idea. Anyway, today, act normal, but keep your eyes and ears open. Got it?"

"Yeah," Emmalee said. "But what are we keeping them open for?"

Mekayla rolled her eyes. "Anything suspicious. Any new information. Obviously."

"Okay. I doubt there will be any of that. Britney's careful."

Mekayla just looked at Emmalee and shook her head, sighing with disappointment. "Em, trust me. You need to pay attention."

It turned out, Mekayla was right.

Just before P.E., Emmalee was hiding in a bathroom stall in the girls' locker room, feet pulled up so no one would know she was there. She just needed to catch her breath, and prepare for another round of classes with people gawking at her like she was some kind of circus freak. Rumors were flying around the school about Emmalee being interrogated by the police. Just as she gathered her courage to face them again, she put her hand on the lock to open the door and heard whispers. Whispers she recognized.

Britney and Kristen.

"Don't be such a worrier," Britney ordered.

"But, what if—"

Britney cut Kristen off. "What if what? You didn't call from your own phone, right?"

"Well, no, but—"

"And you didn't give your name?"

"No."

"Any other identifying information?"

"I don't think so, but—"

"But nothing, Kris. You did the right thing. You helped them find the body of a missing teenager."

What? Emmalee's head swam. They were the reason police had found Gretchen's body? Why would they do that? They were friends with Emmalee, too. They had been at that crime scene. Surely it made them seem guiltier, too?

Her fingers shook on the lock, and she held her other hand over her mouth, trying to keep from sobbing out loud and having them hear her.

"It's just a matter of time until they take care of our little problem for us, okay? So, just stay calm. No matter what."

Kristen didn't respond, but she must have nodded her head because Britney responded with "Good girl. Now let's get the hell out of here."

Emmalee waited in the bathroom stall for several more minutes to be sure they were gone, so she was late for gym and had to listen to Coach Taylor gripe about kids not respecting authority these days. It was hard to care, though, because she kept focusing on the fact that Britney — who'd told Emmalee to keep calm and not draw attention to herself — had as good as sent the cops straight after her.

It would be no time before they found evidence linking Emmalee to the crime. She thought they'd been careful, but she watched enough true crime to know that there was almost always evidence left behind. And what was this little *problem*? Was it her? Emmalee? It had to be.

When she reconvened with Marshall and Mekayla after school, they quickly agreed to meet at the coffee shop again. Mekayla made the point that they wanted to appear normal, like everything was just business as usual.

Once they had their drinks, Emmalee told them what she'd overhead.

"What the fuck? Is Britney trying to get caught here?" Mekayla's whisper was entirely too loud.

"Shhhh!" Emmalee looked around to make sure no one was staring at them. "I think she's trying to get me caught. Remember, there's nothing linking her to this."

"Except your story," Mekayla reminded her. "And the fact that she was with you in the car."

"True. But who's going to believe my story? I'm just the new girl here, the one who's been hanging out with the dead girl's boyfriend, the one whose car — you know." Emmalee scanned the room, hoping no one was watching or listening to them. There were just a few other people, all talking animatedly at distant tables and at the bar. "And besides, Britney wore gloves.

"Em, look. We can't change all that. I get it. But, we can work on finding evidence to help you. And this is actually a good thing. There has to be a way to connect Kristina to that phone call to the police. Then, she'll have a lot of explaining to do about how she knew where to find the — you know." It was Mekayla's turn to look around furtively.

Emmalee sighed. She was glad Mekayla was trying so hard

to help her. God knew she needed it. But, she felt like there was little hope for her regardless.

CHAPTER 32

The next day, on the way to lunch, Britney grabbed Emmalee's arm. "Hey, bitch. You've basically disappeared lately. Come eat lunch with us."

Emmalee's heartbeat sped up. "Oh, yeah, I can't. I have a project with Mekayla and Marshall. We need to work during lunch."

Britney smirked and leaned in. "Just remember to keep your mouth shut. I'd hate for you to get caught, you know?"

Emmalee avoided Britney's eyes. "Yeah. Of course. We're just working on this creative writing project."

"Right, right. Okay, go play school with the nerds." Britney dismissed her with a wave of her hand, then flounced her way to her table full of friends.

"What was that all about?" Mekayla popped a fry in her mouth.

"She wanted me to eat lunch with them." Emmalee sat and waved at Marshall, who looked exceptionally uncomfortable.

"You okay, Marshall?"

"Yes. Why?" he asked quickly. Too quickly.

"Dude. What's up with you?" Mekayla eyed him suspiciously.

"Nothing." Again, way too fast.

"Nope. Lies. Spill it." Mekayla chomped on another fry.

"Really, it's nothing." His face was flushing. Emmalee watched silently as it kept turning darker shades of red and spread to his ears.

Mekayla side-eyed him. "Marsh. Seriously? Your face is an open book."

"Mekayla, you don't always know everything." Marshall's voice raised to a high pitch.

Mekayla laughed. "Yes, I do, and you know it. Now, spill."

He shifted uncomfortably in his chair and took an extremely long drink from his milk carton, then cleared his throat and wiped his mouth with a napkin, which he immediately started crumpling into a very tiny ball.

Mekayla sighed loudly. "Jeez, just tell us already. You're going to give yourself a nervous breakdown."

"Um. Well, I don't really want to start something."

"What the hell, Marshall? In case you haven't realized, something's already started." Mekayla rolled her eyes at Emmalee.

"Marshall, really, you can tell us, whatever it is." Emmalee reached out and put a hand on Marshall's arm, which just made him turn redder.

"I don't want you to get upset, Em." Marshall stared at the napkin he was now reopening carefully.

"It's okay, really. Not much more can happen that will phase me." She squeezed his arm, and when he met her eyes, she smiled at him. "Really, I can take it."

He took a very deep breath, then the words rushed out in a jumble. "I saw them together. Chase and Britney. They were together in the library when I walked in."

Emmalee felt immediate relief. "So?" There was nothing weird about that.

"They were just really close, like maybe too close." He stayed focused on the napkin.

Mekayla's eyes narrowed. "What do you mean, too close?"

"Well, I mean, I think–" Marshall stuttered.

"Think or know, Marsh?" Mekayla's voice was sharp.

"Well, they were there when I walked into the library, then they jumped apart real quick." He was looking between the two girls desperately, wanting out of this inquisition.

"Did you actually see anything specific, Marsh?"

Emmalee's heart clenched. "Like what, Mekayla? What are you implying?" Emmalee felt like she was missing something.

Marshall looked up at Emmalee. "Well, no. I just saw them jump apart, and I just assumed–"

"Great. Don't assume, Marshall." Mekayla let out a long sigh. "Well, that was a lot of drama for nothing."

Emmalee let out a sigh of relief. "She was probably threatening him about something like she does to me all the time. She's a control freak."

Mekayla nodded.

Marshall nodded eagerly. "Yeah, I'm sure that's what it was." His face was still bright red and his hands were shaking. "She did tell me that no matter what I saw, I hadn't seen anything and to keep my mouth shut."

"That sounds like her," Emmalee said, staring at her lunch tray, feeling way too nauseous to eat anything. She hated the idea of Marshall being dragged into this. He'd never been anything but sweet to Emmalee. To everyone, really.

She spent the rest of the day trying to convince herself she wasn't worried about it.

She was still trying after school when she rolled the car windows down and let the crisp November air blow her hair in the wind, cooling her burning skin as she sped down the highway.

Chase had texted her during last period.

> Meet me at our spot after school. I need to
> see you.

She was headed there now, heart in her throat, butterflies in her stomach.

She'd had to lie to Mekayla and Marshall, making up a story about her mom wanting her home right after school. Mekayla had seen right through her, though.

"Just be safe, Em," she'd said, scrutinizing her with those eyes that always seemed to see behind Emmalee's mask. "When in doubt, record everything."

Emmalee had laughed it off. "Yeah, I'll make sure I record myself taking out the trash and doing homework. No worries."

Mekayla had just nodded, eyes clouded with worry. "Let's go, Marsh."

Then she'd tapped out a quick text to her mom.

> Meeting friends for coffee and maybe dinner.
> My phone's about to die so don't worry if I
> don't text back right away.

She'd shut her location off and slipped her phone into her back pocket.

Now, Emmalee's heartbeat picked up speed when she rounded a corner and saw Chase's car parked. She pulled up behind him, and he got out and opened his passenger door for her.

"Where are we going?" Emmalee asked as he'd sped away. She'd assumed they'd stay there like they had before.

"I want to show you something." He grinned over at her, sliding his hand over and squeezing her knee before folding her hand in his. "I'm glad you finally made time for me." He winked, making sure she knew he was just teasing.

She felt something in her stomach unclench, a feeling of safety coming over her.

After about twenty minutes of snaking through smaller, windier, woodsier roads, Chase pulled up to a small cabin. It looked plain but sturdy, made of weathered logs.

When he shut the engine off, he looked over at Emmalee. "I found this place a long time ago and begged my dad to buy it for me to use as a hunting cabin. Mostly I just come out here to be alone and think."

He was bringing her to a space where he liked to be alone? That had to be a good sign for their relationship.

"Come on." He smiled and got out, walking up to the cabin and unlocking it. "It was pretty trashed when I found it, but I did a little work to make it sort of a home away from home."

She followed him inside, gasping at what she saw.

There was a leather sofa in front of a stone fireplace. A thick rug covered the floor between. Behind the little living area was a rustic kitchen, the kind of rustic that looked very expensive. Above the kitchen, a loft sported a massive log-frame bed with dark plaid blankets and pillows.

"A little work? It's beautiful."

"I'm glad you like it." He smiled at her, then slipped his hands around her waist and pulled her close. "God, I've been wanting to do this for days." He buried his face in her hair.

She wanted to melt into him, to let him kiss her, but she could feel her body stiffening, her mind wandering back to what Marshall had seen in the library. She wanted to ask him about it, but she wasn't sure she wanted the answer. And she didn't want to get Marshall in trouble with Britney.

"What's wrong?" Chase pulled back, looking into her eyes.

"Nothing." Emmalee tried to smile.

"You sure?" He stroked her hair back from her face.

"Yeah." She bit her bottom lip, looking down.

He reached out and curled a finger under chin, tipping her face up, and then he kissed her, and it was magic. The heat of it spread slowly through her body, melting her defenses. She let herself soften into him, and he pulled her even closer, hands traveling up and down her back, slipping into her hair, pressing her to him.

After several intoxicating minutes, he pulled away, then wordlessly took her hand and led her up the stairs to the loft.

Her heart beat faster as he turned facing her and slid his fingers under the hem of her shirt, lifting it over her head. Then he pulled his shirt off, put his arms around her again and held her close, their skin touching, igniting her nerves as his fingers traced slow circles on her lower back.

He leaned in close, his breath in her ear, and whispered, "I've needed you so much." Then he gently laid her back on the bed and climbed in, hovering over her, staring down at her for a moment, then taking her mouth again.

Part of her wanted to stop him, to ask him about what Marshall had seen, but a bigger part of her just wanted him, wanted to disappear in him and forget about everything else. She closed her eyes and let that part of her take over.

CHAPTER 33

"Mom, you're overreacting." Emmalee tried to keep her voice calm as she poured a cup of coffee, her back to Nikki, who was seated at the kitchen table.

"You didn't come home last night, Emmalee! That's completely unacceptable. If I was overreacting, you'd be dead. Consider yourself lucky to be alive."

Emmalee knew her mom was mostly joking, but the comment felt like a slap across the face. Her mother must have seen it.

"I'm sorry, Em." She could tell that Nikki realized it was too far. "Look, I'm worried about you. You lost a friend. That's traumatic. And you just haven't been yourself."

Nikki was right about that. Emmalee was definitely not herself lately. She'd never spent the night at a guy's house before, that was for sure. But waking up in Chase's arms was incredible. She felt so safe, warm, cared for. She'd hoped to sneak in without Nikki noticing, but no such luck. At 4:54am, she'd opened the door quietly to find Nikki sitting upright on the sofa, staring daggers at her.

"Mom, I'm 18. You have to let me make some choices for

myself. Besides, it's the weekend. It's not like I have school today."

"Look at me when I'm talking to you." Nikki smacked the table. "Where were you?"

Emmalee took a long sip of coffee, buying herself some time to prepare for the lie. Then she turned around, forcing herself to meet Nikki's eyes. "I was with my friends." Emmalee looked away again, focused on her coffee cup.

"What friends?"

"Just some friends. You don't know them."

Nikki stared at her, eyes narrowed, calculating. "You're right. I don't know any of your friends. Why don't you have them over for dinner? I can order pizzas, we can watch a movie."

Emmalee thought about it for a minute. Maybe it was a good idea. She could regroup with Mekayla and Marshall. And get her mom off her back about where she'd been. "Cool. When were you thinking?"

"Tonight."

Ugh. She was supposed to see Chase again tonight. "Tonight? That's pretty short notice, but I'll see if they're available."

"Let's hope they are because you're not leaving the house for the rest of the weekend." Nikki smiled and stood up from the kitchen table. "We're going to get some work done around here."

Emmalee sighed, not wanting to have to let Chase down. "Great. Sounds like a blast."

It actually wasn't so bad. They'd listened to classic rock as they scrubbed the bathroom, swept and mopped the floors, changed the sheets, washed windows, and polished furniture.

Nikki had put in a grocery order and Emmalee had stocked their cabinets for real, for the first time since they'd moved here, unloading cans of soup, boxes of rice and pasta, fresh fruits and vegetables, and plenty of snacks. When they sat down for lunch, Nikki smiled at her.

"Finally starting to feel like home, huh?"

Emmalee nodded, looking around, appreciating the gleaming countertops and crystal clear windows.

"After lunch, I'm going to take care of bills and a few errands. Finish up your homework before your friends get here, okay?"

"Okay." There was no chance the homework would get done, but report cards didn't come out for a couple more weeks. Instead, she crashed on her bed, daydreaming about Chase holding her last night, making her feel like the only woman in the world.

There was no way he'd kissed Britney.

Her phone pinged.

UNCLE DAN

You on for today?

Crap. She'd forgotten. But there was no way she could leave. And she certainly couldn't tell him the truth. He'd be here in an hour, teaming up with Nikki to get into her business.

Sorry - Tennis match

That sucks. Where at?

Here.

It's raining. You play in the rain?

Shit. Why couldn't people quit interrogating her?

It's indoors.

Wow. Must be some fancy school.

Yeah. Gotta love those private schools.

Sure.

> Next weekend then?

> If I can sure.

Please stop texting. She had too much going on right now.

Three dots kept popping up and disappearing, and her heart wanted to beat out of her chest.

> You okay EmmaBee? I heard about that student at your school.

> I didn't know her.

God, she just kept lying.

> Okay. Call any time if you need to talk - love you

> Love you too

She dropped her phone on the bed and collapsed. Everything was such a fucking mess now.

At four o'clock the doorbell rang. Mekayla and Marshall were standing in the entryway chatting with Nikki by the time Emmalee got to the room.

"Nice to meet you again," Nikki smiled at them, shaking their hands.

Again? What the hell?

"Nice to see you, too, Ms. Sloane."

Marshall just smiled and nodded, letting Mekayla speak for the both of them.

"Okay, Mom, we're gonna go hang out in my room until the pizza gets here."

"Sounds good. I'm actually going to go out and pick it up, along with some sodas and ice cream. I'll be back soon. You guys lock up behind me."

After Emmalee secured the dead bolt, she led Marshall and Mekayla to her room. Mekayla hopped on her bed, stretching out on her stomach. Marshall sat cross-legged on her floor, letting Emmalee take the desk chair.

"So." Mekayla said.

"So?" Emmalee countered.

"You lied."

"Mekayla," Marshall's voice pleaded.

"No, Marsh. She owes us an answer."

"I didn't lie." Emmalee's heart was pounding.

"We stopped by yesterday evening. Just wanted to make sure you were okay, but you weren't here. Your mom wasn't sure where you were."

Emmalee's stomach sank. "You don't understand."

"Then explain it. We're trying to help you, Em. Why lie?"

"It's just—" She buried her face in her hands to hide the blush. "I was hanging out with Chase." She peeked out between her fingers.

Mekayla's eyes widened. "Okay." She dragged the word out way too long.

"Yes, okay. We're friends."

"Friends, right." Makayla just shook her head. "Unbelievable."

"Mekayla, come on." You had to love Marshall, always trying to be the peacemaker.

"Shut it, Marsh. You know I love you, but you're no good at confrontation."

"Confrontation? Is that what this is?" Emmalee was feeling the burn of anger rising in her chest.

"Yes. You lied. I don't care if you hang out with Chase, or whoever else you want to hang out with — though, to be clear, why you would want to is beyond me. I just don't get why you'd lie. This is a dangerous situation, like really dangerous."

Emmalee was quiet. She wasn't sure what to say. How could she explain it? Maybe she should just tell the truth.

She sighed. "Okay. Chase and I are kind of a thing, like seeing each other."

Mekayla's eyes didn't even flicker. "Duh."

"What do you mean, duh?"

"Well, anyone can see the way you practically drool over him every time he's around."

"I do not drool over him!" Emmalee's face flushed.

Mekayla rolled her eyes. "You do. Anyway. I'll never understand it — he's not my type and his girlfriend just died — but you don't need to lie about it."

"It's just that Chase thinks – we think – we can't be open about it because, you know, it would look suspicious. With Gretchen, like you said."

"I mean, Em, yeah. Come on, you did, you know—"

Mekayla didn't have to finish the thought. Emmalee instantly saw flashes of the rain on the windshield, felt the sickening thump, the mud on her hands, under her fingernails. She must have started shaking because Mekayla hopped up and wrapped her in a hug.

"I'm sorry. I'm not trying to be mean. I just want you to be careful." She pulled back to look at her. "And honest. We're your friends. We're trying to help, but if you lie to us, we can't help you."

Emmalee was having a hard time swallowing the lump in her throat. It had been a long time since she'd had any friends who wanted to be there, to help, to know the truth. Not just to get something from her, or laugh at her. But just to be her friend. Tears sprang into her eyes, and Mekayla just hugged her harder.

"She's right, Emmalee," Marshall finally spoke up. "And to be honest, I don't trust Chase."

Emmalee pulled back from Mekayla's hug, looking over at Marshall. His face was red, but he was looking straight at her.

"I know you don't think there was anything weird happening with Britney the other day, but the more I think about it, something just felt off."

Emmalee needed to set him straight, fast. "No, Marsh. I appreciate you worrying, but Chase is safe. Trust me."

He stared at her for a few seconds, almost like he pitied her. "Just be careful, okay? I don't want anything bad to happen to you."

"Speaking of careful, I have a plan." Mekayla sat on the edge of the bed. "But you're going to need some major balls to pull it off."

CHAPTER 34

Emmalee took a deep breath and tried to slow her racing heart. She knocked on the ornate double doors in front of her and waited. She'd messaged Britney asking to talk, and had received just an address in return. Emmalee thought it might be Britney's house, which would be a first.

One of the doors swung open, revealing Britney, sporting an eerie smile.

"Hey, bitch! Long time no see." Britney stepped back, allowing Emmalee entry. "Welcome to my lair." Creepy.

"Hey. Yeah, it's been a while." Emmalee hated the shake in her voice, sure Britney would be able to see through her, right to the phone tucked in her pocket. She paused inside the doorway and took in the surroundings. Everything was glass, marble, mirrors, gold-edging. Everything was untouchable.

"Where have you been hiding?" Britney led the way upstairs.

"My mom's had me under house arrest after the detectives showed up at home." Emmalee stayed focused on the floor.

"Right." Britney didn't look back, just sashayed to the landing, then down a long hallway, stopping at what Emmalee assumed was her bedroom.

"Wow." Emmalee scanned the utterly blank canvas of Britney's room. There was no color anywhere, from the pale wood floors to the bare ivory walls to the fluffy cloud-white comforter.

"Thanks." Britney flopped onto the bed. Kristina was already perched on a chair — also white — at a wide glass desk.

"Hey," Kristina said, waving but not smiling.

Britney patted the spot next to her on the bed. "Here, Em. Sit."

Weird. Emmalee crossed the room, slipping her shoes off and sitting on the edge of the bed, afraid she'd mar the pristine white.

"So, what brings you by, bitch?" Britney grinned at her, teeth bared.

Emmalee tried to keep her voice strong. "I just thought we should talk, compare notes, regroup."

Britney flipped over on her stomach, looking up at Emmalee. "Oh, yeah? Why's that?"

"Well, it's just since they found Gretchen's body and the cops came back again to question me—" Emmalee's voice was shaking again. She had to get it under control.

"Well, obviously. I mean, you were her tennis partner and you're screwing her boyfriend."

Emmalee's face got red. "That's not true." She began picking at a loose thread hanging off the sleeve of her button-up shirt.

"Whatever. I'm not stupid, Em." Britney's eyes were sending warning flares.

"Anyway, I'm just not sure what to do."

They were interrupted when the door opened, and an older man in a suit popped his head in.

"Hey, baby girl. Just wanted to say goodbye before I go."

His eyes roamed over Kristina, Britney, and then settled on Emmalee. She shivered, uncomfortable with the way his gaze raked over her face, chest, legs, and back up again.

"Bye, Daddy." Britney sounded like a little girl.

"Who's your new friend?" Her dad — the freaking Governor, Emmalee remembered — was practically salivating.

"Daddy, we're really busy. Let's chat later." Britney gave him a death stare. He just smirked and winked at Emmalee.

"Definitely later. Bye, ladies."

When he shut the door again, Britney turned to Emmalee, eyes still flashing with anger. "Don't you think it's about time you just tell the cops the truth, Emmalee?"

"God, no!" Emmalee panicked, suddenly unsure if Mekayla could hear. She'd insisted that Emmalee double-up the evidence she collected. She had a voice memo recording and an open call going with Mekayla. She slipped her phone out of her pocket, careful to keep the screen facing her, and pretended to mindlessly scroll.

"Oh? Why not?" Britney cocked her head to the side, watching Emmalee's fingers moving over her phone screen.

"I thought you didn't want me to tell the truth?"

"You mean, you don't want to tell them you buried Gretchen's body after you ran her over with your car?" Britney flashed an enormous smile at Emmalee.

Emmalee took a deep breath. She was sick of Britney always ruling over everyone. She took a page from Mekayla's playbook. "Look, Britney, we all know I'm not the only one involved here."

"Oh, really, is that what we know, Em? Kris, is that what we know?" Britney's eyes looked dangerous, narrowing to slits.

"I don't know anything about that, Brit." Kris looked worriedly between Britney and Emmalee. "Em, I think you're mistaken, right?"

Emmalee's heart leapt into her throat. Now or never. "No. I'm not mistaken." She was going to stand up for herself. Finally. "You swerved the car into Gretchen, Britney. You forced me to bury her and left me to clean up the mess." Her voice may have been shaking, but she felt lighter. Freer.

The feeling didn't last.

"No one will ever believe you, Emmalee. If you weren't such a weak little bitch, you would never have let yourself get into this little predicament." Britney stared at her, her mouth twisted into a terrifying smile. "Kris and I were actually on our way to the gym when you called. You're going with us. Let's go." Britney hopped up.

"I can't. My mom—"

"I don't give a shit about your mommy, Em. We're going."

Emmalee's anger rose. Who did Britney think she was? "No, I really can't. I'm going home."

"Oh, you really can't. I see. Well, I really can't keep the photos of you fucking Chase the other night from going viral." Britney shrugged and smiled at Emmalee.

"What?" Emmalee was confused.

Britney scrolled through her phone then tilted it toward Emmalee. There she was, in bed with Chase in his cabin, leaning down over him to share a kiss.

"How?" Emmalee couldn't catch her breath.

"Does 'how' really matter, Em?" Britney's eyes were wide. "All that will matter is that sweet, innocent little Em is screwing Gretchen's boyfriend. I'll bet the cops would like to see this."

Emmalee lunged for the phone. "You can't do that!"

Britney sprinted out of the way. "Oh, I can, and I will. Now, let's go to the gym."

She didn't know what to do. Refuse? Scream? If she did that, maybe one of Britney's maids would hear her and call the police? But then, that picture – she couldn't imagine living through the hell of everyone seeing that.

Maybe it would be best to just go with them for now. See if she could figure something else out.

CHAPTER 35

Emmalee was shaking in Britney's car. The other two girls were in the front, and Emmalee was in the back, frantically trying to decide what to do next. She was feeling incredibly stupid, going along with them. Over a picture. She was feeling a lot like Gretchen. She wondered if she would be able to text 911 without them seeing.

She was saved from the decision when her phone was ripped from her hands by Kris, who immediately saw there was an open call. "Well, well, what do we have here, Brit? Looks like Em's been on a very, very long call with her little emo friend this whole time."

"What the fuck?" Britney slammed on the brakes in the middle of the highway.

Emmalee scrambled for an excuse. "It was an accident. I must have forgotten to hang it up."

"You fucking liar!" Britney had the phone now, swiping up to see what apps were open. "You bitch!" Emmalee's stomach sank as Britney stopped the voice memo recording and deleted it. "I knew you were up to something with all of your 'What should I do, Britney?' bullshit!"

Emmalee reached for the phone, trying to salvage the message, but Kristina just shoved her hands away.

"Let's see what sweet little Em has been up to, shall we?"

"Britney, no, that's private!" Emmalee tried again to reach for the phone, but this time, Kristina grabbed her wrist, digging her nails in.

"Let's see." Britney scrolled back through Emmalee's texts with Mekayla. "Wow. Em. I didn't know you had it in you." She powered the phone down and handed it to Kristina. "Put that in the glove box. And lock it."

Emmalee's heart sank as Britney hit the gas. She looked around, noticing for the first time that they were not in Ravensville.

"Where are we going?" Emmalee's voice sounded strangled, even to her.

"Just relax, babes. You'll find out." Britney's grin at her in the rearview mirror was terrifying. "Kris, text the boys. 911."

Emmalee dug her nails into her palms, trying to slow her breathing, her heartbeat, her thoughts. This had all gone very, very wrong. She needed to think of a way out.

For the next twenty minutes, she watched the scenery pass, realizing that she was heading in a familiar direction. She felt more and more nauseous as her fears were confirmed, as Britney pulled up in front of Chase's secret cabin in the woods.

Kristina jumped out of the car quickly and opened Emmalee's door. "Come on."

Emmalee hesitated, but Britney pushed her way between Kristina and the door, reaching in and grabbing Emmalee's arm. "Let's go. Don't make this harder than it has to be."

Emmalee heard the sound of an engine. She clambered out of the car and looked around, seeing Bryce's Humvee pull in behind Britney's car. He and Tyler jumped out quickly, looking ready for a fight.

"What's going on, Brit?" Bryce asked, his voice tight.

"I'll tell you inside. First, can you park the vehicles around back?"

"Sure, babe." He cast Emmalee a threatening glare. "You got this one under control?"

"Oh, yeah. She's not going to put up a fight, are you, Em?" Britney grinned at her. Emmalee's stomach twisted. "Cat got your tongue, babes? That's understandable. Get the fuck inside."

Britney pulled a key out of her pocket and headed for the cabin door. Kristina grabbed Emmalee's arm.

Emmalee started moving, not sure what to do, but knowing she didn't want Bryce getting involved. She had no doubt he'd put his hands on her again given the chance.

Inside, she noted the water glasses she and Chase had used were still on the kitchen counter. A quick glance up at the loft showed the sheets and blankets still in a jumble. Her face flushed red. She had no idea what was going on. Why did Britney have a key to the cabin? Why were they here? How did Britney get a picture of her and Chase that night?

Where was Chase?

Britney must have noticed the confusion in Emmalee's expression. "I'm guessing you have a few questions, huh?"

Emmalee nodded.

"Well, see, Em, it's like this. We've all been friends forever. We know each other. We help each other. We share with each other. You, however, are not one of us. Which is why you don't know that this is our hangout. Sort of a clubhouse, if you will." Britney smiled, then reached out and tucked Emmalee's hair behind her ear, chuckling when Emmalee flinched. She leaned in to whisper, "It's not just a little secret hideaway for you and Chase to smash."

Emmalee felt anger rise in her, this time letting it take over. "What the fuck is wrong with you, Britney? Why are you acting like this?"

"Well, let's see. You tried to record a private conversation between us in order to set me up, so I could take the fall for your crime. Does that sound about right, Kristina?"

"Sounds right to me." Kristina looked bored, seated on the couch, scrolling on her phone.

The door opened. Bryce and Tyler finally entered, immediately crossing to where Emmalee and Britney were squared off in the middle of the living room.

"So, what the fuck is going on?" Bryce's jaw flexed.

"This bitch asked to hang out and then started talking to us about Gretchen. While recording it. And, she had a fucking call open with her little nerd friend Mekayla listening on the other end."

Bryce looked at Emmalee incredulously. "You're a brave little bitch, aren't you?" He sneered at her. "You fucked with the wrong person, Em."

Emmalee felt a shiver of fear race up her spine, cold sweat breaking out on her neck.

"Sit down." Britney pointed at the couch.

She looked at the door, but Bryce was between her and it. He saw her looking and shook his head. "I wouldn't try that if I were you." He grinned. "But I promise you, if you do, I'll enjoy it. A lot."

Emmalee shivered and sat down.

"Good girl." He winked at her.

She wanted to throw up, but took a deep breath, trying to take stock of the situation, start formulating a plan. She needed to get out of here. Her thoughts were continually interrupted by the mental ass-kicking she was giving herself for getting in the car with them.

Meanwhile, Britney and Bryce had moved and were whispering in the kitchen. Bryce kept looking over at Emmalee like he was ready to skin her alive. She couldn't hear most of what they were saying, but she heard something about Mekayla and her heart stopped.

Fuck. She'd also put Mekayla in danger. She never should have told Mekayla and Marshall anything.

And then an engine rumbled, a car door banged, and Chase burst into the room.

CHAPTER 36

Emmalee breathed a sigh of relief. Chase looked from Britney to Emmalee and back to Britney again, anger simmering in his eyes.

"Explain." His voice was controlled, angry.

"Chase, I–" Emmalee struggled for words.

"Shut. Up." Chase held his hand up at her, kept his eyes trained on Britney. Emmalee was confused. Was he angry with her?

"This bitch recorded our conversation about your ex-slut, and she also had Mekayla on the line listening in. Not to mention she's been asking a lot of questions about Audrey." Britney's voice had a tattle-tale whine to it that infuriated Emmalee.

"Chase, wait–"

"I said shut up!" he yelled at her, his voice like a heavy hand slapping her across the face. She must have looked appropriately chastised because he turned back to Britney.

"Fuck, Brit. What do we do now?"

"Well, I haven't had time to make a plan yet, but I'd say we need to make sure this one is taken care of first." She hooked a thumb over her shoulder in Emmalee's direction.

Chase nodded, turning back to the door. "I'll be right back."

When the door closed behind him, Emmalee turned to Britney. "I don't understand." It was a lie, but she was grasping for any possible way to calm them all down.

"Oh, you really fucked up, Em. You have no idea." Britney was smirking at her now.

"Listen, Britney, you're overreacting."

"Oh, am I? Please, tell me more." She leaned against the kitchen counter, chin in hand. "I always love a good lesson."

"It's just not a big deal. You didn't say anything incriminating."

"On second thought. Shut the fuck up." Britney smiled at her. "Or we'll shut you up."

What the hell did that mean?

Chase came back in, carrying rope, duct tape, zip ties. No, no, no, no, no.

Emmalee started breathing rapidly, chest heaving. There was no staving off the panic. What exactly were they planning on doing to her? Images of blood, rain, mud, and those eyes flashed in her mind.

He dropped the items on the counter, then looked at her. "Get over here."

"Wait, you don't have to do this!"

"Now!" his voice thundered.

She stood up, moving slowly on shaking legs toward the counter. After a couple of steps, panic took over. She turned and ran toward the front door, managing to get it open – thank God he hadn't locked it — and leapt off the front steps.

She landed wrong and fell in the tall grass. Just as she was scrambling to get up, a hand twisted in her hair and pulled her up.

She screamed, but the hand kept pulling. "Nice try, bitch." Bryce sounded almost gleeful as he dragged her into the house.

Chase pulled out a chair from the dining table. "Sit."

She sat, barely able to catch her breath. "Let's just talk about this, please."

"You're done talking."

He wrenched one of her arms behind her, bending it painfully behind the chair back. "That hurts, Chase."

He didn't respond. He just grabbed her other arm, contorting it until her wrists were together, digging his nails into her flesh when she struggled. Britney handed him a zip tie, and he swiftly locked her hands together. Her shoulders felt like they were going to pop out of their sockets.

"Chase, this really hurts," she choked out. She could feel tears stinging her eyes, a thick lump in her throat.

No response.

Next he grabbed the rope, one of two lengths dangling off the counter edge, and cinched her right ankle to one chair leg, her left leg to the other.

She was shaking uncontrollably now, sobs wracking her body, as he moved in front of her, pulling a long strip of duct tape off the roll. His eyes were black, angry, inhuman as he strapped it around her head, covering her mouth.

When he'd finished, he stepped back and examined her, testing the zip tie and ropes, making sure they were tight enough. He turned back to the others.

"Now, let's make a plan."

Emmalee tried not to throw up while she listened to the whispers of Britney, Chase, and the others over in the living room.

She couldn't make out what they were saying. But she could imagine it involved unspeakable violence. Finally, after whispering for about an hour and frequently looking over at Emmalee, who was trying to keep from hyperventilating, they held Emmalee's phone in front of her face and then read through her text messages with Mekayla.

"Listen to this one!" Britney took on an extra high-pitched, whiny tone. "'Em, where are you? Are you okay?' Oh, my God, what a baby!"

Chase came toward her quickly and ripped the duct tape off.

He leaned down over her and grabbed her face in his hands. "Listen to me very carefully. We're going to get Mekayla on a call, on speaker. You're going to convince her to meet you. Tell her you'll send her a pin. If you don't stay calm and act normal and do exactly what I tell you, you're going to regret it. Got it?"

Emmalee nodded, eyes wide, still trying to calm her breathing.

"Good. Because the regretting will be a long, slow, painful process." He stared into her eyes, and all Emmalee saw there was darkness. "And I will enjoy it."

Emmalee wanted to just shut her mind down. Black out. Not have to deal with this anymore. But, somehow, she'd managed the phone call with Mekayla without completely melting down.

Mekayla had wanted to know why she'd hung up, what had happened. Somehow Emmalee had convinced her that she'd gotten away from them and found some evidence she wanted Mekayla to see.

When Mekayla had asked where they were meeting exactly, Emmalee had just said she'd drop her a pin – no idea where to.

Now, she was frantically trying to figure out what to do. Britney and Chase left to meet Mekayla, and Emmalee was left with Kristina, Bryce, and Tyler. Kris and Tyler were huddled together on a couch, their backs to her. Bryce was leaning down, staring in her face.

"Too bad it had to be this way, Em. We could have had a lot of fun with you." Bryce ran his hand up the inside of her thigh.

"Don't touch me!" Her voice sounded raspy.

He just grinned at her, squeezing her thigh. "Stop me."

"Cut it out, Bryce," Kris said, sounding annoyed.

"Shut the fuck up, bitch, and mind your own business."

Tyler was across the room in a flash, grabbing Bryce by the shirt.

"Don't talk to her that way, dickhead!"

As the guys tussled, Kris yelled across the room. "Stop it, you idiots! We need to stay focused!"

Emmalee closed her eyes, let her mind wander through possibilities, searching deep inside herself. She was back in the cold, on the side of the road, watching her dad's blood pool in front of her, not sure where she was or what to do. Then she was back on the side of the road with Gretchen's body beside her, not sure who she was anymore.

Something inside her burst at that. A sob broke free, and she completely lost it, screaming cries. No amount of them telling her to shut up could stop her. Then Kristina slapped her, and she was stunned into silence. Bryce pressed a piece of duct tape back over her mouth.

"That should keep her quiet."

CHAPTER 37

By the time Emmalee could hear a car engine and see pale lights shimmering on the wall opposite her, it had started raining. She could hear the drops pelting the windows. It was evening now, and dark in the house. She assumed they didn't want to attract any attention if a car passed by. Then the front door flew open and hit something.

"Fuck!" Chase screamed.

"What the hell? Where's that little emo dyke?" Bryce asked.

"She never showed." Britney's voice was eerily calm.

"What the fuck are we going to do?" Chase crossed in front of Emmalee and punched a wall.

"Calm down," Kris said, her voice soft and gentle, like someone trying to soothe a feral animal, which seemed close to the truth right now. "Have Em call her again and see what happened? Maybe she got lost."

"Genius here shut Emmalee's phone down and threw it out the window." Britney's voice was snide.

Chase's face reddened with rage. "Did you want to risk someone finding it? Or her?"

Emmalee's heart sank. Her phone was gone. She was completely, utterly alone in this now.

"Kris, take Bryce and Ty and go look for her." Britney tossed a set of car keys to Kris.

"How do you expect us to do that?" Kris snapped.

"Maybe go by her fucking house? Or that ratchet little coffee shop she's always at?" Britney's voice snapped back. "Why the fuck do I have to be the only one with any fucking brains around here?"

"Fuck off, Brit." Kristina headed for the front door, Tyler and Bryce in tow, the door slamming behind them.

As a car engine roared back to life and the tires squealed over the mud and wet leaves, Emmalee closed her eyes, thankful Mekayla hadn't shown up wherever they'd gone. She just hoped she wasn't at home or at the café right now.

Chase ran his hand through his hair and began pacing from the living room to the kitchen and back.

"Calm down. They'll find her." Britney pulled a glass out of a cabinet and filled it with water.

"Maybe, but I'm sure this little bitch," he pointed at Emmalee, "said something to warn her on that call." He stood in front of Emmalee, glaring. He started to turn away, then reversed and backhanded her across the face, nearly knocking her chair over.

It felt like her cheek bone shattered. The heat of his handprint stung her skin, and she could taste blood trickling in her mouth.

"Calm down, babe. It's okay." Britney walked over to him and put her hands on his face. "Everything will be okay."

Emmalee watched as he let his head droop into her hands, his fingers lifting to curl gently around her wrists. What the hell was happening?

He looked up, and stared into Britney's eyes for a moment, then pressed his lips to hers. The kiss was long and tore through Emmalee's heart, ripping it open. It was true. Marshall was right. Chase and Britney really were together.

Britney broke away first and looked over at Emmalee. "Aww, poor girl. She's so confused right now." She sighed. "You better explain, Chase. Or shall I?"

"I've got it." Chase started pacing, rubbing his hands together. "You see, Em, I know you're thinking that everything I told you was all lies. But you're wrong. My dad really is a prick who cares more about his reputation than his family."

"Mine, too," Britney added, pulling up a chair in front of Emmalee, facing her, grinning like a child.

"Yes, but we'll get to you in a moment. Anyway. Where was I? Oh, yes, my dad. See, when Brit and I discovered we had something here, something real," he gestured between himself and Britney, "he walked in on us in my bedroom. After he politely asked her to leave, he told me I could see her over my dead body. Not only would the breakup with Gretchen be a little messy, but being connected to Britney's family wasn't going to help matters, was it, honey?"

Britney shook her head. "Nope. Cause my Daddy's a pedo." Britney shot a scary grin Emmalee's way, but she could see a flash of anger, hurt, something in her eyes.

What the hell? Emmalee's eyes widened, her mind trying to sort through the revelations.

"I know, right?" Britney put her hands on her face, jaw dropped in fake shock.

"And he had the stupidity of trying to sink his — hmmm, claws — into none other than Miss Gretchen Thomas." Chase stopped pacing to look at Emmalee. "Who you have so kindly removed from the situation for us." He smiled, and she'd never seen anything so grotesque.

Emmalee shook her head, bile rising in her throat. Guilt welled up. Suddenly, it all made sense. Gretchen had been going to the counseling group to process the trauma Britney's dad had put her through. She'd met Camry there, who had wanted to help her, but Gretchen was beyond help. Going public would cause all kinds of negative publicity for her family. And Chase's by association.

She couldn't imagine the sick, twisted mind it would take to act like Gretchen was just an inconvenience. To set Emmalee up to eliminate her as a problem.

If her mouth hadn't been taped shut, she would have told them how sick they were. And reminded them that Britney was at least as guilty as Emmalee. Even more guilty for Audrey. And for what they were doing to Emmalee now.

Instead, she had to settle for shaking her head, her message clear. *No.*

Chase shrugged. "You can deny it, but your car ran her over. Your tire tracks are in the forest. Traces of her blood are on your car. You buried her fucking body, for Christ's sake. Who else could have done it?"

"So, with Gretchen gone, Chase and I can be together. See? It works out perfectly. Really, we should be thanking you, Em." Britney smiled at Chase.

"Once we make sure Mekayla's phone — and Mekayla — have been erased, we'll be set," Chase smiled and rubbed his hands together.

Britney contorted her mouth into a faux frown. "It's sad, though. About Emmalee."

"I know." Chase looked at Britney, frowning back.

Britney shrugged and looked at Emmalee. "If you hadn't felt so guilty and killed yourself because of it, we could all celebrate."

Emmalee's heart started hammering painfully in her chest, and her stomach turned to liquid.

Chase ran up the stairs to the loft.

Britney patted Emmalee's knee. "It's okay, though, Em. We understand. It's so hard being a depressed, guilty little bitch."

Chase skipped back down the stairs, holding a revolver, his hands hidden inside black gloves.

"You know, after our little evening here, Em, I never thought you'd come back on your own, find this gun, and take your own life."

Emmalee was shaking her head, pleading with her eyes for them to just stop. She struggled against the ropes and the zip tie. She was not ready to die.

"No, no, it's true. It's all right here in this letter you're going to write."

Britney had gotten up and fumbled around in a kitchen drawer, producing paper and a pen, laying them on the table in front of Emmalee.

"Now, be a good girl, okay? Britney's going to untie your hands, and you're going to write exactly what we say." Chase stopped talking and placed the muzzle of the gun against Emmalee's ear. She was shaking, tears streaming from her eyes. "If you don't, well, we'll have to take care of it all for you. Not ideal, but we can if we have to, right, babe?"

"Right. It's not the first time." Britney giggled.

Emmalee looked confused.

"Oh! We never told her, did we?" She giggled again.

Chase pondered for a moment, and Emmalee could feel the muzzle of the gun twisting in her hair as Britney cut the zip tie from her wrists. "You know, I don't think we did."

Britney laughed. "Well, let's just say that Audrey's 'accident' was no accident."

"No, it wasn't. Your dad sure does have a thing for your friends, Brit."

"He really does. I guess I wasn't good enough for him anymore." Her eyes flashed, and this time Emmalee could see pain in them.

Her dad had assaulted her, too. Emmalee's stomach twisted into knots. Even in the middle of her fear and anger, Emmalee felt a stab of pain for what these girls – Britney included – had suffered. She couldn't imagine it and wouldn't wish that kind of trauma on anyone.

"Thank God you got that picture of him doing Gretchen at your house last summer. That really helped my sob story, didn't it, Emmalee?" Chase smirked at her. "Of course, it wasn't all that hard to get you hot for me."

Emmalee's mind was reeling. Britney took a picture of her dad assaulting her own friend? This was so messed up. More than Emmalee ever could have realized.

Britney glared at her. "Bryce either. Little slut." Britney tugged Emmalee's hair, jerking her head back, bringing tears to Emmalee's eyes. "I can't wait to watch you paint this room with your own brains."

Chase's lips twisted into another frown. "Easy, Brit." He unclenched Britney's hand from Emmalee's hair. "We don't leave evidence on her. Besides, we'll be out of here before long. Graduation will be here before we know it."

Their voices were beginning to sound faraway, like they were speaking at the other end of a long tunnel. Her mind couldn't handle it anymore, and suddenly she was focused somewhere deep inside herself, hoping for a miracle.

Suddenly, she was ripped from her trance by Chase's shout.

"Wake up, bitch!" She jolted. "That's right. Focus."

Britney freed Emmalee's hands, and she instinctively reached for the duct tape on her mouth, but Chase was too fast.

"No, no, no. Be a good girl." He grabbed her hands and pinned them to her lap, the butt of his gun resting on her thighs. He was staring into her eyes. "It's a shame, you know. You're not my type, but someone could make good use of you." He glanced down at her chest. "You do have some good points." He smirked. Who was this guy? Where was the gentle, sweet, flirtatious jock she'd met just a few weeks before?

He guided her right hand to the table top. "Now, write."

Emmalee picked up the pen, her hand shaking.

"Let's start with, Dear Mom – or whatever you call her." Britney nudged Emmalee's arm. "Come on. Get going."

She held the tip of the pen to the paper, forced herself to write 'dear' in big, loopy handwriting. They might be able to force her to write, but they couldn't force her to make it realistic. Her mom would know immediately that this wasn't Emmalee's normal handwriting. She paused, then added 'Nikki'.

"You call her by her name? Interesting." Chase snickered.

"Wait, no. Give her a new paper." Britney grabbed her face, her fingers clamped around her jaw. "Don't fuck around with us. Call her mom."

Trembling, she started over, wrote 'Dear Mom,' still in the loopy handwriting.

Britney's phone rang. "Did you get her?" Britney paced away, phone to her ear. After a minute, she hung up and faced them. "They didn't find her at her house or the café. They're going to go hang out at Kris's now before someone sees them. Dumb fucks."

"Fuck!" Chase yelled. "Can't anything go right for fucking once!"

Britney turned to Emmalee and ripped the tape off her mouth. "Where would Mekayla go?"

When Emmalee could say nothing because she was too busy coughing, Britney slapped her and screamed, "Tell me! Now!"

"I don't know." Emmalee's voice was rough and choked-sounding from hours not being able to talk, and her swollen cheek.

"Calm down, babe." Chase put his hands on Britney's shaking arms and rubbed them. "We'll figure it out."

Then, he turned his gaze on Emmalee. "Now, write."

The look on Britney's face dared Emmalee to defy them. Emmalee picked up the pen. Britney dictated. "Write this: I'm sorry, but I can't live with the guilt anymore. I was jealous of

Gretchen's relationship with Chase. I wanted him all to myself. So I did the same thing I did to Dad."

Emmalee's hand stopped moving, and she stared up at Britney. How did she know about her dad?

"What are you talking about?" Her voice sounded weak and shaky. She felt a mix of rage and guilt and sadness and fury. She clenched the pen tight and lunged toward Britney.

Britney was quick, though, and grabbed her wrist. "Emmalee, when are you going to learn? You can't win against me. I know what happened with your dad. I read the news articles online." Then she leaned down and whispered, "I do my research. You were just the wounded little bird I needed. Now, keep writing."

Tears were streaming down Emmalee's face. Chase held the gun up to her ear again, pulling the hair back from her face with the muzzle.

"Listen to Brit, Emmalee. We could make this a whole lot worse than it has to be. There are much slower, more painful ways to do this." He gestured toward the knife block on the counter.

"Let's see." Britney again. "Finish up with this: I ran her over with my car and buried her body, hoping no one would ever find it. But I keep seeing her face, hearing her voice. It's like she's right here, taunting me."

"Okay, okay. Wrap it up. You're giving me the creeps." Chase shivered.

Britney laughed. "Alright, let's finish this. Write: I hope you can forgive me, for Dad and for Gretchen." When Emmalee's hand stopped moving again, Chase pushed the gun harder against the side of her head.

Britney continued. "Last few words now, Em. Write: I hope you can find happiness."

Emmalee listened to Britney's words, but she didn't start

writing again. She envisioned her mother, finding out Emmalee was gone, being left alone.

Her husband killed in a bloody crash her daughter caused.

Her daughter killed with a bloody gunshot wound.

Her daughter a murderer.

Something unlocked inside of her. She couldn't do that to her mother. No matter what happened, she could choose not to be a part of their game anymore. She'd spent months afraid to speak up. She was done taking orders from these people. They could kill her, but they'd have to do it on her terms.

"Write!" Chase yelled, smacking her already sore cheekbone with the but of the gun.

She curled her finger under the edge of the paper, lifted it, then tore it in half, then in half again, while Britney and Chase watched in disbelief.

Emmalee was staring down the barrel of Chase's gun. "That was the wrong choice, bitch."

"You still have to die, Em." Britney fake-frowned at her again.

"I'll give you one last choice. Either you pull the trigger or I will." Chase's steely eyes bored into hers.

Emmalee pushed down the fear and focused on owning this choice. "I'm not going to do it. You're the one who's going to have to commit this murder."

She saw his eyes flicker. That was the opening. He didn't really want to do this.

"Shoot her, babe."

Chase's eyes flicked over to Britney and back to Emmalee, his hand shaking now.

"Do you want to be a murderer, Chase? Do you want to be responsible for killing someone?" She saw flashes – her dad's face. Gretchen's face. The blood. The broken glass. The mud. Tears stung her eyes. "Trust me, you don't want that on your conscience."

He just smirked, but he'd lowered his eyes from hers.

She held her wrists up. "Plus, they'll know I didn't kill myself when they see these rope burns and bruises." She thought back to the day Gretchen died. Someone had planted that shovel and tarp. Chase had left the house before them. "And I'm sure your fingerprints are all over the tarp and shovel."

She was reaching him. She could see the wheels turning.

"Don't listen to her. She's just lying to save herself." Britney's face was beginning to contort in anger. "And you wiped your prints, right?"

Chase didn't respond.

"Right, Chase?" Britney's voice was sharper. "Tell me you didn't fuck this up."

Nothing.

Chase just renewed his stance, holding the gun straighter, staring at Emmalee. She could see him calculating.

She stared back, trying to reconcile herself to the fact that this was her last moment on Earth. She was sorry for all the messes she'd made. Sorry she wouldn't have the chance to atone for her mistakes. But maybe she deserved this. Maybe dying here would be payback for all of the damage she'd done.

But the gun never went off. She opened her eyes again. Chase closed his and dropped the gun to his side.

"Maybe there's a better way."

"What the fuck are you talking about!" Britney screeched. "Just fucking shoot her!"

"But they'll know she didn't do it. They can tell those things now."

"Bullshit. You're such a fucking baby." Britney reached for the gun, but Chase knocked her arm out of the way then pointed the gun again at Emmalee, his eyes steely, jaw tight.

"Chase, don't!" Emmalee pleaded.

He just stared at her, clearly still confused. The muscles in his jaw were working overtime.

"Chase, listen to me. Britney will get in trouble and so will you."

Chase's eyes closed and his arm went limp, dropping his hand to his side again.

This time, Britney took hold of the gun easily.

"No!" Emmalee screamed. He was giving up, letting Britney do his dirty work.

Now Britney leveled the gun at her head. Emmalee squeezed her eyes shut, her entire body tensing.

"Say hi to Gretchen for me."

A gunshot exploded and Emmalee's ears started ringing.

But there was no pain. Emmalee slowly opened her eyes. Britney was just standing over Chase, where he lay on the floor clutching his chest, eyes wide, face white, blood seeping through his light blue shirt.

She looked over at Britney, who was grinning at her.

Emmalee scrabbled at her ankles, furiously trying to undo the ropes, but they were knotted so tight.

Her head was wrenched up by the hair again, and this time, Britney shoved the muzzle of the gun against Emmalee's forehead.

"Finally, just you and me." Britney's voice sounded strangely relaxed.

Emmalee was shaking. She couldn't make sense of what had just happened. She hated what Chase had done to her, to Audrey, to Gretchen, but she didn't want him dead.

"I know. More questions, right, Em?" Britney leaned down and sniffed her hair. "I can smell the fear on you."

"Britney, please," Emmalee whimpered. "I'll tell them you shot Chase to save me. You'll be a hero."

Britney laughed. "There's no fucking way I'm letting you walk away from this. You have to take the fall. I sure as hell won't be doing that."

"But I thought you and Chase were –"

She jabbed the gun at Emmalee's forehead again. "Chase was the means to an end, like all of you. He was just horny enough to do anything I wanted. Until you scared him just now. And now you're going to have killed Gretchen and Chase." She grinned. "And yourself."

"But why?" It made no sense. "If you didn't love Chase, why hurt Audrey and kill Gretchen at all?." Emmalee was quickly becoming more terrified than she'd ever been. If Britney wasn't acting out of love, then that meant it was something far worse.

And far scarier.

Britney laughed. "Why does anyone do anything?"

She paused, as if waiting for Emmalee to answer.

When she didn't, Britney whispered, "Because they can."

Emmalee shivered, teeth chattering now.

Britney shrugged. "The first time, it was an accident, really. Audrey and I were arguing. She wanted to go to the police about my dad. When I told her I'd ruin her life if she tried, the little bitch slapped me, so I pushed her. But, God, the sound of her head hitting the floor. I'll never forget it." Britney closed his eyes, reliving the memory.

She opened her eyes again and shrugged, sighing. "She didn't die. But it shut her up." When she smiled at her, the evil in it chilled Emmalee to her core.

"Then when Gretchen fucked my own father, I got excited. I mean, I was angry at first. I've never been good enough, and Gretchen has always been perfect. That's all I ever heard growing up. 'Be more like Gretchen.'" Britney was mocking someone now. Her mom? Her dad? "'Gretchen gets good grades. Gretchen wins beauty pageants. Gretchen has a killer body.'"

Britney pushed the gun harder against Emmalee's forehead.

Emmalee sobbed.

"Honestly, Chase was even more fun. Do you know how much fun it is to twist someone's mind until it snaps?" Her eyes were glowing now. "Chase was like warm butter in my hands.

Not only did I give him what Gretchen wouldn't – fucking prude – my Daddy's the Governor. There's no college, no job, no position out of reach with Daddy on your side."

"You're sick." Emmalee's voice was shaking.

Britney frowned. "Call it what you want. But this –" She spread her arms, gesturing to the bloody mess on the floor, to Emmalee tied to the chair. "This is my masterpiece."

"You don't have to do this," Emmalee pleaded. There had to be some little bit of humanity in her.

Britney sighed and hung her head. "No. I don't."

Emmalee breathed a sigh of relief.

Then Britney lifted her head and stared at her. "But I want to." She was grinning when she lifted the gun again, pointing it at Emmalee.

This was it, she thought.

Then Chase made a gurgling sound that distracted them both.

Britney looked confused. She cocked her head and turned to Chase again. "Tough little bitch, huh?"

Chase was still alive!

Britney swung her arm toward Chase again.

This was Emmalee's chance, and for once, she didn't hesitate. Didn't overthink. Didn't worry. No one else was going to die because she was too worried about herself.

She heaved herself up onto her feet, still tied to the chair, and thrust her arm out with every ounce of strength left in her body, aiming the pen she still clutched at Britney's neck.

When the pen sunk into flesh, Britney gasped and grabbed at it. She pulled it free with a sickening, squelching sound, and her body jerked back. Her back slammed into the edge of the countertop, and the gun slipped from her hand. She clutched at the hole in her neck that was now spurting fountains of red between her fingers.

Emmalee dove for the floor, ignoring the chair still attached to her ankles. The ropes and corners of the chair legs were digging into her flesh, but she ignored the pain, scrambling for the gun and twisting her body back toward Britney.

Incredibly, Britney hadn't given up. One hand still holding her neck, blood leaking between her fingers, she reached for Emmalee, catching hold of her wrist as Emmalee fought to squirm away.

Britney was weak, though, and in the scuffle, the gun went off, scaring both of them. In the split second Britney backed away, startled, Emmalee pointed the gun at her, staring into her eyes. Normally so sure and confident, Britney's eyes were now confused.

Time slowed down. She saw another pair of eyes. Her father's. Staring at her that night in the cold and ice. Empty, lifeless. The moment rushed back to her in startling clarity.

She'd been 16, and they were living in D.C. at the time, but they were visiting her mom in Fayetteville, North Carolina, over a long weekend, where she was assisting in a training course. Emmalee wanted to get home early, on Sunday instead of Monday, because one of her friends was having a birthday party, and she wanted to go.

They'd been in D.C. for three years. Her mom had agreed to take a position teaching at the War College, her dad was covering D.C. politics for the *Post*, and Emmalee was finally feeling like she fit in and belonged somewhere, not just with her parents. She'd even found the cutest sweater and the perfect friendship bracelet for her best friend Lilly and was hoping she might just get her first kiss from Xander, the cutest boy in 10th grade.

There was a problem, though. It was unseasonably cold for North Carolina and an ice storm was predicted just as Emmalee wanted to be setting out for home. To make matters worse, her dad's thumb was broken, so his driving was a no go. Which would normally be no big deal. Emmalee had her permit. She'd driven them to North Carolina after all. However, her mom and dad had argued, Mom wanting them to stay until the weather cleared, Dad understanding Emmalee's plight, also arguing that if they waited for it to clear, she'd have to miss a day or more of school as well. Best to head out now before it got too bad. Besides, it would give Emmalee a chance to practice driving in bad weather.

Emmalee was so excited that her dad won. Especially because he'd reminded Nikki that it was her job that had made it hard for Emmalee, and that their daughter deserved a chance to spend time with her friends before they moved again. She sort of shut that part out of her brain, though. She wasn't ready to think about leaving her home, again, and starting over, again.

As they'd set out, her mom hugged her tightly, then leaned in the passenger window, frowning at her dad. "Be safe, you two. If it gets too bad, just pull over." Emmalee rolled her eyes. Her mom could be so dramatic.

Minutes later, they were on the freeway, listening to the Beatles, when the first drops of rain started to fall. It was no big deal. Emmalee's dad suggested they pull over at the next rest area, but Emmalee whined and convinced him she'd be fine. She didn't want to be late, or worse, miss the party altogether.

The next thing she knew, she was waking up in the cold.

When she finally realized what had happened, when she saw her father's lifeless blue eyes staring at her, his blood dripping on the icy ground, she screamed. Not out of fear. Not even out of loss. But out of a keening, soul-eating guilt that it was all her fault. If she'd listened to her mom, if she hadn't been selfish, if she'd just not worried so much about a stupid party, if she'd pulled over when her father said to, her father would still be here.

Instead, she was fatherless. And she and her mom had to go through his things, discarding and donating. Emmalee kept his favorite book, a tattered copy of *The Catcher in the Rye*, and a couple of his flannel shirts that were soft and almost threadbare from years of wear and way too big for her, but she loved them dearly.

They moved to Georgia for a year. She assumed her mom just couldn't stand to stay in D.C. with all those memories. Emmalee thought she was also punishing her daughter for killing her husband. In Georgia, she connected with no one. She kept to herself, avoiding the lunch room and the library, content to cozy up to her grief and guilt. She was invited to a few parties at first, but the very idea of a party just made her blood run cold. Eventually, the other kids decided she was weird and either made fun of her or ignored her.

The present moment zoomed back to her. Here she was again. Another person's life in her hands. Two people's lives this time. She could put the gun down and let Britney kill her. She deserved it.

For her dad.

For Gretchen.

But then again. Britney would kill Chase, too.

If she pulled the trigger, she'd maybe save Chase.

Suddenly, the choice seemed so simple.

She fought the urge to close her eyes. She needed her eyes wide open as she made this choice.

She squeezed the trigger.

Britney collapsed on top of her, and all Emmalee could do was scream.

CHAPTER 38

Police officers swarmed the cabin, digging through drawers, opening cupboards, dusting for prints. A paramedic examined Emmalee's bruises and abrasions, and wrapped the ankle she'd sprained when she'd fallen still tied to the chair.

She just sat there, watching everything happen around her. It all seemed so surreal.

After Emmalee had crawled her way out from under Britney's body, she'd hurried over to where Chase lay on the floor, barely clinging to life. She'd pressed her hands to his chest, trying to stop the bleeding. She could see his lips moving and leaned down to hear what he was trying to say.

"Sorry." He barely got the words out before his eyes closed.

"Chase!" she'd screamed. She listened, but couldn't hear any breathing. She had no idea what to do. She needed to call for help, but her phone was God knew where. She forced herself to dig in Chase's pockets and found his phone. She cringed, using his limp finger to unlock it. She called the first number that came to mind.

"Mom!" Emmalee had sobbed.

"I'm on my way, Em."

Then it seemed like hours before Nikki burst through the door, gun drawn.

Now, a hand shook her shoulder. "Emmalee, talk to me. Why didn't you tell me what was happening? You almost died!"

"I know, Mom." Emmalee grimaced. "Maybe that wouldn't have been so bad."

Nikki's eyes went wide. "What the hell are you talking about?" There was a note of hysteria in her mother's voice.

"I've never told you the truth about that night, Mom." She took a deep breath.

"What night?" Nikki's eyes were wide.

"That night, the night Dad died." Hot tears started falling, stinging her split cheek. "We were only on the road because I just had to go to that stupid party."

Nikki's eyes filled with tears. "Em, it was just an accident. None of us knew what would happen." Nikki reached out to touch Emmalee's arm.

Emmalee pulled her arm away, putting her hands in her lap and twisting her fingers together nervously. "I know. But I never told you. When the ice started, he told me to pull over, that it was too dangerous." Emmalee tried to swallow to keep back a sob, but it broke through anyway. "If I'd just pulled over, like he said, he'd still be here, and none of this would have happened."

Nikki sat silent, stunned. "So you think that – and all of this –" She gestured at the cabin full of police officers – is your fault?"

Emmalee nodded and a fresh wave of tears rolled down her face.

"And you think you deserve to die for it?"

"Yes."

Tears filled Nikki's eyes, and Emmalee's heart wrenched in two. Her mom was supposed to be strong one.

"Well, maybe. I don't know. I've done everything wrong,

starting that night. I was too selfish to pull over. Worried what my friends would think if I didn't show up." Emmalee choked on another sob and Nikki pulled her into her arms.

"Emmalee, you can't blame yourself for that. Your dad could have forced the issue, but he didn't. If he'd really thought it was that dangerous, he would have made you pull over."

Emmalee swiped at a fresh wave of tears. "Don't, Mom. I know you blame me, too. For the last two years, I've watched you drink yourself into a coma every night. The nights you were home, anyway." Emmalee shuddered, her throat aching. "You could barely stand to be around me after Dad died."

Nikki pulled back and leaned her elbows on her knees, staring at the porch step under her feet. "If you want to blame anyone, blame me for that night, Em. I should have fought harder to keep you there, but I was so pissed off at your dad for always making me feel guilty about work."

"But, Mom—"

"No. You listen to me now, Emmalee. I wasn't drinking because I blamed you. I was drinking because I blamed myself. And drinking and working were easier than facing you every day, trying to figure out what I could possibly say to you to make it all better. And your dad was right. I did put work first." She paused and dropped her head. "I *do* put work first. And you've suffered for that. So much." Nikki's shoulders shook.

Emmalee didn't even know what to think anymore. "Mom, don't. Really. It's not your fault."

"It is. After your dad died, I should have focused on getting us therapy, spending more time together. Anything but drinking and leaving you alone. I watched my parents drink and medicate themselves to death. I never wanted that for you. Now look what I've done to you."

"What do you mean? What you've done to me? I insisted on going to that party." Emmalee stood up now, anger rising. "I begged Dad to let me get back for that stupid party. I got in that car with Britney. I did what she told me to. I dug a grave for Gretchen with my own two hands." She held her hands up in front of her face, shuddering at the blood stains on them. "I hid it from you, the cops, everyone. I got in that car with Britney again today to protect myself from some pictures getting out. I shot Britney and killed her, Mom! The responsibility for those choices is mine. Not yours." Emmalee's voice was almost a screech now. "You can feel bad for drinking. Or for working too much. Not being home as much as you could have and maybe should have. But you don't get to take the blame for my choices."

"Emmalee–" Nikki stood and reached for her again, but Emmalee backed away.

"No." Emmalee turned.

Nikki didn't listen. She followed, standing right next to Emmalee again.

"Listen, Em. Whatever happened – whatever happens – we're in this together. Okay?"

Emmalee felt Nikki's fingers curl around her own.

"Ma'am, I'm afraid I'm going to need to take her to the station."

They both turned and looked at the officer.

Nikki squeezed Emmalee's hand. "I'll be there right behind you, Em."

The interview took hours. Her mom wasn't allowed in the room with her since she was eighteen. Emmalee's heart had broken as she imagined her mom reading the report later, learning of all of the horrible choices Emmalee had made in the past months – the parties, the alcohol, the sex. Gretchen. All the lies.

Then there had been the written statement, the collection of her clothing, the booking, fingerprinting.

And then she was alone. In a cell. She huddled on the hard

cot, back against the wall, knees against her chest, and wanted to cry. But there were no more tears.

She was locked up, but she finally felt free of all the secrets and the lies. She bowed her head, resting her forehead on her knees.

And then she breathed.

CHAPTER 39

"You have a visitor, Sloane." Emmalee pried her eyes open, squinting, trying to orient herself. She looked around at the grey cinder block walls and recalled the night before. How she'd nearly died. How she'd murdered someone. Not by accident. Not maybe. By choice. How she'd been arrested. How she was facing a prison sentence and the end of her life as she'd known it.

"Come on. Get up." The corrections officer rattled keys in the lock and swung the door open.

"Who's here?"

"Hell if I know. Come on now."

Emmalee padded down the starkly lit corridor to a large room full of those little booths she'd seen on TV, where inmates talk on the phone to someone on the other side of a pane of plexiglass.

"Down at the end."

She moved slowly down the aisle, past several booths, and stopped at the last one. She turned and her heart leapt at the sight of Mekayla seated on the other side. She gave her a weak smile, and Mekayla started to cry.

Emmalee sat down and picked up the phone, tapping on the glass to get Mekayla's attention. When Mekayla picked up her receiver, Emmalee urged her not to cry. "Really, it's okay."

"I'm so sorry, Em." Mekayla let loose another sob.

"Seriously, Mekayla, don't." Emmalee's heart was breaking. She'd hurt so many people in this. "I shouldn't have ever dragged you into this."

"I got myself into it, remember?"

Emmalee shook her head. "No. This is my fault."

Mekayla sniffled. "It's Britney's fault, actually. Britney's and Chase's."

"But I went along with them. I was too afraid to do the right thing from the start."

Mekayla stared at her through the glass for a moment. "I'm just so glad you're alive." She sniffled again and wiped her eyes.

"Me, too." Emmalee smiled. In that moment, she realized that for the first time in more than two years, she really was glad to be alive. "I have a question I've been wondering about. How'd my mom and the police know where to show up?"

"When I talked to you and you sent me that pin, I just knew something was up. There's no way Britney was just going to let you go when she found out you were recording that conversation. I drove straight to your house and told your mom what was happening. Since she's in the military, I figured she could help."

"Yeah, but how did you guys know where I was?" None of it made sense.

Mekayla smiled. "Easy. I took a screenshot of your location on Snapchat when I heard Britney and Kristina take your phone."

"I'm so sorry, Mekayla." Tears slid down Emmalee's cheeks. "They knew it was you. They wanted you to meet them so they could—" Emmalee shuddered. "I could have gotten you killed, Mekayla."

"But I'm still here. And you're the one who saved my life, really."

Emmalee shook her head. "It could have been so much worse."

"Well, it wasn't. So just stop it." Mekayla grinned. "Now, I have some news."

"Okay." Emmalee's heart clenched, wondering what it was.

"Chase was arrested." Mekayla waited for the news to land.

"Wait, what?" Britney shot Chase point blank in the chest. He wasn't breathing.

Mekayla nodded. "The bullet didn't hit his aorta. They did emergency surgery, and he's going to have a long recovery. But he'll make it."

Emmalee's face crumpled, and it was her turn to cry again. "He's not dead."

"It's okay, Em. He won't be able to hurt you again."

"No," Emmalee said, shaking her head. "I mean, she was going to shoot him again, but she didn't."

"Because you stopped her. You saved him." Mekayla pressed her palm against the glass.

Emmalee raised hers and pressed it against the glass as well.

Now they were both crying, and it felt good to have a friend she could cry with.

"I suppose you'll have a great article now. Maybe a series for the school paper." Emmalee laughed through her tears.

Mekayla smiled, sniffling. "Shut up. Don't be ridiculous. It's going to be my first book, obviously."

The girls grinned at each other.

"Time's up." The corrections officer was closing in on her.

"Thanks for coming, Mekayla." Emmalee meant it.

"Thank you for surviving, Em." Mekayla smiled and put the receiver down.

It was a long, lonely walk back to her cell, but Emmalee felt lighter than she had in a long time.

CHAPTER 40

The walk into the courtroom a few weeks later was frightening. She was shackled at the ankles and the wrists, which nearly gave her a panic attack as she relived the memory of being tied to the chair at the cabin.

But, she worked to control her breathing and kept her head up. No more trying to hide.

Today she would receive her sentence for obstruction of justice. Her mom had hired her a lawyer, in spite of Emmalee's insistence she didn't need one. The woman had visited Emmalee at the jail and told her she had a good chance at acquittal. They could make the case that she'd been acting under duress. Emmalee was done letting other people take the blame for her choices, so she agreed to plead guilty to the obstruction charge instead, and the prosecutor took conspiracy to commit murder off the table.

Chase would likely go to prison for conspiracy. Mekayla had recorded the phone call on her end and handed that over to the police, so they knew Emmalee hadn't been at that cabin by choice. The ligature marks on her wrists and ankles proved that as well.

Chase's and Britney's fingerprints were on the gun in addition to Emmalee's, and it was registered to Chase's father, who had hired a high-powered attorney. Chase was trying to get off by claiming temporary insanity. But, Emmalee's lawyer told her that would likely never convince a jury, not when Chase's phone history had revealed a long, drawn out affair with lots of scheming between him and Britney.

And it didn't hurt that Kristina, Bryce, and Tyler were all making plea deals themselves, giving information on how manipulative and violent Britney and Chase were.

Still, Emmalee felt good about her decision to just plead guilty to something she knew she'd done and accept the consequences. It felt like the right thing to do. And it felt like a little sliver of justice for her father's death. And for Gretchen's.

When the judge told her to rise, she rose. When he gave her the sentence, two years in a state penitentiary, she felt the crushing weight of it, but she stood tall and accepted it without flinching.

She wouldn't finish high school. She wouldn't start college with Mekayla and Marshall. She choked down the tears that threatened to spill over.

Then she was led out of the room, still in shackles, trying to ignore Nikki's eyes. And tears. Nikki was crying for a girl who didn't exist anymore. Emmalee hoped one day she'd like the Emmalee she was becoming even better.

EPILOGUE

The sun was bright. Emmalee looked up at it, enjoying the feel of the heat on her face. She never took the sun for granted. Not anymore.

"Ready?" Emmalee looked over at Mekayla and nodded. Over the past five years, their friendship had only grown stronger. Mekayla had visited her in prison nearly every month, sometimes with Marshall, sometimes alone. They'd talked about Gretchen and Chase and Britney and Audrey, whose parents eventually decided to take her off life support. And Emmalee's dad. Mekayla had insisted Emmalee write that book they'd talked about. It was a bestseller now, all of the profits went to a charity they'd established to help teens facing tough choices.

Emmalee nodded. "I'm ready."

The two women headed down the sidewalk of a Virginia suburb toward the first high school they'd visit this week.

Inside the red brick building, she climbed the stage and looked out at a sea of faces. Some of them eager, some shy, some bored, some laughing. All of them young.

She didn't listen to the person introducing her, a principal, she assumed. Instead, she went inside herself, preparing.

She thought back to those days in Ravensville, how they'd ripped her apart, killing the empty person she'd become after her father died. She'd shrugged that shell of a person off, though, and built a new one, one who knew herself. Knew her own worth. Knew it was a joy to be alive.

The principal finished talking, and Emmalee stepped up to the microphone, scanning the audience. She breathed a sigh of relief when she found Mekayla and Marshall. Uncle Dan was next to them. They were all smiling at her, giving her a thumbs-up.

She glanced over at the doorway and locked eyes with Lieutenant Sloane. Nikki gave her a quick salute and smiled. Tears sprang to Emmalee's eyes, but she smiled through them.

A hush fell over the crowd. All those faces, all looking at her now. She took a deep breath, rubbing the locket she wore with her father's picture inside it.

And then she told them everything.

DID YOU ENJOY THIS BOOK?

Thank you for reading! I hope you enjoyed reading Emmalee's story as much as I enjoyed writing it. If you did, why not leave a quick review? Reviews help readers find my books. They also help me keep writing them.

Want to know when my next book is available? Join The Storytelling to get my monthly newsletter. You will also get a special bonus - a Spotify playlist for *Killing Emmalee*. Sign up at:

www.elle-wallace.com

ACKNOWLEDGMENTS

I never thought I'd get to this point, where I was writing my own acknowledgements for my very own book. It's been a long time coming, and I have so many people to thank.

Mom, thank you for all the years of believing in me and supporting my storytelling, from who said or did or wore what in Kindergarten, or reading my school stories and poems, watching the horrible plays I made up for family gatherings, or reading this book multiple times to help me find all of the errors. You are my hero in every possible way.

Ryan, Danny, Jessica, and Alex, thank you for all of the years of supporting me and believing in me. Jessica, thank you for all of your readings of this book and hours on the phone helping me hash out plot problems.

Tucker and Clover, thank you for not only your support, but also the inspiration. Tucker, your writing pushed me to finally finish mine. Clover, your unstoppable drive to make your dreams come true have inspired me to do the same.

Cristen, thank you for the inspiration. Watching you chase your writing dreams gave me the courage to chase my own.

Helaina, thank you for reading an early draft of this book and giving me the confidence to keep moving toward publication. You have no idea how much your words meant to me.

To my original Creative Writing crew (Shelby, Nat, Lauren, Bella, Thomas, Peyton), NaNoWriMo 2023 was rough, I know, but it was the start of Emmalee's journey, and your daily encouragement has helped make the book what it is today. Thank you for taking the journey with me.

To my 2025-2026 students, you have been incredible. Michaela, Grayson, Miley, Bella, I can't thank you enough for fielding all my, "How would teenagers say this?" questions. 6th period Freshman English class, to name a few, thank you for pushing me. Auni, thank you especially for "bullying" me to stay committed to my goals. Cane, thank you for always asking me if I was ever going to publish my freaking book.

To Lindsay Ribar, thank you for the incredible feedback in your developmental edit. Your input helped me unearth Emmalee's story and voice.

To my Writers in Progress friends, Alaura and Jules, thank you for all the talks and encouragement and accountability. I can't wait to read your books.

To Rae, Poppy, and Donna, thank you for all of your encouragement. When we first started meeting, I had no faith in my ability to actually edit this manuscript, and here it is, a real book. You all played a huge part in that journey - just watching all of you accomplish so much made me want to rise up and do it.

To Ken Crossland, thank you for the exquisite cover art. I had no idea what I wanted, but somehow, you found it.

To Sarra Cannon and all the Hearties, thank you. The Heart Breathings Community and courses and resources have helped me so much on this journey to launch my writing career. I am forever in your debt.

To all of my readers — past, present, and future — thank you for helping me make my dream of having my stories in people's hands come true.

ABOUT THE AUTHOR

Elle Wallace grew up with a story always waiting to be told. As a child, she once felt so sorry that ants didn't have books to read that she sat down and wrote them some — and she hasn't stopped writing since.

Killing Emmalee is her debut novel — a young adult thriller that explores the raw,  tangled journey of growing up. Elle hopes young readers find in its pages both the thrill of a gripping story and the comfort of feeling truly understood.